A GANGSTER AND A GENTLEMAN

ALSO BY KIKI SWINSON

Playing Dirty
Notorious
Wifey
I'm Still Wifey
Life After Wifey
Still Wifey Material
The Candy Shop
A Sticky Situation
Wife Extraordinaire
Wife Extraordinaire Returns
Cheaper to Keep Her series
The Score
The Mark

Anthologies
Sleeping with the Enemy (with Wahida Clark)
Heist and *Heist 2* (with De'nesha Diamond)
Lifestyles of the Rich and Shameless (with Noire)
A Gangster and a Gentleman (with De'nesha Diamond)
Most Wanted (with Nikki Turner)
Still Candy Shopping (with Amaleka McCall)
Fistful of Benjamins (with De'nesha Diamond)
Schemes (with Saundra)

ALSO BY DE'NESHA DIAMOND

The Diva Series
Hustlin' Divas
Street Divas
Gangsta Divas
Boss Divas
King Divas
Queen Divas

Published by Kensington Publishing Corp.

A GANGSTER AND A GENTLEMAN

KIKI SWINSON
DE'NESHA DIAMOND

Kensington Publishing Corp.
http://www.kensingtonbooks.com

DAFINA BOOKS are published by

Kensington Publishing Corp.
119 West 40th Street
New York, NY 10018

All Kensington Titles, Imprints, and Distributed Lines are available at special quantity discounts for bulk purchases for sales promotions, premiums, fund-raising, and educational or institutional use. Special book excerpts or customized printings can also be created to fit specific needs. For details, write or phone the office of the Kensington special sales manager: Kensington Publishing Corp., 119 West 40th Street, New York, NY 10018, attn: Special Sales Department, Phone: 1-800-221-2647.

ISBN-13: 978-0-7582-5183-1
ISBN-10: 0-7582-5183-1
First Kensington Trade Edition: October 2012
First Kensington Mass Market Edition: December 2016

eISBN-13: 978-0-7582-8191-3
eISBN-10: 0-7582-8191-9
Kensington Electronic Edition: December 2016

10 9 8 7 6 5 4 3 2 1

Printed in the United States of America

Contents

I Need a Gangsta

Kiki Swinson

Prologue

The Day of the Interview

The courtroom was pin-drop quiet and packed to capacity. The jury foreman stood up, the rustle of his suit making everyone in the room feel tense. He cleared his throat. The judge asked the foreman if the jury had reached the verdict. The foreman said yes and unfolded a piece of paper. He opened his mouth and the words seemed to come out in slow motion.

"We the jury, in the case of the *Commonwealth of Virginia versus Melody Goldman*, find the defendant not guilty of the charge of first-degree murder in count one of the indictment."

A loud round of groans and moans filtered around the room.

"Order!" the judge shouted, banging his gavel.

Silence came once again. The foreman continued apprehensively. He could feel the evil eyes bearing down on him. "We the jury also find the defendant not guilty of the charge of manslaughter in count two of the indictment," he finished.

The courtroom erupted in pandemonium. There were screams and moans. Reporters were running out of the courtroom so they could be the first to break the news. Melody Goldman grabbed her defense attorney in a long, tight embrace as relief settled on her shoulders like a cloak of comfort. She swiped away the happy tears from her face and mouthed, "Thank you," to her attorneys. In her mind, justice had been served.

Melody could hear the news reporters and tabloid media personalities screaming, "Melody Goldman may have just gotten away with two murders! The verdict has shocked the nation!"

Melody was ushered out of the courtroom, shrouded by her team of attorneys. They had done it. Melody was a free woman. Once they hit the courthouse doors, throngs of reporters moved in for the kill.

"Ms. Goldman! How did you do it? How did you get away with murder?" reporters screamed as Melody tried to get out of the building. She kept her head low, hiding her face with her arms. She didn't want anyone to see that she was smiling.

The replay of my courtroom scene almost brought a smile to my face again. I sat in the network studio watching myself on the big screen. The network had chosen to use the scene as an opening for the piece they were doing on my life. Next I heard the correspondent rehearsing her opening statements. It was all fascinating, to say the least.

"Tonight on *Date Time*, we bring you the story of Melody Goldman. Once a beautiful, wealthy, and widely popular socialite among the elite in the Tidewater area, Goldman narrowly escaped serving time in prison for heinous acts of murder that she says she was wrongly accused of, although Tidewater police and prosecutors have a different view on things. Tonight you will hear Goldman tell the story of how she went from a dazzling socialite who flaunted her position as the wife of criminal defense attorney to the stars Richard Goldman to the most hated woman in the United States. Police say she was aptly dubbed the black widow, who got away with not one but two murders. We will take you through Melody's life, starting with her humble beginnings in the roughest neighborhood in Virginia Beach, through her whirlwind love affair and marriage to one of the most renowned defense attorneys in the United States, to her current life as a wealthy widow who says she enjoys every day of her life after coming so close to losing her freedom. Stay tuned as we bring you the story of Melody Goldman, a woman who, by her own account, got caught between a gangsta and a gentleman."

I smirked to myself as I listened to Michelle Moyer, the host of the television special that would be featuring the rise in my celebrity and my even higher rise to grace, as she rehearsed the opening for our interview. The smirk turned into all-out laughter as I thought about the comment that I had gotten away with not one but two murders. It was nervous laughter, I have to admit, but I was thinking, *You damn right I got away! I was the real victim. Those motherfuckers did themselves in. It was not me. Period.* And now the world would know the truth about my story. I'd walked away from being convicted of horrible crimes, but not before I was put through some shit myself.

I folded my arms across my chest as I thought about the entire ordeal. Folding my arms was something the show's producers had asked me not to do during the taping. Well, I was feeling defensive—that's what my psychiatrist often told me whenever I folded my arms and twisted my lips in his presence. I didn't care that people didn't believe my side of the story; I knew the truth. I was going to tell it like it really happened. Not like the media had made it out to be when everything first happened. After listening to Michelle Moyer rehearse several times, I didn't think what she was saying about me was too bad; at least she didn't call me what everyone else had been calling me in the media—a jealous, scorned, gold-digging murderer who wanted revenge.

Michelle finished her intro and was ready to get down to business with the interview. She smiled at me as she settled into her chair directly across from me, and members of the crew put the finishing touches on her makeup. It was a phony smile, forced through her porcelain veneers. I could feel the envious vibe she was sending my way. It was clear that even Michelle Moyer, one of the top news correspondents in Virginia, was jealous of the still-fabulous Melody Goldman. I guess *still fabulous* was a bit of an understatement. I was new and improved. I mean, my natural beauty was still apparent even after all of the stress I had endured. I had stepped up my game from my old usual $500 weave to lace front wigs imported directly from India just for me. I kept my nails done with weekly manicures, and my skin was even more radiant than it was before my little run-in with the law. I say *run-in* because that's just what it was. I am Melody Goldman—didn't they know that? I was simply not to be fucked with. I also refused to take full responsibility. I would always maintain my innocence.

"Are you ready?" Michelle asked, still flashing that fake-as-a-three-dollar-bill smile.

I inhaled deeply. "As ready as I'm gonna get," I answered, exhaling. I hadn't really talked about all of the intricacies of my story since my trial. In fact, I had definitely pushed some things into the far reaches of my mind, but today, like I promised when the network agreed to pay me $200,000 for my story, I was going to tell everything, raw, uncut, and in their faces.

"O-okay, Ms. Goldman, or do-do you prefer Melody?" Michelle stumbled over her words.

"Melody is fine."

"Melody, you are one of the most talked about women in America. Many people say you literally got away with murder. Although you say you didn't do it, this can't be how you planned your life. You can't walk down the street without someone recognizing you. You've even received death threats. I mean . . . ," Michelle started, her trailed off statement leading me down her little path.

"No, definitely not. As a little girl, I always knew I would be famous, though. I also knew I'd be just as fabulous as I am today," I began.

"But did you know you'd be infamous?" Michelle blurted out, cutting in before I could say anything else. Her words struck me like a gut punch. I grabbed the edges of the chair and gripped them tightly. I was more determined than ever to tell the story now. I opened my mouth and thought about how it had all gotten started.

1

One Year Earlier

It was a usual day in the neighborhood for me. Just like any other day, I woke up as the wife of Richard Goldman, a wealthy criminal defense attorney to the stars. I had started out my day like any other—manicure, pedicure, hair appointment, a little shopping, some calls to other attorneys' and doctors' wives, and, finally, a check of my phone's calendar to see if Richard would be traveling or if I would have him for myself, which had become a rare occasion for us. Shit! I had almost choked on my words when I looked at the date. I immediately felt like shit when I read the date and realized it was Richard's birthday and I had forgotten. He had been traveling and working late hours so much, I often forgot what day it was. I had immediately gotten on my phone and called our personal shopper, Almonté. Luckily, Almonté had a free block in his schedule and agreed to meet me at Neiman Marcus to help me pick out the perfect gift for

Richard. I figured I wouldn't call Richard to say happy birthday right then because he'd probably figure out that I had just remembered his birthday at three o'clock in the afternoon. Instead, I planned on surprising him with the perfect gift and the perfect lingerie so he could have his best gift—some of me. I was hoping that my body would be on his mind and not the fact that I had really forgotten his day.

Almonté and I moved through Neiman like two gazelles being chased by lions. We made quick work of picking out a gift for Richard, who, by the way, was very hard to shop for because he had everything you could possibly think of. But we'd finally found a few things that were exclusive enough for Richard's taste—a new pair of Salvatore Ferragamo loafers that hadn't even been put on the floor yet and a pair of David Yurman cuff links with black and canary diamonds in them. Those were both small, but the big gift was the hot La Perla number I found to wear. I was super excited. I loved to buy things for Richard. It just made me feel like I was doing something other than sitting around looking pretty and spending his money.

When I pulled up to my front door, I was brimming inside with anticipation. Richard's car was there, and I couldn't wait to see his face when I showed him what I got for his birthday. More importantly, I couldn't wait to show him what I was going to do to him for his birthday. I shivered just thinking about the dick. Richard's shit was addictive and one of the many reasons I had sacrificed so much to be with him for the rest of my life. I knew that being with Richard meant a safe, secure, financial future for me. Or so I thought.

Giving up my job as a paralegal and my law school studies seemed to be a small sacrifice when I met and fell in love with Richard and his dick. I loved making love to my husband, and with his clientele growing, and him being gone a lot more, I hardly got any dick lately. I was actually salivating thinking about it, and I made a mental note to remember to tell him that I would be accompanying him on at least one or two of his business trips per month. I was tired of being home alone. "Here I come, honey bunny," I sang as I parked the smoke-gray Audi R8 he had leased for me to drive for the next two years. That's another thing. My husband was extremely intelligent and financially savvy. He thought it was a waste to finance a bunch of cars when I always wanted to change cars like underwear.

I hopped out of the driver's seat and rushed inside our home with the beautifully wrapped gifts in hand. Sweat beads were lined up on my forehead, threatening to ruin the glue on my new hair, that's how bad I was rushing to get to my man. My heart sank as soon as I stepped inside our grand foyer. I almost tripped over bags on top of bags. I groaned loudly, because that could only mean one fucking thing. But he'd just got back! *Where could he be going again?!* I thought to myself, exasperated and disappointed all in one. I eyed the bags good. That's when I noticed that it wasn't just his usual traveling bags by the door; there was much more this time. I crinkled my eyebrows because Richard had every piece of his Louis Vuitton luggage set by the door and then some. There were at least seven bags and two garment bags. He even had his Gucci duffel that he used for the gym packed to capacity. Shit, it looked like he was packing and never coming back. I dropped the Neiman Marcus bag, my purse, and my keys on the baby-grand bench. I slipped out of my heels and proceeded through the house to find out what the hell was the deal.

"Honey, I'm home!" I sang out, trying to keep my voice steady as an uneasy feeling crept up on me. My voice echoing off the walls and high ceilings made me feel even more dread. You know when you just know something is not right? Well, instinctively, I felt something just wasn't right.

"Richard?" I called out as I walked slowly toward the spiral staircase. "Richard, honey, where are you?" I called again, growing more frantic. Finally, he appeared at the top of the staircase. I looked up, my eyes as wide as dinner plates. I swallowed hard when I saw the look on his face. To this day, I remember it as something more evil than I'd ever seen, even from my mother, who hated my guts and often wore a scowl whenever she looked at me. The devil himself was dancing in Richard's eyes.

"Happy birthday, baby," I said, flashing a fake-ass smile. I was trying real hard to stamp down the sick feeling in my gut. Richard just looked at me steely-eyed and stone-faced. He was holding one of his many watchcases in his hand. Strange to say the least. *I know he is not emptying his watch-cases!* I remember thinking.

"I . . . I . . . got something for your birthday, and I got something special planned for us. You . . . you . . . weren't going to travel again, were you?" I stammered. His glare just had me feeling uneasy. I couldn't stand it anymore. I needed to know what the hell was up.

I didn't want to jump to any conclusions, so I waited for him to tell me what was going on. We stared at each other for at least thirty long seconds. "Richard?" I said, breaking the eerie silence. "Why do you look like that? The bags? It's your birthday . . . What the . . . ," I said, my voice cracking.

"Look, Melody, I was going to tell you," he said, lowering his eyes. He started fiddling with the watchcase. "There's no easy way to say something like this . . . ," he continued. His voice was even, stern.

I started shaking. What was he talking about? He couldn't even look me in the eyes, which was a bad fucking sign. I could feel my heart squeezing tight inside of my chest, but I didn't say a word.

"I'm leaving. I'm having all my things moved out today," Richard rambled, nearly devoid of any emotion. I couldn't find one shred of remorse in his words or in his face. I felt like a bell had gone off in my head. There was loud ringing and I felt off balance. What did he just say? Leaving. Moved out today. I screamed inside of my head. My legs started to shake. Caught off guard by his sudden betrayal, I slumped against the staircase wall for a second. I felt like the wind had been knocked out of me too. At first when I opened my mouth to say something, nothing came out.

"Why?" I finally whispered breathlessly as I caught my balance.

"Don't make this harder than it has to be, Melody, with all of the dramatics," Richard said coldly. Another slap-to-the-face statement. He couldn't be serious. I was thinking this shit was a joke. I laughed a little bit.

"Richard, are you mad because you think I forgot your birthday?" I asked. Tears were right at the rims of my eyes. I couldn't help it. My heart was hammering so hard I felt nauseous, and I was scared to death. *I can't lose my husband,* was all I kept thinking. He had to be playing a cruel joke on me.

"No. I'm leaving. It's over, Melody. It's been over," he replied dryly.

"No! No!" I screamed as I bolted up the staircase toward him.

"I'm not going to do the drama queen thing with you. This is not one of those stupid reality shows you watch," Richard said, turning his back on me. I was huffing and puffing when I reached the top of the steps. I ran after him as he walked away dismissively. I felt the need to be face-to-face so he could look me in the eye and tell me why he had really packed up his shit. I mean, we hadn't had the perfect marriage, but damn, it hadn't been so bad that he'd want to pack up his shit and leave me.

"Richard, don't you turn your back on me!" I

growled, leaping toward him. He whirled around, and I bumped into him. His large barrel chest was heaving up and down like he was the one who had just gotten the bad news. I backed away a few steps. I wanted to look into his face, his eyes.

"Richard, what do you mean you're moving out? Leaving? What the fuck is going on?" I cried as I searched his cold eyes for answers.

"Melody, you act like you don't know. I mean, we haven't had sex in months—or did you not notice between all of the shopping and bullshit party hopping you've been doing?" Richard snapped.

I felt weak. How fucking dare he!

"What are you talking about? I did everything for you! I only go out when you're on one of your fucking many business trips or working late!" I screamed. I could feel my face filling with blood. "I could give it all up! I won't shop. I won't party! Richard, this is too drastic. What are you thinking about? We are happily married!"

"Face it, Melody. I'm just not in love with you anymore. It's over," he told me sharply, and then he stepped by me and headed down the steps. It was like he didn't even want to be in the same breathing space as me. My heart felt like it had exploded. Vomit crept up my throat, and I hunched over from the cramps that trampled through my stomach. I honestly could not believe that my husband of ten years had just uttered the words that he didn't love me anymore and gave me my walking papers. I felt an overwhelming sense of desperation.

"Richard! You are not going to just say some shit like that and think it's going to be that easy!" I screamed at the top of my lungs.

I raced down the stairs after him. I wasn't about to let him just walk out of our fucking house without a fight. Part of me wanted to show him that I still wanted to work on our marriage, but another part of me just wanted to hurt him, claw his eyes out or scratch his smooth face.

"You bastard! You just gonna say you don't love me anymore? Huh? Do you realize what you're doing?" I spat, on the verge of hysteria. "After everything I've done for you, Richard!" My face was now a mess of makeup and tears.

He was totally ignoring me. He walked past the bag with his gifts inside and kicked them slightly, like he had just done with my heart. I felt like I had to try a different approach. The desperation was mounting. He was walking swiftly around our parlor, gathering up the pictures he had of himself along with a couple that he had of his parents from the mantel over our fireplace. I was hot on his ass. I was panting—hyperventilating was more like it.

"Richard, please! I'm asking you, do not do this! I need you! I love you!" I sobbed. That was my attempt at trying the loving, desperate wife approach. Richard was acting like I didn't exist. I grabbed his arm roughly, more desperate attempts to keep him from doing this.

"Answer me, Richard! Say something! Say we can work this out," I demanded with a death grip on his bicep.

He yanked his arm away from me and gave

me a shove. "Melody, don't reduce yourself to these type of antics," he shot coldly, his glare enough to back me down a bit. Then he turned around casually, giving me his back again. "What do you want me to say? I told you, there is nothing to explain, nothing to save, nothing to talk about. I don't love you and I'm leaving," he said, finishing his verbal murder.

I stomped my foot. "Nothing to talk about? Nothing to say? After every-fucking-thing I did for you? After everything I gave up for you?" I hollered, feeling the veins in my neck throbbing against my skin.

Richard had the nerve to laugh at me. He was actually laughing at what I had said. This motherfucker had forgotten. He had really forgotten that I had given up my college career, my dreams of being a lawyer, to work long, hard hours in his fledgling fucking law firm when he didn't even have so much as one fucking client. I had spent hours and hours typing briefs, scouting out leads, reading press releases, anything it took to build his firm. I was the bitch who went out and recruited soon-to-be stars to hire Richard. I had used some of my past modeling connections to get him some leads on clients, like rappers and actors who had gotten into trouble with the law. Now he was standing there telling me we had nothing to talk about. In my book we had plenty of shit to talk about. I charged into him like a raging bull.

"You fuckin' ungrateful bastard. You are not just going to leave me like this!" I screeched. I started throwing wild punches at Richard's chest. He grabbed hold of my wrists roughly. I could feel his strong hands bearing down into the bones of my wrists. I would've never believed my husband would ever put a rough finger on me.

"Let's not do this right now, Melody. It is so unnecessary," he said through clenched teeth, releasing me roughly. He had the nerve to try to walk away. When he tried to pass me to go into the kitchen, I blocked him. Now I know what people mean when they say they felt their world crumbling before their eyes. My heart was aching and I needed to express it. "We will do this now. Because you're not leaving until you do. You owe me that much, Richard!" I roared, throwing myself in his path.

He sighed loudly. "I knew I should've just never come back. I should've just left all this material shit here. I knew you would act the damn fool," he gritted.

In a knee-jerk reaction, I reached up and slapped his face. I was immediately sorry.

He folded his face into a scowl. "I'm out of here!" he growled. He started moving away from me again. He looked like he wanted to just kill me. I grabbed on to him from behind. Clutching on to him for dear life. "Richard, I'm sorry. I'm sorry for whatever I've done. Please just tell me you won't leave. Not today! We can sleep on it. Let's make love—it will fix everything." I continued to sob.

Richard let out a loud, cacophonous laugh. "You just don't get it, do you? I've just outgrown you. You don't satisfy me anymore. It's as simple as that," he hissed, his words dripping with venom. He was trying to hurt me. That much I had figured out. For some reason, the man I had sacrificed my entire life for wanted to stab me in the chest and turn the knife round and round.

Trying desperately to see his eyes through my tears, I said, "No. Don't say that. You know you don't really mean that. You told me that we were best friends, remember? And that we were partners for life." I started rambling, recalling things from early in our relationship.

He laughed at me again, this time more evilly than before. "You think I just stopped fucking you because I was traveling or working? Think about it, Melody. Men take pussy even if they're dead-dog tired. You had to know," he said, followed by a short chuckle. It was like it was a real big joke to him. I was flabbergasted.

"But I tried to give you your space. I didn't want to crowd you since I know you've been traveling. I tried to be understanding of the fact that you were either gone or working late hours with your new partner at the firm every night for the past year. Remember, you're the one who's always complaining that you're tired," I said, and then I fell silent. It was like something hit me like a hammer on the head. I had solved the mystery without even doing anything. My own words had brought clarity to the situation. I immediately covered my mouth. Richard had tried to make me feel like I was crazy when I met his new partner, Christina Cox, and immediately became suspicious of their relationship.

A whole year of suspicion and numerous

speculations had just been confirmed by my own words. "Oh my God, Richard. How could you? You're having an affair with Christina, aren't you?" I shrieked. My eyes lowered into slits, and I bit down into my bottom lip until I drew blood.

"I'm out of here! No more of this bullshit!" he snapped. I jumped in front of him again as he headed toward the front door.

"You fucking piece of shit! I can't believe you're leaving me for that bitch!" I yelled. It was like an evil force took hold of me. Without even thinking about it, I jumped straight on his back and started pounding on his head. "You son of a bitch! I knew it. All of this time you tried to make me feel like I was crazy!" I screamed as I pounded on him. He was whirling around, trying to get me off of him. "I knew deep down in my heart that you were sleeping with that whore behind my back. I'm gonna kill your ass!" I spat, trying to bite his fucking ear off. He struggled for about a minute and a half to get me off his back.

"Get the hell off me, you crazy bitch!" he yelled.

And when he finally was able to wrestle me to the floor, I was crying uncontrollably and panting. Richard was out of breath too. But it didn't prevent him from bailing out the front door.

"I'll be back to get my shit later," he snapped with finality.

I was too exhausted to fight him anymore. I was emotionally and physically drained. I lay in a heap on the floor. "You tell that home-wrecking bitch I'm gonna kill her when I see her!" I roared into the air about two seconds before he closed the front door. The entire scene was like some shit out of *Waiting to Exhale.* It was the kind of shit that happened in movies, not to me. I kicked and flailed my arms like a baby missing her best toy. I felt like dying. After about an hour of staring into space with tears running out of my eyes as if they were faucets, I was struck by a sudden burst of energy. I sat up like a woman possessed by an evil spirit. It wasn't over. I wasn't going to let it be over. I swiped the tears off my cheek and stomped over to Richard's bags. He wanted to act like this was a movie, well so would I. I opened our front door and began tossing all of his shit outside. I did that until sweat covered my entire body. "This is just the beginning, Richard Goldman!" I screamed from the door. I didn't give a fuck who heard me. I was a woman possessed. And by the time all of this was over, the entire neighborhood and the city would know what a low-down husband I had.

2

The night Richard left me, I cried and cried until I made myself so sick I was throwing up nothing but my stomach acid. I didn't even have enough energy to go up to my bedroom that first night, so I slept curled up in a fetal position by the front door, a few feet away from the bag of gifts I had bought for him. It wasn't until the next day that I was able to drag myself to the bedroom. I lay in bed, tossing and turning, replaying Richard's betrayal in my head over and over. My emotions ran the gamut from sorrowful to all-out rage.

Finally, after three days of a mentally debilitating roller coaster, an unnerving calm suddenly came over me like a warm blanket. I bolted up in the bed as if possessed by a demon. Suddenly, I mustered enough strength to pull myself out of bed. "Melody, you're better than this," I gave myself a pep talk as I stood on wobbly, weak legs. With a mission in mind, I showered and set out to try and piece my life together as best I could. With my face painted with extra foundation to cover the huge bags under my eyes, I slipped into a lady Brooks pantsuit and my favorite Gucci pumps. I wouldn't say that I was my usual stunning self, but I looked decent enough to go out in public.

The first thing I planned to do was go to the bank and check on my financial stability. Richard had come completely out of left field with the whole leaving thing, so there was no telling what else he had up his sleeve. I needed to make sure I had money, just in case. I had depended solely on Richard for ten long years for everything—including the drawers on my ass. He had doled out money to me in a monthly allowance of $5,000. It was good enough for me. I could shop, party, take girlfriend trips or whatever I felt like doing for the month. Richard also paid all of the bills for the house and for my car lease. I didn't have to worry or want for anything. It worked. All along I had always felt our arrangement was a fair deal for what I had sacrificed to help him before he became wealthy.

When I met Richard, I was working as a low-paid paralegal in one of the largest law firms in Virginia. I had just started law school, and I was focused on becoming an entertainment lawyer. I also did modeling stints in the evenings to pay for school. I was strikingly beautiful. When I walked the streets, I turned heads and that was a fact. My five-foot-seven-inch statuesque frame and caramel, blemish-free complexion garnered lots of attention and made it pretty easy for me to make a few bucks with print ads and some low-level catwalk stints. I was fully independent and loving it. I had escaped my childhood, and at twenty-five, I had my own apartment, my own car, and I was holding my own in general. I wasn't thinking about a man. I had watched my mother put men before me all of my life.

As a kid, I was determined to make my own way and never to depend on a man. I was also determined to show my mother that I could do it without her. Sometime over the years, the lines got crossed and shit got blurry for me. Meeting Richard had changed my "I-am-woman-hear-me-roar" attitude so fast I couldn't even remember how it all happened. Richard had come into the law firm for an interview on a rainy afternoon. He was soaked, yet I couldn't take my eyes off of him. He was fine in a Boris Kodjo type of way. He had smiled at me and asked if I could show him where he could clean up before his meeting. I had snickered at him, because he had looked kind of worked over. I gave him a roll of hand towels and told him the secret of using the bathroom hand drier to dry his shirt, tie, and suit jacket. We exchanged glances and smiles the entire time he was there. I was immediately smitten, but I never thought he would want me—the office paralegal. Richard was half black and half white, and he had taken the best attributes from both races. He stood six foot two inches tall and kept his body chiseled. His teeth were straight and magazine-quality white. He was articulate, well dressed, and as charming as a fucking fairy-tale prince. Even if I had tried to play it off like I didn't like him, my face flaming over each time I looked at him would've given it all away.

Richard asked me out once he'd gotten the job at the firm. I accepted and the rest is history. At first, we worked together, pretending we didn't know each other. Sometimes I think our acting was so bad that we had blown our own cover. The pretending didn't last long. Richard had been brought into the office of one of the firm's partners and warned about their fraternization policy. That night, over wine and sex, Richard decided that I would quit the job as he prepared to go off and start his own firm. At first, I was very leery about giving up my paycheck and independence to turn around and depend on Richard. I voiced my fears to him, and he assured me I could go to school full-time and not have to worry. Richard had put his hand over his heart and swore to me that he would always take care of me. I don't know what I was thinking, being that I had never trusted anyone, not even my own mother, but I followed my heart and did what Richard had asked. Besides, at the time, going to school full-time seemed like a good plan.

Then Richard came up with the idea that I would start running his fledgling office as he began to get his own practice off the ground. It was too much to handle—the demands of law school and working more than fourteen hours a day helping Richard. Needless to say, I eventually quit school. Again, Richard promised I wouldn't have anything to worry about. He swore before God that he would take care of me for life. As soon as he made his first big case, Richard proposed. I was elated. It seemed like he was definitely making good on his promises. No more dealing with my trifling-ass mother and no more working like a slave. Richard was taking care of everything just like he'd said he would. In the end, I had given up everything—my apartment, my car, my job, and my dreams. I was just Mrs. Melody Goldman, wife of Richard Goldman, Esq.

I took one last long look at myself in the mirror before I stepped out of my door. I exhaled and prayed for the best. I wasn't sure what I would encounter at the bank. With his erratic behavior, there was no telling what the hell Richard would do. Most of our accounts were joint, but Richard had some solo accounts.

I pulled back the door, and the sunlight hurt my eyes. "Damn, Melody, you stayed in the house way too long," I grumbled, fishing in my purse for my shades. Just as I covered my eyes and got them to focus, I noticed a man on my lawn. I crinkled my brows and looked down over the top of my shades. "Hey!" I screamed out at the man. He was banging something into the ground. He looked up at me, waved, and continued to bang. I stomped down the porch stairs and stormed toward him. "What are you doing?" I huffed as I approached him. He looked at me like I was from outer space. "Answer me! Why are you on my lawn?" I snapped, eyeing him evilly.

"Miss, the owner of the house is putting it up

for sale. I am here putting in the for sale sign," he said with an attitude, as if I should've known why he was there.

"Who sent you?" I barked. It was the only thing I could say. I felt like melting into the well-manicured grass. Here I was saying it was my house, but I didn't know the shit was being put up for sale. My cheeks flamed over right away.

"Uh . . . a Mr. Richard Goldman," the man read from a paper he'd pulled out of his back pocket.

A flash of heat came over my body so fast I snatched the piece of paper from the man and ripped it into shreds. *Fucking Richard! Bastard!* I screamed in my head.

"That's what I think of your fucking sign! Get the fuck off my property!!" I screamed, jutting an accusatory finger at the man.

The man backed away as if he were being attacked by a rabid dog. He stumbled toward his pickup truck, which read RE/MAX. I rushed over and picked up the red, white, and blue tin sign he'd left lying on my grass. "And take your fucking for sale sign and shove it up your ass!" I hollered as I used what energy I had left to toss the sign into the street. The loud clang of the tin sent a chill down my spine, and not in a good way. I had come completely undone. My first day out trying to pick up the pieces of my life and this is what I have to deal with. I hated Richard at that moment.

My face was painted with a scowl, my wig was loose, and I was sweating through my damn clothes. My chest heaved up and down wildly. "He wants to sell the fucking house right out from under me, huh? I got something for Richard's ass," I mumbled to myself as I rushed back toward our three-car garage. I hit the garage door opener that was connected to my keys and waited for the door to go up. When the door was fully up, I almost dropped down. Another fucking low blow. My car was gone! I whirled around in a circle, feeling lost and crazy. It couldn't be possible. There was no way someone could steal my car from a locked garage. "What the fuck? It can't be!" I bellowed. I felt like some unknown force had snatched my breath away. I walked into the garage slowly, feeling like my legs weren't even connected to my body.

All of the cars were gone. That's when I knew exactly what had happened to my fucking car. I slumped down atop the garden-tools box. My legs were too weak to stand. "How did he . . . ," I whispered, holding my head in my hands. I had been home since the day he'd left me. I had not heard Richard come like a thief in the night and take away my car and both of his. He must've used his garage keys and not the opener or else I would've heard him. Then again, we lived in a million-dollar estate that was over 12,000 square feet. Our bedroom was at the back of the house; I would've never heard him as I lay in my bed depressed and distraught crying so much that at times I couldn't even breathe.

"Arrghhh!" I screamed, throwing my shades across the garage. I jumped up from the toolbox and pulled out my cell phone. My first instinct was to call Richard and curse him out, but I had something better for him. He wanted to play dirty, so I was going to join his game.

"Yes, I need a car at . . ." I huffed out my address. I couldn't stand still as I waited for the car service to pick me up. As I climbed into the back of the Lincoln Town Car, I could feel the adrenaline surging through my veins. "You wait, Richard Goldman. You will regret this shit," I mumbled, drumming my nails on the door armrest. The driver looked at me strangely through the rearview mirror. "Just drive! And hurry the fuck up," I snapped at him.

By the time I reached Richard's office building, I had thought of so many evil things I could do to him that I almost forgot to hand the driver my credit card. I fumbled in my bag and handed him my debit card. I tapped my foot anxiously as I waited for him to swipe my card. "What is taking so long?" I snapped. "Swipe the shit and let's go!" The driver looked at me through his rearview mirror. He looked shaken, scared even.

"Mrs. Goldman, I'm sorry. This card is declined." He handed me my card.

My face grew dark and folded into a scowl. "That's impossible. Try the shit again," I barked, banging on the back of the seat. "I don't have time for games. Are you sure your machine is working? I have plenty of money in the bank. There is no way my card would be declined," I said through clenched teeth.

"I tried it about ten times. . . . It is declined," he said.

He looked scared as hell. It didn't sway me at all. I was too pissed to even handle it. I dug around in my bag and handed him three more cards. "Here! See, I have fucking cash in the bank!" I screamed as I threw the cards at him over the seat. He looked at me like I was crazy and started swiping all of the cards.

"Look . . . you can look at the machine yourself," the driver said. "All of these cards are declined as well. Mrs. Goldman, just pay with cash and we can forget about it."

I felt flush with embarrassment. I never carried cash. I didn't have anything on me except my debit cards and credit cards. "Just wait right here. My husband's law firm is right through those doors. I will get some cash and come back," I said feeling defeated.

"I can't really wait, Mrs. Goldman. . . . Is there someone you can call to come outside and give you the cash?" the driver said.

I could tell he didn't trust me and he was irritated. "You're just going to have to wait!" I snapped, grabbing the door handle roughly and rushing out of the car.

"Mrs. Goldman, I'm going to call the police!" the driver yelled to my back.

"Oh, shut the fuck up and wait," I mumbled under my breath. This whole thing was humiliating enough; I didn't need his ass threatening me.

I stormed into Richard's office. As soon as I stepped in, his assistant, Deana, stood up like she had a fucking spring in her chair. A look of horror came over her face as if I were Freddy Krueger. Deana's mouth went into a perfect O. She was clearly shocked as shit to see me.

"Melody . . . um . . . hi . . . um . . . ," Deana stuttered as I continued past her. She couldn't get from behind her desk fast enough to block my path to Richard's office. "Melody, you can't. Wait! Don't go in . . . ," Deana yelled at my back.

It was too late. I had made a beeline for the door, and there wasn't a fucking soul who could stop me.

"Richard!" I screamed as I damn near kicked in his office door. I froze as soon as I stepped over the doorsill.

"Melody . . . I tried to tell you," Deana huffed from behind me.

I saw that bitch right there before my eyes. My heart felt like it had exploded in my chest.

"Ohhh, baby!" Christina Cox cooed. Her bare back was to me, and her legs were gaped wide open. Richard's face was buried between Christina's legs, and her head was thrown back in ecstasy. The scene almost made me faint. I doubled over for a quick second, but suddenly I was filled with a white-hot rage that I couldn't control.

"Richard, you fuckin' piece of shit," I growled as I lurched forward.

"Oh my God! How did she get in here?" Christina screeched, jumping up off the desk. They had been so into their shit that they hadn't heard me at first.

"Melody!" Richard shouted as he jumped up, his face wet and disgusting. I was seeing nothing but red. Christina tried in vain to cover herself.

I was on her within a few seconds. "You home-wrecking bitch!" I spat as I grabbed a handful of her naturally long, silky hair. I yanked her toward the floor. Her titties and ass were splayed out on the burgundy carpet that I had helped Richard pick out for his office. "You wanna fuck my husband, huh, bitch?" I yelled as I punched her in the face.

"Oh my God! I'm so sorry, Mr. Goldman!" Deana wailed. She was crying.

"Get off of her, Melody!" Richard barked as he grabbed me around the waist. I kept a firm grasp on Christina's hair, so each time Richard pulled me, I pulled Christina's hair. I was trying to rip that bitch's hair completely out of her scalp.

"Aggh! Help me! She's ripping my hair out!" Christina belted out.

"You damn right, bitch! You fuckin' traitor! I was the one who helped get you hired. I treated you like a sister, and this is what you do? You fuck my husband and ruin my fuckin' marriage?" I screamed at the top of my lungs. Tears of hurt and anger started involuntarily pouring out of my eyes. I slammed my fist into Christina's face again.

"Let her go, Melody! Deana, call security!" Richard yelled. He was trying with all of his might to pull me away. He wasn't strong enough to handle the strength I had acquired from the adrenaline rush. I started bucking against him, still keeping a tight grasp on Christina's hair.

"Richard, let her go so she can let me go. Please!" Christina begged.

I slammed her body again. She was hollering like I was killing her, which is exactly what I wanted to do to her ass. Richard finally let me go. I swung Christina around by her hair and punched her in the face again. This time blood sprayed out of her nose and onto my clothes.

"Help me, Richard," Christina choked out.

Richard didn't touch me again. Like the fucking punk he was, he had to call in his guard dogs. I finally felt at least four security guards bearing down on me.

"Let her go, Mrs. Goldman," one of the guards commanded. The other barrel-chested guard pried my hands off of Christina and lifted me off my feet.

I started kicking and screaming. "Richard! You and your bitch will pay for what you did to me! You motherfucker!" I screeched.

"Get that crazy bitch out of here," Richard hissed.

All I could see in his eyes was pure hatred for me.

"This is not over, Richard. You will not get away with what you're doing to me. You will reap what you sow, motherfucker," I continued to scream at the top of my lungs. I kicked and flailed my arms like a wild animal. The security guards carried me out of Richard's office, but it wasn't easy. I was putting up a fight that surprised even me. "All of you will be sorry. I helped build this fucking firm. You can't get away with this, Richard!" I screamed through my heartbreak and devastating embarrassment.

They tossed me out of the doors. I went tumbling to the ground like a piece of trash. "I'm sorry, Mrs. Goldman, but you will not be allowed back on the premises," one of the guards said as he prepared to shut me out.

"Fuck you. I built that firm. All of you will pay," I screeched, lifting myself off the ground. Just as I turned around, I was met by the Virginia Beach police. Three officers were walking toward me, looking like they were ready for battle.

"Oh, now he called the cops on me too?" I said, trying to straighten out my rumpled clothes. That's when I noticed the car service driver right behind the police officers.

"Are you Mrs. . . . um . . . Melody Goldman?" a tall, white officer asked as he read from his memo book. I eyed him evilly and shot the car service driver the look of death.

"Why do you need to know?" I asked, my voice cracking and shaky.

"That is her," the car service driver said, pointing in my direction.

"Mrs. Goldman, you are under arrest for theft of services," another officer said as he grabbed my arm. I tried to dip away from him, but I wasn't fast enough. He had latched on to my arm with a death grip.

"What? You can't do this! Wait, I can go get the money from the bank," I hollered, trying to yank my arm out of his grasp. It was too late. They had all put hands on me already. I dropped down to the ground and began fighting again. They were too strong. Within seconds they had my hands pulled roughly behind my back, and I was being carried like a slaughtered animal into the back of the patrol car.

"Every fucking body will pay for what has been done to me. Everybody!" I screamed, and began to cry. It was like I was caught in the worst nightmare and couldn't wake up. I could not believe how drastically my life had changed within a matter of days. I had gone from sitting on top of the world to being in the pits of hell.

3

"Ms. Goldman?" a police officer said from the other side of the holding cell bars.

I jumped to my feet. "That's me," I said, anticipation in my voice. I was praying Richard had had a change of heart and was there to get me out. I had been told if I paid the fine, I could get out of that jam, and they would consider dropping the disorderly conduct charges they were throwing at me for punching and kicking the police officers.

"You get your one phone call," the officer said dryly.

My shoulders slumped in disappointment. No such luck. I was quickly aware that Richard hadn't had a change of heart at all. I just had a phone call. My mind was racing a mile a minute thinking about who I would call to get me out of this jam. There was no way I could've called any of my friends, who were all wives of doctors and lawyers. I got stomach cramps even thinking of their reactions to me telling them I was locked up. Oh, I would've been the talk of the town. Those bitches probably would've had a dinner party just to discuss the fact that I had gotten arrested. I shook my head in despair, concluding that those fake-ass friends were not an option. There would have just been too much explaining to do about my situation. I wasn't ready to face the fact that my husband had left me in such a disrespectful way, much less tell those high-horse-riding bitches my business. As I contemplated my options, I realized I had no one outside of my life with Richard, except for my sister Paulette. I stood at the phone, frozen with a mixture of fear and apprehension. Paulette's face came into focus in my mind's eye.

"Goldman, are you going to make your call or what? If not, let me take you back to the holding pen," the officer barked at me.

I jumped into action. "N-no . . . I'm going to make the call," I stammered. That settled it. Paulette was my only hope. I barely remembered Paulette's number. I hadn't spoken to her in over six years. She and I were never really as close as sisters should have been. That was all thanks to my evil-ass mother. She always drove a wedge between my sister and me by blatantly favoring Paulette over me. My mother used to tell my sister I was ugly and she was beautiful. She would buy Paulette dolls and treats, while she didn't buy me anything. She would make Paulette tease me with her new things too. I would suffer in silence, hurting deep down inside. As a kid, I secretly hated Paulette because of how much my mother loved her. Paulette grew up thinking she was superior to me. Sometimes we would get close, but if my mother saw that, she would work her way back to making Paulette and I archenemies.

When I married Richard and we became well-off, I basically turned my back on my sister. I had already stopped fucking with my mother way before Richard came along, but I had always tried to keep in touch with Paulette. After Richard, I just poured all of my time and energy into him. I was aware that Paulette was struggling to pay for college and I told her in no uncertain terms to deal with it. I was only doing to her what my mother had done to me. Now I was sorry. None of it had been either of our faults.

I dialed the last number I could remember for Paulette. All along, I was silently praying. "Please be the same number, please, please," I whispered as the line rang on the other end. After the fourth ring, I shifted my weight from one foot to the other. My heart was hammering. Paulette was my last-ditch hope; if she didn't answer or had changed her number, I would be doomed. "C'mon, c'mon," I chanted under my breath as I held the phone tightly.

"Hello," Paulette breathed into the phone, as if she had been sleeping. A hot wave of relief washed over me and I exhaled.

"Hi, Paulette!" I said with fake excitement, my voice rising three octaves. I had never been so happy to hear her voice in my life. I didn't want to sound distraught just yet, but the feeling was definitely there.

"Who is this?" Paulette grumbled.

Shit, I had forgotten we hadn't spoken in so long that she might not have recognized my voice. I closed my eyes tightly.

"Oh goodness . . . it's Melody. Your sister," I sang, trying to sound as pleasant as possible. I really wanted to just melt from embarrassment. My own sister didn't recognize my voice because my dumb ass had not called her in so long.

"Who?" Paulette groaned.

"It's me, Melody, your big sister. You forgot me already?" I replied, anxiety lacing my words. I let out a short chuckle, although my voice was filled with uncertainty and anxiety.

"Yeah . . . ," Paulette said hesitantly.

"Look, Paulette, I know you haven't heard from me in a while—" I started.

She quickly cut me off. "A while? A while? Try almost ten years!" Paulette snapped. I could tell she had sat up in her bed. I could just imagine the scowl she was wearing on her face too.

I laughed nervously. "I know, right? It's been too long. I can explain when I see you. Listen, I don't have much time. Something has happened and I need your help," I rambled, the words slipping out like rushing water. I could hear Paulette sucking her teeth and blowing out air like she had sprung a leak.

"Please, Paulette. I wouldn't call if it wasn't an emergency," I pleaded, on the brink of tears.

"That's what I'm saying. You're only calling me because you need something. Same ol' Melody," Paulette snapped.

I could tell she was getting ready to hang up on my ass. "Wait! Please, Paulette. If you just come get me, I promise to explain everything. I promise to make it up to you, Paulette. Right now is not the time to bring up the past. I would do it for you. I swear I would. I'm sorry for everything, but now is not the time. . . . You're all I have," I croaked out between sobs. I just couldn't hold the tears back another minute. "I'm in jail. Please, Paulette." She was blowing out exasperated breaths and sucking her teeth while I pleaded my case. Then there was a long pause. I felt frantic inside.

"I'll think about it," Paulette said in a low voice. Then she hung up the phone. I broke down.

The officer who had been waiting for me grabbed my arm roughly. "That's it, Goldman. Let's go," he grumbled.

I dragged my feet slowly back to the holding cell, and for the first time in over ten years, all I could do was pray.

I had dozed off with my head up against the holding cell wall when I heard them calling my name. "Goldman! Goldman!" I jumped up like someone had thrown ice water in my face. I rushed over to the bars.

"Someone came and paid the fine. Lucky you," the officer droned as he pulled back the cell door.

I couldn't help but smile. I rushed behind him, ready to get the hell out of that horrendous place. When I stepped behind the large desk in the police station, I caught a glimpse of Paulette pacing in the lobby. I never thought she looked more beautiful. She had put on a few pounds since the last time I had seen her, but her smooth almond complexion and five-foot-six-inch curvy frame still made her a bombshell. Although she just had on a pair of jeans and a fitted wifebeater, she still looked like an angel in my eyes. I was so damn grateful to see her. She had not only paid my fine, but she'd waited for me as well. My heart melted at the thought of Paulette coming to my rescue after everything I had done. I felt awful too. I wondered if I would've done the same for her had things with Richard and I still been good.

When I was released, I rushed toward Paulette. She heard my heels clicking on the floor and whirled around. I smiled at her, but she didn't so much as crack a smile. Her face was stony and the look in her eye was downright evil.

"Thank you," I sang, extending my arms for a sisterly embrace. It was phony, but it was all I could offer right then.

Paulette threw her hands up, halting my request for a hug. "Melody, I'm really not in the mood for all of that. I mean, it's not like shit is all good between us," Paulette said dryly.

I knew that she was right. I dropped my arms. I understood just where she was coming from. I had really cut Paulette and my mother off right after I married Richard. Although I already had my own place when I met Richard, Paulette often visited me and I would still sometimes go by my mother's house when she wasn't feeling so evil. The more involved I got with Richard, the less I visited my mother and sister. After I finally confided in Richard how my mother treated me as a child, Richard had demanded that I just forget about them. He assured me that he was the only family I needed.

At first, I stayed in touch with Paulette as best I could. I would call once a month to check in on her. But Paulette was loyal to our mother, and she would tell her all of my business, so eventually I cut Paulette off as well. I kept tabs on her, though. I knew she had graduated from Norfolk State and that she was a registered nurse at Sentara Leigh Hospital. Sometimes I would go by the hospital and just peek at her. I loved my sister, but I couldn't get past the disdain for my mother, so I stayed away from Paulette too. Even though Paulette was always made to feel like she was the chosen daughter, and as kids she'd exercised her position as the chosen one, I still had love for her deep down inside.

We walked to Paulette's car with awkward silence between us. Paulette looked at me strangely when I stopped at the passenger side of her car. "What? You need a ride home too?" Paulette asked angrily, rolling her eyes.

"I don't even have a car right now and probably no home either," I rasped. My mouth was desert dry.

Paulette sucked her teeth and hit the key fob to let me into the car. I slumped into the passenger seat.

"So what! Your knight in shining armor, Mr. Big-Time Defense Attorney to the Stars, left your ass for dead?" Paulette asked, chuckling evilly.

I hung my head and swiped tears from my

cheeks. Her words stung. "You know, Paulette, I never meant to walk away from you. But you of all people should know that I couldn't take how Diane treated me. You were always her favorite. She called me names, beat me, made me go hungry, and when we got older, she would even lock me out of the house for spite. What was I supposed to do when I finally found an escape from her?" I replied.

Paulette was quiet. I could see her biting down into her lip, thinking about what I was saying. She knew I was right. She'd been there. She'd seen firsthand how my mother abused me. "You were there when she beat me so badly with that broomstick that she knocked out my front tooth, or did you forget about that? What about when she made me stand up for an entire night? I couldn't sit or lie down. C'mon, Paulette, you were there. When I finally found Richard, I felt like someone had saved me. He was demanding just like Diane, but in the beginning, he treated me like no other person ever had. You have to understand that," I said sternly. It was the truth. My mother was probably the reason it was so easy for me to give up everything for Richard. I just needed somebody, anybody, to love me.

"That shit between you and Mommy didn't have anything to do with me, Melody. After you got rich and moved into your big house, you forgot where you came from. You forgot you had a sister, until now. I guess it's a lucky thing that I'm not a selfish bitch like you or else you would've stayed in jail," Paulette gritted. She wasn't trying to hear my pleas. I couldn't blame her. I knew somewhere deep down inside she understood, though, and that was the reason she'd come to help me in the first place.

"I know. I'm so sorry," I said. I had to be humble, although I was burning up inside. Paulette had dredged up things I had worked hard for ten years to suppress. Paulette knew damn well why I left. It just wasn't the time to dwell on the past.

"Can I just stay with you tonight until I can sort out what I'm going to do next?" I asked, almost begging. She didn't answer, but she drove straight to her house. When we pulled up, I don't think I had ever been so grateful to see the Salem Lakes condominiums in my life.

4

"Oh, Richard, I know you're sorry, baby," I whispered through tears as Richard hugged me tightly. I pulled away from him and looked into his eyes. "I've missed you so bad. I just want you, baby. I just want to feel you inside of me. I want to love you forever," I said softly, leading Richard over to the bed. He didn't say a word. I knew he was sorry because he had tears in his eyes. I laid him down and began undressing him. His dick greeted me as I removed his boxers. It was so hard, so thick, so lovely. I took it in my hands and stroked it. I wanted it to fill me up. I wanted it to fill the void Richard had left in my heart. Richard closed his eyes and threw his head back. He relaxed onto the bed. Once all of his clothes were off, I climbed on top of him. I leaned over him and began kissing his neck, his face, and then I thrust my tongue down his throat. Richard was breathing hard and so was I. "I love you. I know you're sorry, Richard. I know you don't want Christina over me, baby," I said, panting. Richard kept his eyes closed. He wouldn't say anything. I just wanted him to say sorry. I wanted him to tell me he loved me. I slipped my hands under the pillow. "I'm going to give it to you now, baby," I whispered. Richard grunted.

"Look at me," I said softly. "Please, Richard, baby, look me in the eye," I cooed. He opened his eyes slowly. Richard's eyes went wide as tea saucers. I placed my hand over his mouth roughly. Richard was paralyzed with fear as he stared down the barrel of the shiny black 9mm Glock I had recently purchased just for the occasion.

"Did you think I would forgive you for what you did to me, you piece of shit?" I spat.

"Mmm," he moaned. I put my finger on the trigger and began to pull it back. Richard opened his mouth to scream. *BANG!*

"Huh, huh, huh." I jumped up out of my sleep, covered in sweat. I was shaking all over from the nightmare. It was always so real. I looked around the room frantically and touched myself just to make sure I was really awake and it was really a dream. I had been having the same dream night after night. It was a recurring nightmare—me killing Richard. Every time it was in a different way. I had to wonder if it was a recurring obsession in my subconscious. I flopped back onto the pillow when I realized where I was. Paulette had allowed me to take up residence in her guest room. After our initial dustup about the past, she and I had had a long talk. We had opened the floodgates of confessions and memories. Some good and some bad. We had made it a habit of sitting up at nights when she got home from work and exchanging stories about the past couple of years of our lives. We quickly buried the hatchet. It was easy without the influence of Diane, our hateful-ass mother. Paulette cried and so did I when we spoke about how Diane had all but tortured me as a kid. Paulette said she was just scared to make Diane mad at her; that's why she'd always done Diane's bidding and always treated me like shit.

Paulette was doing things to try and cheer me up, to take my mind off Richard. She even accompanied me to the bank, where I was devastated to find out that Richard had closed all of our accounts and cut off my monthly allowance. Paulette and I also weren't able to retrieve any of my belongings from my home when she'd driven me back there. That bastard Richard had actually had the doors padlocked and had put the house on the market. He did leave me a nice little envelope taped to the door. The note on the front said, "Melody, I knew you'd come, so I left this for you." Inside was the prenuptial agreement that I had signed way back when like a dumb bitch. When Paulette had asked me why I was stupid enough to sign a prenup, I had to admit I had been too head over heels in love to read carefully when Richard had urged me to sign it.

Paulette took me to see a friend of hers who was one of the best divorce attorneys in Virginia. The woman had raised her eyebrows as she looked over the paperwork. She sighed loudly and folded her hands on her desk gravely. "Melody, I'm sorry, but with your signature on this paperwork, you locked yourself out of everything once the divorce is finalized," the attorney had said. She continued to explain things, although I could no longer hear what she was saying. I left her office in a stupor. Paulette explained to me that basically, the papers summed up the fact that unless Richard suffered an untimely death while we were still married, I wouldn't get a fucking red cent. He would have to die while we were still legally married in order for me to get his assets and cash in on our joint insurance policy of three million dollars. After hearing the full explanation, my knees had buckled. Paulette had to help me get back into her car. She had tried in vain to comfort me all the way back to her condo. There was no use; I had cried and screamed and threw tantrums, but Paulette and I both concluded that there wasn't shit I could do—unless I was going to kill the motherfucker to collect the money.

"Mel?" I heard Paulette shout as she arrived home from work.

I had been lying in bed for yet another day, going through my bouts of sorrow, then anger, but never acceptance. I still could not believe Richard had done me so fucking dirty. He had portrayed himself as the perfect gentleman. Always refined and debonair. That motherfucker was no better than a two-bit street thug with the way he treated me.

"Mel? You up here?" Paulette called out again.

I wanted to hide under the covers and tell her to go away. I knew Paulette would just keep on, so I gave in. I got out of the bed and opened the door. "Yeah, I'm here. What's up?" I answered her, trying to hide the fact that I had just recently been crying.

"Girl, you better get it together and get out of this house before you go crazy," Paulette said with concern.

"I don't feel like even getting up to go to the bathroom, Paulie. For real, I am so devastated. Without you . . . I don't know . . . ," I started, with the waterworks not far behind. Paulette threw up her hand and cut me off. She wasn't trying to hear me with the pity party.

"We said we wasn't dwelling on no past bullshit, right? Then stop it," she chastised. "He is not the last man, nor the last dick on earth, Melody. You are a beautiful woman in the prime of her life. C'mon, I'm going out tonight and you are too," Paulette said demandingly. Then she let a warm smile spread across her face. "It has been ages since we went out together. C'mon, it'll be fun," she urged, giggling. She was just trying to get me out of my slump. I appreciated it, but I just couldn't imagine even washing my ass, much less going out around a bunch of strangers.

"I am not going out! What the hell am I supposed to wear?" I snapped. I thought it was cruel of her to even suggest we go out, since she knew all of my shit was gone.

"Your ass ain't above wearing your sister's clothes, Melody. What, you think I can't keep up with your style?" Paulette chided. I was quiet. She sucked her teeth. "You better follow me to my closet, then, girly. Shit, you think I don't have Gucci stilettos you can borrow?" Paulette said snidely.

I felt my cheeks flame over. She could tell I was thinking that she could never keep up with my style or my previous lifestyle. That was how I had become accustomed to thinking. That everyone else was beneath me. I felt awful.

"That's not what I meant, Paulette. I'm just depressed, that's all," I said apologetically.

"Well going out is the perfect cure for being depressed. You'll enjoy being out with people who live in reality . . . not like those hoity-toity bitches you're used to hanging with. Those bitches who have no life outside of what their husbands give them. I can picture y'all now sitting in a fucking bar, all decked out in Hervé Léger, Christian Louboutin, and turning y'all fucking noses up at every chick and every dude in the place. Grown-ass women with the mean girl's syndrome," Paulette rattled off cruelly.

I felt ashamed again. She was right on the money with her assessment. My so-called friends and I would go out, all dressed up, and not even dance. It was all about the fashion statement or just to see which one of us would repeat a dress or pair of shoes. Real superficial shit now that I think about it. It was all we had to do while our husbands were on travel, fucking their secretaries or, in my case, fucking their work partners.

"We danced sometimes," I lied, embarrassed because Paulette was absolutely right.

"Yeah, right, bitch!" Paulette quipped. She sucked her teeth. "Melody, you can tell that shit to somebody you can pay to believe it. Just c'mon and let's go pick out something to wear so we can hit the damn town," Paulette replied.

I followed her into her bedroom. I wanted to just hug her ass over and over again. She had no clue how grateful I was to have her at a time like this. If I ever came into some money again, Paulette was going to be the only person I took care of. She was also the only person I had left in the world.

When Paulette and I stepped into the club, I could feel all eyes on us. It was the effect of the outfits we had managed to put together. I had been pleasantly surprised by Paulette's closet. Her shit wasn't shabby at all. She had a lot of labels I once owned myself, and more impressive to me was the fact that she had bought them with her own hard-earned money. Paulette had chosen an orange and purple Hervé Léger minidress for me. When I put it on, the shit looked like it had been tailor made for me. I grabbed a pair of Jimmy Choos from her shoe wall to top the outfit off. Paulette wore a Lanvin silk dress with a plunging neckline and some Giancarlo Lorenzi pumps. The aqua-green color of her dress complemented her skin so well she seemed to glow. We were a pair of fine-ass sisters if I did say so myself. Once we were inside the club for a few minutes, Paulette finally spotted who she was looking for.

Paulette waved at her friend Trina who was meeting us here. We walked over to Trina, who was sitting at a lounge seat with a small table in front of it. Paulette and Trina hugged, and I just fell back. Paulette introduced us and I just cracked a fake halfhearted smile. I immediately got a bad vibe from Trina. Something about her didn't sit right with me. Maybe it was that she was dressed like a cheap hoochie and her wig was horrible. I shook off the bad thoughts about Trina. I was making a snap judgment, something I had also grown accustomed to doing since being married to Richard.

I think my immediate disdain for Trina had more to do with the fact that I was jealous that my sister was paying attention to someone else. The music in the club was hitting. It made me want to move my body, but I was so used to being a stuck-up snob whenever I went out, I just sat down and struck a pretty pose. As Paulette and Trina yapped on about nothing, I had a fleeting thought about Richard. It was like he just popped into my head. I locked my jaw and closed my eyes for a minute. Once again, I could see Richard lying dead, bleeding from his head. I popped my eyes open real quick. *Damn. Do I want his ass dead that bad?* I thought.

"Melody, what do you want to drink?" Paulette whined in my ear, breaking up my violent thoughts.

I shrugged.

"You're so damn boring!" Paulette chastised. She took the lead and ordered us our first round of drinks. Of course she was paying. I didn't have a fucking dime, and it made me feel a bit uncomfortable. I was carrying a damn Marc Jacobs clutch that belonged to my sister, and it didn't have one dollar in it. As the night wore on, I wanted to just scream. Being out had not helped me to get my situation off my mind. Plus, Trina was annoying to me. Her voice was high-pitched and ghetto. She smacked her lips a lot, and after a while I began downing drink after drink just to tune that bitch out. Trina was also loud, so we were attracting more attention than I thought was necessary.

There were lots of eyes on us. Even the eyes of the hood rat dudes I would never give the time of day. "I'll be right back," I told Paulette in an annoyed voice. When I stood up, I could feel myself swaying. I was feeling really good; the liquor coursing through my system had me feeling like I had no cares in the world. I stumbled into the bathroom. Inside, I looked at myself and smiled evilly. If Richard could see me now, moving on, having fun—totally different from the conservative boring trophy wife he had cultivated. After a few minutes, my face changed. Who the fuck was I kidding? I wasn't happy. Standing here in my sister's borrowed clothes. No fucking money in my pocketbook. No clue on what my next move would be for my life. At thirty-five years old, was I going to go back to school and try to build my own life? Probably not. Shit, how was I going to pay for law school now? I guess I could start over as a paralegal . . . but once I said I haven't worked in ten years, what would a potential employer think? These thoughts had me boiling inside. I balled my hands into fists and clenched my jaw. My chest rose and fell with anger. "You will pay, you fucker!" I gritted under my breath. My head was swaying with anger and liquor.

I rushed out of the bathroom, still wobbly as hell. I just wanted to go home now. I couldn't stand being out anymore with all of the recurring thoughts about Richard. "Ugh!" I grunted as I ran headfirst into someone. I hit the person so hard I almost fell. "Oh my God! I'm so sorry!" I slurred. I put my hand over my mouth. I had run into a guy and spilled his drink all over his crisp white shirt.

"It's a'ight, Ma," the guy said smoothly as he simply brushed his shirt off.

"I can't believe I ruined your shirt," I said apologetically. I wanted to reach out and try to clean it, but I thought better of that idea.

"No worries . . . there are more where this came from, baby girl," the guy assured me, his deep voice making me want to take a good look at him. When I finally scanned his face, I felt slightly flush. *Damn!* I thought. He was fine in a rugged thug type of way. I was immediately aware that I was blushing like hell. He was the complete opposite of Richard, which may have been why I felt an instant attraction to him.

Richard was a gentleman for the most part, but this guy was definitely, in my assessment, a gangsta.

"I'm Scotty. All my friends call me Lil Man," the guy said, extending his hand for a shake.

I batted my eyelashes and exhaled. Damn. He was so fucking attractive.

"I'm Melody. My friends call me Melody," I said, chuckling at my own joke.

Scotty smiled and we both laughed. I took in all of his features. Scotty stood at least six feet tall, and he sported a low Cesar haircut. I could see that he had tattoos covering most of his arms like sleeves and some coming up out of his shirt on his chest and neck. The thing that stuck out the most were the deep dimples in both of his cheeks. I guess those beautiful dimples stuck out because they were so cute while everything else on Scotty was so fucking gangsta.

"Well, since you spilled my drink all over me, come to the bar and let me replace my drink and get you one," Scotty replied, placing his hand on the small of my back.

It was a bold move. It also made me even more attracted to him. A man who could take charge was right up my alley right then. His touch seemed electric. I smiled and followed his lead. His walk was so rugged. Scotty was like the gangsta I would never usually have an attraction to, but right away I was smitten with him. As we slid onto the bar stools, I watched Scotty order our drinks. His slang and swagger all pointed to "bad boy." I smiled wickedly as something evil crossed my mind. I was thinking Scotty was just the kind of dude I need to fucking send Richard to hell where he belonged.

"So what's a sophisticated lady like you doing in a club out here?" Scotty turned to me and asked. "You definitely ain't like most of these clucking-ass broads up in here."

"I'm hanging out with my sister," I answered, nodding toward Paulette and Trina.

Scotty laughed. "You know Trina? Damn, you don't look like you'd be friends with that ho," Scotty said directly.

I almost choked on my drink. He had just said what I had been thinking all night about that ugly chick.

"Correction. My sister knows Trina," I quickly added.

"So, wassup? You got a man?" Scotty asked, getting right to the point.

I liked that. He was a no-holds-barred type of guy.

"Nope. Almost divorced," I said, feeling the anger well up inside of me just thinking of Richard and the word *divorce.* I knew that was the next trick up Richard's sleeve; I just didn't know how soon he was going to try that bullshit.

"Awww, sorry to hear that," Scotty replied.

I chuckled. I could feel the liquor completely taking hold of me. I jumped off my bar stool and moved real close to Scotty. So out of character for me. I was tapping into my inner bad girl. I put my face close to his seductively. "There is nothing to be sorry about. My husband is a piece of shit and so is the bitch he left me for," I whispered. Then I kissed Scotty on the side of his face, dangerously close to his mouth. I was teasing him. I was completely out of character and loving it. Maybe this is who I really was deep down inside. The person I had suppressed just to satisfy Richard.

Scotty huffed seductively. "Mmmm, I like that," he said, placing his hand on my ass in a bold move. I didn't protest one bit.

"Good. Because I think I want to keep you around. I hope Lil Man is just a nickname and they don't call you that for a reason," I said, grabbing a handful of his dick through his pants.

Scotty didn't even flinch. "Nah, Ma, Lil Man is the name I got from being in the game since I was ten. Niggas on the street couldn't believe how much of a man I was since I was so little. I was regulating niggas twice my size, and I was kind of ruthless. I didn't have shit to lose back then. In my hood, I was the fucking man. So they started calling me Lil Man. Trust me, baby, my other man ain't little at all," Scotty said, grabbing his dick for emphasis.

We did the mating dance for another twenty minutes. He was touching me inappropriately, and I returned the favor. I was whispering all types of reckless shit in his ears, and he was offering to fuck me right there on the bar. It was a lot of fun. Scotty seemed more and more like somebody I needed to have around . . . just in case. I had three more drinks and told Scotty all about Richard. He said he was twenty-seven years old and had grown up on the streets of Park Place. He told me how he was no stranger to violence and a quick hustle. In my mind I thought all of those factors were perfect. With the liquor completely taking over all of my senses, I took Scotty's phone number and promised to call him. I was thinking devious things, some of which had to do with letting Scotty fuck the shit out of me, others having to do with Scotty helping me collect on the debt owed to me.

Paulette and Trina came rushing over once they saw me and Scotty all cozy at the bar. Paulette grabbed my arm and pulled me aside. "Melody! How are you fucking sitting between some stranger's legs, kissing all over him? You don't even know him," she whispered harshly.

I was feeling too good to let her break it up. I just laughed at her. "Stop being so snobbish. Remember you were the one who told me to loosen up . . . so I did. Now come let me introduce you to my new friend, Lil Man," I slurred, snickering like a schoolgirl.

I introduced Paulette and Scotty, and instantly I could see the tension between them. Paulette rolled her eyes and barely extended her hand. Scotty chuckled at Paulette and looked at me as if to say *What's up with this bitch?* Paulette stomped away and told me she would be waiting for me outside. I looked at Scotty; he didn't even seem fazed by my sister's rude display.

I giggled; of course, that was the liquor.

"You coming home with me or going with the evil sister?" Scotty asked me boldly. I couldn't let him take that much control. Tipsy or not, I was still thinking, plotting, planning, little did he know.

"No, I'm not going with you, bad boy. I have to honor my sister. But you can give me your number and we can see each other again," I told him.

"Let me put my shit in your cell," Scotty replied.

"No . . . just write it down the old-fashioned way," I demanded. I wasn't trying to give him my phone number. Something told me that Scotty was going to be the perfect loser to have in my corner. He puffed out a breath of aggravated air, but he wrote his number down anyway. I kissed a little white napkin and left my lip prints on it. I stuffed it down the front of Scotty's pants. "Maybe next time it will be my real lips down there," I said seductively. Then I sauntered away, switching my ass for good measure. I definitely would be calling Scotty very soon. The way I saw it, there was no reason for Scotty to have my number if I would be using him to do my dirty work. That would be too risky. Too much evidence would be out there for the taking. Shit, I wasn't that drunk.

When I approached Paulette, she looked like she was steaming mad. I just kept a lazy, alcohol-induced grin on my face.

"What was that all about, Melody?" Paulette gritted as we got into her car.

"It was about moving on, getting redemption, and claiming what is mine," I said seriously. I was tired of Paulette asking me so many questions.

"That dude is no good. Trina told me he is a two-time loser who has done some serious time in prison. She said he has no regard for anybody and walks around with an I-don't-give-a-fuck attitude," Paulette relayed.

I rolled my eyes.

"Is that how you want to move on? A rebound with an even worse loser?" Paulette asked, her tone serious and motherly.

"Yeah, I bet Trina is just jealous because Scotty knew that bitch was a big-time ho," I shot back.

"Ho or not, she knows that you are treading on dangerous ground fucking around with a nigga like that. The last thing Trina said to me was that Scotty or Lil Man or whatever he calls himself will shoot his own mother over a dollar," Paulette warned.

Perfect. Just what I want, I screamed inside my head. I remained silent. I could feel Paulette looking over at me.

"You better be careful . . . that's all," Paulette said with finality.

I closed my eyes to tune her out. No, Richard better be careful, I was thinking.

5

"Damn, baby, you look so fucking good. You got my shit on rock," Scotty whispered as I pranced in front of him, removing my clothes stripper-style. I licked my lips seductively and pinched my bare nipples. He couldn't take his eyes off of me.

"Ssss," he hissed as he grabbed a handful of his rock-hard dick through his pants. "That shit is getting me right. Play with your pussy now," he grunted.

I turned around, spread my now-bare ass cheeks, and teased Scotty by putting two fingers inside of me.

"You want this?" I whispered, slowly taking my fingers out so he could see how moist they were.

"Whatchu think?" he answered, panting now.

I could see sweat glistening on his forehead.

"What you gonna do for me if I give you this?" I asked, turning so he could see my newly shaved pussy clear as day.

"Anything. Shit, anything you want," he

groaned. He was moving his hand up and down on the large lump in his pants.

I walked over to him, straddled him, and began grinding my pussy on his dick. "Wait, let me take it out," he whispered. "I want to feel your shit skin to skin."

I laughed. I had Scotty almost begging for it now. I met him eye to eye, opened my mouth, and began tonguing him down. I pushed him down on the bed roughly, then moved off of him. He opened his eyes wide. I wrestled with his belt buckle and a smile eased across his face.

"Damn, I love a woman who can take charge," he moaned.

I had Scotty completely naked within a few minutes. The session was for both of us. I hadn't had good dick in a long time, so Scotty would be satisfying my craving, and at the same time I was spinning my web and casting my spell over him. I grabbed his swollen dick roughly and yanked it. Then, with a big smile spread across my face, I took all of him deep into my mouth.

"Shit!" he hissed. I bobbed up and down on his dick, spitting on it and taking it so deep I gagged on the head. Scotty was breathing hard. That excited me, so I started pulling my jaws in around his dick harder and harder. I grabbed a handful of his balls and massaged them. He was making a weird noise, so I knew he was close to coming. I moved my mouth from his dick abruptly. "Why you stopping?" he groaned.

"You can't come just yet," I said teasingly. I retrieved a condom from his little nightstand. I rolled it over his throbbing dick. I looked down into his face as I lifted one of my titties, extended my long tongue, and licked the tip of my areola.

"Goddamn, you are sexy as fuck!" Scotty growled, sounding almost beastly. He jumped off the bed and grabbed me roughly. He pushed me down onto the mattress and climbed between my legs. I closed my eyes as he ran his dick up and down my pussy, over my clit and then near my pussy hole.

"Don't fucking tease me. Give me that shit," I hissed. I was definitely a new person. No more conservative housewife. Granted, I had had a few drinks, but I was also motivated by something far greater. "Ahhh," I moaned as Scotty buried his dick deep inside of me. "Agh!" I screamed as he picked up speed and began pounding into my pelvis. His dick was so big I could feel that shit up against my cervix. He was grunting like an animal as he banged at a feverish pace.

"Your shit is tight as hell!" Scotty growled into the space behind my ear. He was sweating and grunting. Nothing like making love to Richard, which had become very dry and boring in recent years.

"Turn over!" Scotty barked, pulling his dick out and flipping me onto my stomach. He urged me onto my knees. He rammed his dick into me doggy-style. Our skin slapping together was like music to my ears. I let out a loud gasp and then a scream. Scotty grabbed on to my hips and grinded me from the back. He leaned onto my ass and back and put his hand around the front of me while he fucked me like crazy.

He started rubbing my clitoris vigorously. "That's gonna make me come," I whispered. That shit felt so good. The pressure from the back, plus the clitoral stimulation was more than I could bear. "Aggh!" I belted out as I had the hardest orgasm I'd ever experienced in my life.

"I can't take that shit, Ma," Scotty groaned, and then he called out in ecstasy too. I had drained his dick. He had also drained me. We both collapsed onto the bed, soaked in sweat. I was still panting. Scotty reached out and grabbed me close to him. "Yo, that is some of the best pussy I've ever had. I can't let you get away from me," he confessed, still trying to catch his breath.

I chuckled. I had broken through that bad-boy persona. I knew pussy would do it.

"You thought having an older woman was going to be all missionary style? Us older ones have much more experience," I told him.

"I can't believe your husband was stupid enough to fuck around on you, yo," Scotty said.

I so loved his slang. I also loved the fact that he had brought up the topic.

"I gave up everything for him. A job, my own place, my schooling. I worked long hard hours helping him build up his law firm, and that was all I got in return—fucked," I said sorrowfully. This was my chance. I had to get Scotty on my side.

"Damn, I ain't never had no chick do shit for me. Including my own moms," Scotty confessed.

"Aww, baby, I'm sorry you had a rough life. I would do anything for you. We can do everything for each other. One hand washes the other, you know," I said, kissing his chest.

"I would do anything for you, too, Ma," Scotty answered. Then he squeezed me tightly and got ready to fuck the shit out of me again. That was just what I wanted to hear, but I wasn't going to say anything to him just yet about the plan I had come up with. In due time. I was still in the gaining-trust stage with Scotty. A few more encounters with me and I felt like I could have him eating out of the palm of my hand.

After I began seeing Scotty on a regular basis, things at the condo changed. It was a constant battle with Paulette and me. Paulette was acting just like our mother with all of her complaining and ranting and raving. She hated Scotty, and every chance she got, she let me know. She absolutely hated for me to have him in her house too. Paulette had told me on more than one occasion that she didn't get good vibes from Scotty. I felt like a teenager being chastised for her choice in a boyfriend. I even slammed the guest bedroom door on Paulette a few times while she shouted at me. I had to admit, I was really acting like a teenager in love. I would sneak Scotty in late at night when Paulette was asleep and let him leave before she got up for work. Paulette was often annoyed with how I dressed. All of the new clothes I had purchased with money borrowed from her were definitely out of the norm from my usual style. Paulette would just roll her eyes and suck her teeth. She was also fed up with what time I came in the house and with me seeing Scotty in general. I didn't care one bit. I knew she wasn't going to throw me out. Besides, I couldn't tell her that seeing Scotty was a means to an end. I wasn't going to involve Paulette in my plans. I figured if she didn't know anything, she would be truly innocent if things went awry. The less she knew, the better.

A few times while I was seeing Scotty, he'd driven me around his neighborhood. When he said he'd grown up on the rough side of Tidewater, I'd thought, *How bad could it be?* It was horrible. I watched crack addicts and drug dealers mingle outside like it was all right. Scotty told me he was "collecting his money" whenever he jumped out of his truck and ran up on some of the little boys standing in huddles outside of rundown houses. I knew immediately that meant he was a drug dealer. Damn. I had really gone from a gentleman to a gangsta. Exciting! But equally dangerous. One time I watched Scotty beat a guy almost to death right in front of everyone who was outside. I couldn't even speak to Scotty when he'd gotten back in his truck. He was dripping with sweat, and his eyes were flashing with fire. That had solidified it for me. Scotty was the type of guy I needed in my corner. *Ruthless* was an understatement when it came to describing Scotty—or Lil Man as he liked to be called on the streets. I was sold. Scotty was going to be my personal hit man.

* * *

I was preparing to meet Scotty the day that my divorce papers were served on me. Richard had figured out that I was staying at Paulette's house. He'd probably had someone following me or something crazy like that. When the process server rang the bell, I came to the door wearing a big smile thinking it was Scotty. My facial expression quickly turned dark when I saw who was standing at the door.

"Mrs. Melody Goldman?" a short, fat white man asked. He was sweating profusely and held a bunch of papers under his fat arm and some in his hands.

"Yes," I said apprehensively, crinkling my eyebrows in confusion. He moved closer to me.

I shrank away from all the nasty sweat dripping from his body.

"Okay, good. Here you go," he wheezed, shoving the stack from his hands into my face. I looked at him, bewildered. Before I could read the paperwork, he puffed out, "You have been served." Then he dropped the clipped stack of papers into my hands. As fat as he was, he got away from me fast as hell. Then he was gone in a flash.

"What the fuck?" I snapped at his back. He had run down the steps so fast that he'd made it to his car before I could even really get the words all the way out. I read the top of the papers: *Petition for divorce.* Then I saw *Richard Goldman, Petitioner.* I felt like someone had stabbed me in the heart. "Motherfucker," I grumbled. I stumbled backward a few steps. My legs felt lead heavy, and my heart was hammering a mile a minute. I knew it was coming, but I don't think I could've ever prepared myself for the reality slap of seeing it in black and white. I could feel angry tears welling up in the backs of my eyes. Just as I made it back across the door threshold, I heard a voice.

"Hey, baby! What's good?" Scotty sang out from behind me. I turned around slowly, still holding the papers in my trembling hands. When Scotty saw my face, he looked at me strangely.

"What's up, Ma? Who fuckin' with you?" he asked sternly, taking in the look of horror I was wearing like a mask. He grabbed the papers out of my hand. "What's this? Is it this that got you looking all fucked up?" he asked as he examined the stack.

I looked at him with tears welling up in my eyes. "That motherfucker filed for divorce already. It hasn't even been two months since he fucking left me high and dry. Now this. He is trying to do it as fast as possible because once the divorce happens, I won't get anything. Nothing for all of the years I put in. Not a fucking dime!" I roared. Scotty closed the door behind us. I flopped down on the couch, exasperated. He sat next to me and put his arm around my shoulders.

"Scotty, unless Richard dies before our divorce is final, I won't get anything. Can you believe he would be worth three million dollars to me if he was dead, but if he lives and marries that bitch, I will die poor?"

"Damn, that's real tempting. Shit, off a nigga and get three mil? You good, Melody. I would have that nigga on ice fast as lightning," Scotty replied, letting out a funny, nervous laugh.

I looked up at him, my eyes still watery. "You serious?" I whispered.

"Huh?" Scotty asked, his eyebrow furrowed. He moved his arm from around me like I had suddenly transformed into a poisonous snake.

"I mean, are you serious about it? We could work together, Scotty. You have the street resources to do something like that, and I would make sure you got your money afterward. We could be together forever after shit dies down too. I can't die broke. He left me with absolutely nothing. I told you I can't keep living with Paulette," I said pleadingly.

Scotty stood up. His hands were out in front of him like he was surrendering. He was shaking his head. "Whoa . . . you a cop or some shit?" he asked, leery. He looked scared.

I had to think fast to put him at ease. I needed him now more than ever.

"Would a cop be fucking you on a regular basis? Would a cop be holding divorce papers from a piece of shit who tried to ruin her? C'mon, Scotty. This is the only way we can get the money. I can't be anywhere near it when it happens or nobody wins. It can be like a car accident, something that won't bring any suspicion," I told him. My words were coming out rapid-fire. I was desperate to convince Scotty. It was my only chance. Scotty seemed to relax a bit. He was rubbing his chin. I could tell he was contemplating it.

"You dead-ass serious, ain't you?" Scotty asked, sitting back down on the couch.

"I am the sole beneficiary on a three-million-dollar insurance policy. I am as serious as fucking cancer," I said sternly. "I am willing to give you one million," I said, looking Scotty directly in the eye so he knew I was serious and sincere.

His eyes lit up like a Christmas tree. "Well, fuck, let's do it then," Scotty exclaimed, clapping his hands. "Shit, I done mirked niggas for far less cake than a mil," Scotty told me.

I smiled. All of my hard work in recruiting his ass had paid off. Scotty was down for the plan, and I didn't even have to badger him into it. I immediately started explaining to him some of the ways it could go down without drawing suspicion. We hashed out our plan, and we even came up with a plan B just in case. I explained to Scotty that he would have to lie low and stay away from me for a while after he took care of Richard. I told him that if anything happened to Richard, the first person the police would come see was me. It was just the natural order of things; spouses were always the first suspects. Scotty said he understood, after he fucked my brains out right there in Paulette's living room.

I had to bring the insurance paperwork down from the guest room and show Scotty that I meant business. It was a good thing I had been able to call National Benefit Life and get a copy of the policy a couple of weeks prior. Scotty was a full believer after he reviewed the paperwork and saw that I was indeed the sole beneficiary on the three-million-dollar policy. I had him on my side. Now all I had to do was trust that soon, Richard and his bitch, Christina, would no longer be a problem.

6

I couldn't sleep for the three days that I hadn't heard back from Scotty. All types of things ran through my head. First, I thought he might've gone to the police and snitched on me. I quickly dismissed that idea when I remembered that Scotty despised the police. Next, I thought Richard might've figured shit out or that he was out of town and couldn't be found to carry out the plan. Lastly, I thought Scotty just had a change of heart and I would never hear from him again. After the fourth day of no contact, I finally got the news.

Paulette's house phone rang and I didn't answer it. Generally, I didn't make a practice of answering her phone just in case our mother called. I had no desire to speak to that bitch. But the calls continued to come so frequently that I grew suspicious and finally walked over to the base and looked at the caller ID. It was Paulette calling. I picked up.

"Melody!" Paulette screeched on the other end of the line.

Her shrieking voice sent a pang of fear through my body. "Paulie, what's the matter?" I huffed, not realizing I had placed my hand over my heart.

"It's Richard! I was in the ER and they just brought him in. Melody, I don't think he's going to make it," Paulette told me. She wasn't crying, but she was frantic.

"What do you mean? What happened?" I gasped, feigning concern and shock.

"He was in a horrible accident. They said a woman was in the car with him. They both might not make it," Paulette relayed.

An evil smile spread across my face. I could just fucking kiss Scotty if he was in front of me. He had followed the plan.

"Oh my God! I can't believe this," I replied, still acting as if I were in shock. I started to whimper like I was crying. Paulette would have no way of knowing they were tears of joy.

"I think you're his only next of kin since you're still legally his wife. I know Richard did some dirty deeds, Melody, but I think you should come down here right away. The situation is pretty bad, and these doctors are going to be looking for someone to talk to very soon," Paulette said gravely.

"I'll be there. Like you said, I am his next of kin," I said in a low whisper. Hell yeah I was going there. I wanted to be the first to get the news of Richard's demise, which meant I was about to come into some huge cash flow. I had dollar signs flashing in my eyes as I quickly slipped into my clothes. Paulette had been leaving me her car and carpooling to the hospital for work, which was a good thing. My hands were shaking like crazy. It was one part excitement and one part fear. I just needed everything to go smoothly and I would be a rich woman very soon.

When I arrived at Sentara Leigh Hospital by taxi, I have to admit I could no longer control the tremors that had taken over my entire body. I had to even suck in my bottom lip to keep my teeth from chattering. I guess the shakes were good; it made for a better show as the distressed wife.

Paulette greeted me with a tight hug and a low whisper: "I'm so sorry. I'm here for you." She ushered me to a waiting area. She hugged me tightly for the second time and told me she was going to get the doctor to come in and talk to me. Paulette returned with the doctor who'd treated Richard.

"Mrs. Goldman, I am Dr. Ruskin," he said, extending his hand. I was impressed that he was a tall, handsome, black doctor. I gave him one of my sweaty palms and dabbed at my eyes with the other hand. He exhaled and lowered his eyes. "I'm very sorry, Mrs. Goldman. Your husband did not make it. His internal injuries were too grave, and it didn't make sense to operate," Dr. Ruskin said sorrowfully. I put my hand over my mouth and stumbled backward. It was an Academy Award–worthy performance if I do say so myself. Paulette helped me ease into a chair.

"Shhh," Paulette comforted, and I sobbed. I had to cover my eyes with the tissue to hide the fact that there were no real tears coming out.

"I know this is very hard," the doctor said, placing a soothing hand on my shoulder.

"Are there any details of how this happened?" I asked, muffling my voice and face behind the tissues. I wanted to know how Scotty had pulled it off.

"Well, the police are conducting an investigation. Your husband and what appeared to be his colleague were traveling together. The police can probably tell you better than I can exactly what happened out there," Dr. Ruskin explained, squeezing my shoulder. I swear, if I wasn't doing such a good acting job, I would've smiled. Dr. Ruskin excused himself, saying he had to make some notifications and speak to the "other" family. Christina Cox's family had arrived at the hospital right after me. I couldn't feel sorry for their home-wrecking daughter. Fuck her and her family.

Paulette offered to leave work early and drive me home. I thought it was best that she did too. It just made it all more believable. I figured if anyone ever came questioning me, Paulette would be able to say I was at her home when the accident happened. She would be able to testify about how distraught I was to find out the news, and she would also be able to say she'd stayed with me the entire night after I got the news of Richard's death. I leaned on Paulette as if I were unable to walk. She helped me to the car, all the while comforting me. A few of her nurse friends came up to us and offered their condolences. I croaked out "thank you" and "that's very kind of you" a few times. Inside, I couldn't wait to get to the fucking car. Enough was enough. Shit, I wanted to be in private so I could fucking celebrate all alone!

"Isn't it just crazy how things happen, Mel? I mean, Richard did you so wrong the past few months. He tried to leave you penniless, cheated on you, just left you for dead. Look how God can turn the tables. Who would think that he would be the one left for dead for real with the same woman he did you wrong with. It's like karma just wrapped itself around his ass and that was it. So tragic," Paulette said once we got into her car.

She was so right. Things always had a way of working themselves out.

"It is crazy. But I am a firm believer in what goes around comes around," I said with no tears and no remorse. I had done a complete 360 from the crying, sniveling wife. I knew my words sounded harsh and angry, but I just didn't care anymore. Paulette shot me a look. I could see her out of my peripheral vision, but I just stared straight ahead. I wasn't going to pretend that I was mourning anymore.

As soon as we pulled into the parking lot of Paulette's condo, my heart felt like it had seized in my chest. Scotty was standing outside, pacing nervously. This motherfucker just looked guilty. I got cold inside as feelings of dread mixed with anger filled me up. *What the fuck is he thinking?* I screamed inside my head. I could only hope at that point that Scotty wouldn't be dumb enough to say shit in front of Paulette. Paulette got out of the car first. I opened the passenger side door slowly. Paulette was all over it within minutes. She hated Scotty; we all knew this. Seeing him there at a time like this sent her over the top. She stalked over to where Scotty was standing.

"Look, my sister just found out that her husband is dead. She's not up for no ghetto trash today, so visit her another time! Or better yet, get the fuck out of her life for good and let her heal properly!" Paulette yelled at Scotty, jutting her pointer finger at him like a mother chastising a child.

I saw the look on his face turn dark, evil even. I had to intervene before Scotty said something we would both regret. I rushed over to them and got in between them.

"It's okay, Paulette. Really, I'm fine. You . . . you go inside and let me just explain everything to Scotty," I stammered. My nerves were standing on edge. I gave Scotty a look that said, *Keep your fucking mouth shut.* He laughed at Paulette. Then he screwed his face up and spit on the ground next to where she was standing. He just barely missed spitting on her hospital clogs.

"I think your sister is a big girl. Let her tell me she don't wanna see me. You should mind your own business. . . . Oh wait, you ain't got no man, so you don't have no business," Scotty said cruelly.

Paulette pursed her lips and was ready to go in on him. I pushed her along.

"Really, Paulette, I got this. Go inside. I'll only

be a minute." She rolled her eyes and reluctantly began walking away.

"Fucking loser," Paulette grumbled as she turned and headed inside.

I stormed over to Scotty. "What are you doing here so soon?" I hissed, looking around suspiciously. All of the street smarts in the world couldn't explain his dumb-ass behavior right then.

He squinted his eyes into dashes and got real close to me for emphasis. "I just wanna make sure you know I kept my part of the deal. I'ma give you until next week to tell me when the insurance company gonna pay out and when I'ma get my loot," Scotty whispered, holding on to my arm roughly.

I could smell that he had been drinking and smoking weed as the scent of his breath shot up my nose and straight to the back of my throat.

"I'm going to keep up my part of the deal. Now, you need to be fucking smart and lie low, stay away from here. Trust me, the cops will be coming to see me today or tomorrow. We can discuss the details later when the heat of everything dies down. I will come find you, trust me," I growled.

I saw a few people walking down the street. They were Paulette's nosy-ass neighbors. I had to think quickly on my feet. I leaned into Scotty's chest and acted as if I were crying. I wanted to make sure that if those neighbors were watching, they got a good show. They would only be able to tell the cops that in the days after Richard's untimely death, they had observed me being nothing but torn up. Besides, I was still the distraught widow who had just found out her husband was dead.

Scotty let me play my role. Then he embraced me and squeezed me tight. "Don't fucking play any games. I am not the one to be fucked with, Melody," he gritted in my ear. I nodded. "Take this phone and make sure you stay in contact with me. If I don't hear from you soon, I will be back," he whispered harshly, placing a small prepaid cell phone into the back pocket of my jeans. My heart was racing painfully against my chest. I was starting to think maybe Scotty was too much of a gangsta to get into business with.

The days after Richard's death were like a media whirlwind. The newspapers were reporting headlines such as ATTORNEY TO THE STARS KILLED IN CRASH, and ATTORNEY AND HIS ALLEGED MISTRESS DEAD IN HORRIBLE CAR CRASH, and the best one of all, FAMED CRIMINAL DEFENSE ATTORNEY AND HIS LOVER MAY HAVE SUFFERED A KARMIC FATE. I had been keeping up with all of the news reports while I set about planning Richard's memorial service. Some were saying that Richard's death might've been foul play, but thankfully, none of them had named me as a potential suspect. Also, thankfully, I had put in my claim in the insurance company before all of this shit broke in the news.

Just like I expected, the homicide police detectives came knocking. I wasn't shocked to see them; in fact, I had been practicing my spiel, my behavior, and my instant ability to cry. There were two detectives, one male and one female. I instantly didn't like the female. I didn't like her tone or the way she kept looking at me like I was guilty. They asked me a slew of questions, all of which had to do with my whereabouts on the day that Richard and Christina crashed.

Once they were convinced that I had an alibi, they started asking questions about the recent goings-on between myself and Richard. The female detective seemed to key in during this line of questioning. Her tone was plain and simply accusatory. I had the jilted, cheated-on wife syndrome down pat. I used my ability to cry on cue as I told them the story. I played the distraught role very well. From what I could tell, the male detective didn't seem suspicious, but the female still gave me the chills. She just wouldn't let the fuck up. I wasn't going to let her break me, though. I kept up my act. The male detective, who seemed to feel sorry for me, did finally tell me that the brakes on Richard's Jaguar might have been cut. He also said that Richard's female companion, who I knew was Christina, had apparently suffered a gunshot wound to the head prior to the accident. The detective threw it out there that they were looking into a possible murder-suicide theory. The word *suicide* made my heart rate speed up. Suicide would mean no insurance payout. The detectives kept talking, but those little pieces of information they had given me had made my stomach cramp. I was finding it hard to keep my cool, but surprisingly enough, I did.

"Who would do something like that?" I asked, feigned shock lacing my words. I shook my head and acted as if I were searching the recesses of my mind to help them. "I didn't know my husband to have many enemies," I informed them. The detectives asked me if I thought any of the "thuggish" rappers Richard represented would want to hurt him. It felt like a lightbulb went off above my head like in the cartoons. That was a great road of suspicion to send them down. How stupid could they be? I took their suspicion and fucking ran with it.

"Well, I do remember this guy, a rapper named Hard Rock, arguing with Richard because he hadn't beat his last aggravated assault and gun charges. Richard had seemed very stressed out after dealing with that guy. I remember feeling that our safety might be in jeopardy as well. Richard told me that guy was a pathological liar and he was dangerous," I lied, adding shit to the story that I knew they could never verify. "You don't think he . . . ?" I asked, widening my eyes and placing my hand on my chest in a clutch-the-pearls manner. "Do you think Hard Rock would have done something to Richard? I mean, they told me he died in an accident," I said. I covered my face and began to cry again.

"We're sorry for dredging up these feelings, Mrs. Goldman. We are just trying to make sure we do our best to rule out everything," the male detective said apologetically.

"Everything is a possibility. All we know is that your husband's death might have been foul play. It doesn't seem to us to be a regular car accident," the female chimed in dryly, understating the circumstances. She acted like she wasn't buying my behavior or my story. If it wouldn't have blown my act, I would've cursed that bitch out. "Mr. Goldman didn't stand a chance in that car," the female followed up. She clapped her memo pad shut and rolled her eyes. "We'll be in touch," she said, standing up like she had run out of patience.

The male detective followed her lead. My insides were churning from nerves.

"Um . . . please keep me abreast of the developments," I said in a shaky voice. A fine sheen of sweat broke out on my forehead and some rolled down my back. I guess every plan had a snafu. I just prayed that this little investigation wouldn't hold up my insurance check. Now it was all about waiting for them to deliver the money.

7

I was leaving Paulette's condo to attend Richard's memorial service when Scotty ran up on me again. He scared the shit out of me, and I almost shit my pants. I had never seen him lurking. He grabbed me from behind like he was hugging his long-lost girlfriend. "My baby. Just the beautiful woman I was looking for," he chimed.

I wrestled away from him, whirled around, and looked at him like he had lost his fucking mind. I was too shocked to even get my words out right away.

"What's up, Melody? Or Mrs. Goldman, the grieving widow," Scotty said, smiling snidely as he grabbed on to the back of my arm. I looked at him evilly and wrestled my arm away from him. If he only knew I was wishing the devil's fucking wrath on his ass right about then.

"Stop fucking touching me, Scotty! What are you doing here right now?" I growled, unable to make my eyes go from round as marbles to their regular almond shape. "Get out of here before my sister comes outside," I hissed, looking around nervously.

"Nah, you got the situation fucked up. Why haven't you been answering my calls to the phone I gave you? Seems to me like you tryna avoid a nigga. I did the deed. Now it's time to pay up," Scotty responded roughly.

He was seriously blowing my mind. How fucking hungry can you get? I rolled my eyes. "Look, I've been busy planning this funeral and trying to get the check from the insurance company. Why are you being so paranoid, Scotty? I mean, you are putting us both out there. You being here right now is going to blow the whole shit out of the water. Why can't you just relax and wait?" I said gruffly.

Scotty's facial expression was stoic. I swear, it was like I was speaking to a two-year-old who couldn't understand English. He let out a maniacal laugh. My heart was racing so fast I felt light-headed. I could see now that I had fucked around with the wrong gangsta for sure. That was my greed.

"See, the way I figure it is you was using a nigga and now you finished wit' me. For real, for real, I think you had this shit mapped out from day fucking one in the club. Spilling your drink on me, flirting and fuckin' me like you did. What was that all about? Roping a nigga in, huh?" Scotty snapped, his lips bunched into a pucker.

I swallowed hard and shifted my weight from one foot to the other. He was reading my card. There was no way I could risk him going against me. He was already a loser used to prison; I don't think I would look good in the prison clothes bunking with an inmate named Big Martha.

"That's ridiculous. Now is not the fucking time to discuss your feelings about me not returning your goddamn phone calls, Scotty. You coming around here is not good. Now get the fuck out of here before you bring unwanted attention to us," I growled, standing my ground. Showing any signs of weakness to a street dude like Scotty was a big no-no—even I knew that.

"Nah, you can't get rid of me that easily, baby girl. I'ma be at your husband's funeral. I'ma be right there when that undertaker calls you in the office to sign off on them papers . . . you know, the insurance release papers," Scotty gritted. "What? You thought a nigga like me ain't know the process and shit. C'mon, you so used to fucking with the perfect gentleman that you was sleeping on Lil Man," Scotty said snidely.

He wasn't as dumb as I had pegged him to be. My legs were shaking. I squinted my eyes into slits and moved closer to where he was standing. I reached down low into my lungs to find my deepest breath. "If you keep coming around, people are going to start talking. Your ass is already fucking lucky we getting the money at all since you fucked up and cut the fucking brakes on his car. That wasn't the plan. You don't think that shit looked suspicious to the cops? Then you shot Christina—what fucking part of the game was that?" I hissed through clenched teeth, my breath hot on his face. He didn't have a chance to respond before Paulette seemed to be up on us all of a sudden. I was too enmeshed in chastising him that I had not even heard her coming. Scotty stepped back from me a few feet like I had scared him. Then I noticed Paulette; he had obviously seen her coming. I inhaled and swiped the front of my black dress down. I stepped back from Scotty and placed my dark shades back over my eyes. I softened my facial expression, back to grieving wife. This up and down with emotions was starting to make me really crazy. I suddenly had an instant headache.

"Melody, I am really sorry again for your loss. I just came by to give you a card and send my love," Scotty fabricated on the spot. He handed me an envelope, which I was pretty sure didn't contain a fucking sympathy card. I reached out with shaking hands and took the card. I could only imagine what the fuck Scotty had inside. Paulette eyed him up and down evilly. Then she sucked her teeth and chuckled at Scotty in disgust.

"What? You didn't expect a nigga like me to give the grieving widow a card? Gangsta niggas have hearts too," Scotty snapped at Paulette before he walked off with his usual bad-boy swagger. I exhaled a windstorm of relief. I held my head up high, trying to get my equilibrium back from my nerves having me shaking all over. Scotty's behavior had been spooking me out. I was starting to think paying him that amount of money was a bad idea. Judging from how bold he had been coming around, I wasn't so sure he would be able to hide where he'd gotten that large amount of money. Scotty would probably take a million dollars back to the hood and show off so bad the police would definitely come sniffing. I surely misjudged his ass. The plan may not have been that well thought out after all. There was no turning back at that point. During the entire ride to the memorial service, my mind raced with ways to get rid of my little problem that they called Lil Man. First things first, I had to go buy myself a gun. That was the one good thing Richard had taught me—how to shoot. I had spent lots of days at the gun range just to pass time, but I had begun to believe all of my practice was going to come in handy, probably sooner than I had anticipated.

Scotty kept good on his threatening promise. He showed up at Richard's service and sat in the back of the funeral chapel with dark shades covering his eyes. I could feel the heat of his gaze on me the entire time. Maybe I was paranoid, but I could've sworn some of the other people scattered throughout the room were some of Scotty's thug friends. I couldn't be sure. I mean, some of Richard's clients were similar to Scotty in appearance too. The detectives also showed up at the service. Let's just say I wasn't doing too well being surrounded by piercing gazes and suspicious smirks. Everyone there thought I was sick because I'd lost my husband; I knew better. I was sick because the heat in the room was too much to handle with my hired hit man and police detectives sitting only a few feet away from each other.

After the memorial service, I was ushered out of the chapel to the funeral director's office. I had told them I'd rather take a few minutes to sign the paperwork while everyone loaded into the limousines for the burial rather than come back. I wanted the process started as soon as possible. I could see out of my peripheral vision that Scotty had followed us into the hallway. I caught a quick glimpse of him watching me before I stepped into the office. This nigga was playing hardball for real. The funeral director kept asking me if I was all right, if I needed water or something. My hands were shaking so bad I could hardly sign the papers. But I finally made it through the process. I nervously signed the release paperwork for the insurance check and obtained original copies of Richard's death certificate. I needed those to close the deal on several of his bank accounts, the house he had tried to sell from under me, and a few other assets he owned. I was about to claim what was rightfully mine all along.

It was so much to handle and if Richard weren't already dead, I think I would've killed his ass again.

When I left the office, Paulette was waiting for me so we could get into the limo to the cemetery. She had a funny look on her face. I already knew why too.

"Melody . . . this guy Scotty is starting to spook me. He is waiting outside again. Is there something you want to tell me?" Paulette asked, stopping in front of me. She gave me a look that said she was growing suspicious.

"Don't be silly. He is just being there for me. I know he is a little rough around the edges and he is not the type of man you're used to me dating, but I really think you're overreacting, Paulette," I quickly answered. She was getting on my nerves with all of this motherly behavior. I had one fucking mother and I hated that bitch. I was thinking Paulette better stop the bullshit before I put her ass in the same category.

"Well, Trina called me last night. She said he might be going around spreading rumors that he knows what really happened to Richard," Paulette whispered. "I think he is trying to say you might've had something to do with Richard's accident, Melody."

My eyes dimmed and I could feel blood filling up in my face. "Don't believe that jealous bitch Trina," I whispered back harshly. "Now either move out of my way or come on. Please, Paulette. Stop with this shit. Now is not the time or place. Can I go bury my husband without all of this drama?" I snapped, pushing past my sister. Paulette immediately looked apologetic. She was hot on my heels and didn't bring the subject up again. My ears were ringing. *What the fuck is Scotty out there doing and saying?* I thought. He was definitely a problem that was getting out of hand.

8

Within a week, I was in New York at the National Benefit Life Insurance Company collecting my check. It was a little less than three million after Richard's memorial service and burial fees were subtracted. I didn't care because once I finished liquidating all of his accounts, the house, and the cars, I knew I would be coming out way on top.

Once the check was in my hands, I felt overwhelmingly powerful. I felt vindicated, although I had to admit I still had mixed feelings about Richard being dead. I mean, he had done me wrong, but deep inside, I still held on to the fact that he was the first man I really loved.

With my check in hand, I had gone into the ladies' room at the company and did a little dance. I even kissed the check. It was all mine, every red fucking cent that Richard owed to me for the years I had given up was finally in my hands. There were no more mixed emotions, no more sorrowful thoughts about Richard and his bitch Christine.

I immediately thought about Paulette. I felt bad about how I had to sneak out on her while she was at work. I did leave her a note. I explained that I was forever grateful for everything she had done for me and that I was not going to leave her high and dry ever again. I promised her that as soon as I cashed the check, I would repay her for all that she did and then some. I told her that I couldn't tell her where I was but that I would contact her soon.

I really meant what I had said too. I was going to hook my sister up; that's for sure. I was eternally grateful for how she had bailed me out and stood by me when things were really grave for me. It was more than I could've asked for. I even thought about just buying Paulette a beautiful house and paying off all of her student loans. That idea came from the fact that I couldn't stand to think she would be giving my evil mother some of the money if I just sent Paulette a check. I was definitely spending the money before I got it. I felt so good. I slipped the check into my bag and smiled at myself in the oversized bathroom mirror. "You are one bad bitch, Melody Goldman." I smirked.

I had to give myself a lot of credit. I had been very good at thinking on my fucking toes. The fact that I had managed to get out of Virginia to come to New York without Scotty's ass following me was just one prime example of how smart I was. That bastard had followed us to the cemetery, to the restaurant where I held the repast, and back to Paulette's after Richard's services. The only thing that ran Scotty away from stalking me was when the detectives came by Paulette's condo a few days later to ask a few more questions. I guess Scotty got spooked when he saw the cops. That was the little opening I needed. I had been waiting for one small window of opportunity to give Scotty's ass the slip, and it came in the form of two pain-in-the-ass Tidewater police detectives.

When the detectives left Paulette's house that morning, I had jumped into her car and followed them out. I knew Scotty was watching me like he had been doing for days. I also knew he wouldn't dare follow the police or me, so long as I was following them. Once I lost his ass on the streets, I rushed to an Enterprise and rented myself an ugly-ass minivan. It was the most unsuspecting car in the lot. From what Scotty knew of me, he would've never guessed I would be caught dead in a minivan. With my nerves on fucking edge, I drove all the way to New York City without even stopping to take a piss. It was a close call too. The whole drive I thought about how mad Paulette was going to be with me. She would think I was just a selfish bitch who used her during my time of need. She would be halfway right. I needed to use her for a little while, but this time I wouldn't forget what she had done for me. I promised myself and God that I would call Paulette or send her another note letting her know where her car was once I got everything settled and done with. Then I thought better of it. She was a big girl; once she reported her car missing, it would be found and returned to her. I was just going to repay her for what she'd done for me and send her a little something for herself. She could either be happy with that or fuck it.

I checked myself into a swanky boutique hotel in downtown New York City after I left the bank. Good thing I had taken a few bucks from Paulette's stash. Another grimy thing I had to do as a means to an end. She wouldn't even miss it after I sent her some money. There was so much red tape trying to open up an account without anything except a driver's license and old credit cards bearing my name. There were at least fifty telephone calls to verify shit. But after all of the jumping through hoops, the bank manager helped me open a few accounts that would separate the money that I was going to use for everyday living and the money I would save.

When that was solved, I hit yet another snag in my plan to take my money and run out of the country. I didn't have my damn passport. Everything had been left inside of my house when Richard had padlocked me out. I had to go about the process of reapplying and getting a new passport. An almost impossible feat without my birth certificate and Social Security card, which now I also had to reapply for. Good thing most stuff could be done over the Internet these days because there was no way I could risk going back to the Tidewater area to get a birth certificate and Social Security card. Needless to say, it was going to be a few weeks before I could run out of the country. I could only imagine what Scotty was doing. I pictured him rounding up a posse of thugs to hunt me down. The idea made me shudder. But the thought of all the money being mine cleared away my fears.

After two days in New York, I thought it would be best for me to hop to another city. I decided to drive to Washington, D.C. I figured it was as good a place as any to set up a post office box so I had an address for the government to send me my birth certificate and Social Security card. I didn't think Scotty would think to look for me there either. I mean, he knew the insurance company was in New York, so being there was risky. He had been blowing up the phone he'd given me. I finally decided to listen to all of the messages he had been leaving. I pulled out the Trak phone and began listening to the full voice mail box. I closed my eyes as I heard Scotty make a million threats. But the last message he left sent a cold chill down my spine.

"Melody, you fucked with the wrong nigga. I'm outside your sister's house right now, and I guess if I can't get to your snake ass, I'll have to get to your bitch-ass sister. You better get in touch with me or else the next time you see this bitch she'll be pushing up daisies," Scotty barked. Hearing him threaten my sister took my breath away. My heartbeat sped up and I couldn't even think straight. I was a nervous wreck. I didn't think Scotty would ever go there. I should've known, though.

"Shit," I cursed to myself. I needed to contact Paulette right away. I was going to tell her to stay away from her condo for a while, demand that she go stay with Diane. In a risky move, I called her house from the W hotel in D.C. I was pacing the floor as the phone rang. My stomach was in knots.

"C'mon, Paulette, answer, please," I whimpered as I walked circles into the rug. "You finally decided to check on your sister," a voice filtered through the line. I almost fucking fainted when I heard Scotty's voice come through the telephone. I quickly hung up the phone and dropped onto the floor. There was no way I could let him hurt Paulette. I would just die if I put my sister in danger after everything she had done for me. I was sobbing trying to figure out what I would do. I came up with the idea to call him back and tell him I would bring him the money. I needed to act like I was never trying to give him the slip. I exhaled a few times, trying to will my nerves to calm down. I swallowed hard and dialed Paulette's phone number again. The line connected.

"Melody! You have to help me! He said he is going to kill me if you don't give him what is his. How could you do this to me, Melody?" Paulette cried into the phone.

Tears immediately began pouring from my eyes. "Paulette, I'm so sorry. I never thought he would hurt you!" I screeched into the phone.

"You fucked with the wrong one, bitch! I saw the letter you left here. You never had any intentions on giving me my paper," Scotty growled into the phone.

I could still hear Paulette crying in the background. "Scotty, listen to me. I was going to give you your money. I just needed to sign the check and get it cleared. I only left town to do that. I was going to contact you, but I couldn't risk the police seeing you or anything. Please don't hurt my sister. I have your money, Scotty!" I yelled. The room was spinning around me. I flopped down onto the hotel bed. I couldn't stand any longer. "Just tell me what you want me to do. I can come back to Virginia and meet you with your money," I rasped out. If that was what I had to do in order to protect Paulette, then so be it. I didn't have a good feeling in the pit of my stomach at all.

"Yo, you got twenty-four hours to arrange to meet me with my money. If I don't hear from you, this bitch right here dies," Scotty growled.

"I will be there," I assured him. "Please, Scotty, she doesn't have anything to do with all of this. She doesn't even know anything about it," I cried. He started laughing. That same crazy, maniacal laugh that had scared the shit out of me before Richard's funeral. This motherfucker wasn't working with a full deck at all.

"She knows everything now. She's a witness, so you better think about that shit," Scotty hissed. Then he disconnected.

I hung up the phone. I rushed over to my bag and pulled out my Glock. I was going to save my sister. Scotty thought he was the only mother-fucker who could get gangsta. He had another think coming to his punk ass. I checked out of the W and headed back to the Tidewater area. Scotty had better pray for his sake that I find Paulette with not a hair harmed on her fucking head.

9

As soon as I got back into Virginia, an ominous feeling came over me. It was like an instinct and I couldn't keep my teeth from chattering. I switched the radio station in my latest rental car to the local station. As soon as I turned on the radio, it was like divine intervention. The first station I turned to was the local news station. "Police are investigating what appears to be the senseless murder of a local nurse. Paulette Mitchell was found strangled to death in her Salem Lakes condominium. . . ." I didn't hear anything else. It felt like a loud bell had been rung in my ears. Blood was rushing through my veins so hard and fast I was burning up all over my body. I swerved the car off the road and came to a screeching halt.

"Nooo! Oh God no!" I begged, banging my fists on the steering wheel so hard I broke the skin on my knuckles. "Agghh!" I screamed and screamed until the back of my throat burned like I had just swallowed a stick of fire. I couldn't even catch my breath. "Paulette! Oh God! Paulette, I'm so sorry!" I just continued to scream for what seemed like an eternity. "Scotty, you will fucking pay! You will fucking pay!" My voice echoed around the car. My chest heaved up and down uncontrollably. I had to take deep cleansing breaths in order to stop the spinning in my head. My hands were trembling like crazy.

I finally pulled myself together enough to speak calmly. I set out to dial Scotty's phone number. I had to stop dialing seven or eight times because I could not get myself calm enough to act as if I didn't know anything. I needed to be my old self. It was the hardest thing I've ever had to do because my insides were churning with a mixture of pain and anger. I swallowed a golf-ball-sized lump that was sitting in my throat and dialed his number once more. This time I didn't hang up. I waited for him to answer. I was biting down into my lip so hard I drew blood. The metallic taste of it made me feel animalistic. I closed my eyes and could see myself ripping Scotty's fucking head off and shitting down his neck. Even as I imagined my revenge, I was afraid that he'd go after the other people in my life. I pumped my left hand in and out, trying to get my anger under wraps. The vein in my neck was pulsing fiercely against my neck when I heard Scotty's voice.

"I didn't think you were really gonna call me. I guess you weren't bluffing," Scotty finally answered. No hello or nothing. I closed my eyes tightly, trying to keep my emotions in check. *Bluffing, motherfucker? You thought I was bluffing, so you killed my sister?* I screamed inside my head.

"Where do you want to meet, Scotty? I have something for you . . . something you definitely deserve," I said as calmly as I could.

"Whoa, whoa, slow your roll. Now you calling the shots? I thought you was the one who dipped out on a nigga after the deed was done," he said, being a smart-ass.

I exhaled and swallowed the words I really wanted to say to him.

"We can meet on my terms in my hood. Meet me at the corner of Princess Anne Road near the Longshoremen Hall. Don't try no funny shit or else your sister is gonna get it," Scotty told me.

I bit down into my tongue, drawing more blood. Tears sprang into my eyes when he mentioned my sister. He knew what he had done already. Fucking piece of shit! I had to make sure he didn't hurt anyone else.

"I'll be there as soon as the sun goes down. Come alone or the deal is off. Just like you got people, I got people, too, Scotty. I have your money, so don't try no bullshit or else nobody wins," I rasped. I reached down and touched the gun that sat on my lap. Scotty or Lil Man or whatever he wanted to call himself was going to regret the day he ever crossed paths with Melody Goldman.

"All I want is what's mine, baby girl. We ain't got no beef," Scotty said, chuckling like it was one big fucking joke. That shit sent embers of fire through my body. I couldn't wait until it was time to meet up with him. I hung up, my anger palpable. There was going to be hell to pay!

I cried the entire day over what happened to Paulette. I didn't know where to go. I couldn't go to her house. My old house was locked up and on the market. I definitely wasn't going to my mother. I was wracked with guilt. I felt responsible for Paulette's death and to a certain extent I was. There were so many ways I could've handled things without getting her in the middle.

It was finally time for me to go to the meeting place. Of course it was in the seediest fucking place in the Tidewater area. At that point, I didn't care. I had obviously arrived first, which is how I had planned it. I sat in the car, swinging my leg in anticipation. I watched as Scotty pulled up in his all black Tahoe. His windows were tinted so dark he could've had anybody hiding in the back. I felt uneasy, but thoughts of Paulette kept me from running away. This was something I had to do. If I had gone to those lengths to take revenge on Richard, I don't know what the fuck made Scotty believe I would let him slide for killing my sister. I watched him get out of the Tahoe and stand in front of it. He had his hands shoved down into the pockets of his jeans. I crept out of the car, removed my shoes, and moved stealthily like a lion sneaking up on its prey. I knew then that Scotty had been slipping. He didn't see me yet. He didn't know what car to expect or anything. Some street thug he was. You would think he would've asked so he could have the jump on me instead of the other fucking way around. He was too busy murdering a fucking innocent woman to ask any questions of me. I put my gun in my strong shooting hand and extended it out in front of me. Just like Richard had taught me. I slowly eased up on Scotty from the side. He never saw my ass coming.

"Don't fucking move, you piece of shit," I hissed, placing the cold steel of the 9 mm Glock to the side of his head. Scotty started laughing nervously. He went to take his hands out of his pockets. "I said don't fucking make any moves," I growled. He could see out of the corner of his eye that my finger was in the trigger guard.

"Damn, it's like that, Ma? Not even three months ago you was riding my dick into the sunset." Scotty smirked. He was trying to make jokes to mask his fear. Maybe he was trying to throw me off. I could tell he was scared because I could see his shirt fluttering from his rapid heartbeat. There was nothing that could deter me from this mission.

"You killed my sister, you fucking devil. All you had to do was wait for what was coming to you, but you couldn't wait," I gritted. I could feel the tears coming. My nostrils flared as I fought back the tears. Showing weakness could be deadly in a situation like this.

"I didn't kill your fuckin' sister. I didn't touch her," Scotty said, his voice cracking with fear.

"Oh no? I heard on the news she was dead—strangled to death. You're the only motherfucker who would do something like that to Paulette.

Did you really think you would get away with killing her and then come here and collect my fucking dead husband's insurance money? You are dumber than I thought!" I hissed.

Scotty suddenly jumped and turned toward me. He scared the shit out of me. "Agh!" I screamed.

He hit me in the face and I almost lost my balance. The pain of the hit reverberated through my skull. Scotty rammed into me with all of his might. He reached out and tried to grab the gun out of my hands. "You bitch! You was trying to—" he growled as we struggled over the gun. I refused to let go. I knew my grasp meant the difference between my life and death.

"Let go!" I shouted. Scotty was still trying to overpower me. I started recalling all of the gun-retention techniques Richard had showed me on our many trips to the gun range. Who knew that shit would ever come in handy? Scotty held on tight to the hand that had the gun. He was overpowering me so much I couldn't even get my finger out of the trigger guard. I felt when the slack went out of the trigger. The little click let me know that the gun was about to go off. I dropped my hand and pushed it away from myself and into Scotty's body. "You better let go . . . ," I started to warn. Scotty didn't listen. One more touch of that trigger and . . . *BANG!*

One shot pierced through the night. My body shook from the powerful shot. I could no longer hear anything as my ears began to ring painfully. My eyes popped wide open and my mouth formed into an O like I was going to scream but nothing came out. Next, I felt the weight of Scotty's body as he began falling to the ground. He was making this sickening face as if he was in great pain. I could tell he was saying something, but the ringing in my inner ear prevented me from hearing what he was saying. I was trying desperately to get him off of me, but he was strong. He was fighting me. He had a death hold on me. His eyes were wide. I couldn't believe that he was still trying to fight me for the gun.

"Get off of me!" I growled, trying to use my other hand to mush Scotty's face and get him off of me. My finger was still stuck in the trigger guard. Scotty grabbed the gun again; this time he put his dead weight on it.

BANG! Another involuntary shot rang out. That time I was more prepared for it. And that time Scotty's body completely went limp. His grasp on me loosened right away, and he slid down the front of me, onto the ground. His mouth hung wide open like he was about to scream in pain. His eyes were also open, gazing up at me eerily.

"Oh my God," I whispered, clasping my free hand over my mouth. I felt a little urine leak out of my bladder. I whirled around. The park was empty, but I could see headlights in the distance. The gunshots had not even made a difference. I guess in that part of town they were used to hearing shots ring out. My body didn't feel like my own. I wasn't cool at all. I broke and ran straight back to the car. I couldn't believe how lucky I had been that Scotty didn't have anyone hiding in the back of that Tahoe. I would think a thug like Scotty would have dudes posted up around our meeting place just in case I decided to do just what I did. I kept shaking my head, thinking he was really stupid.

Although I went there with intentions of killing him, I was not prepared for the reality—the smell of the blood, the look in his eyes, the feeling of shooting the gun had all caught me off guard. I guess I wasn't as ruthless as he was since he had strangled my fucking sister. When I reached the car, I yanked the door open and slid into the driver's seat. My chest heaved up and down like somebody was using a pump on my ass. My hands were shaking so badly that trying to reach for the steering wheel was difficult. I could not pull out of the spot. I looked down and saw Scotty's blood all over the front of my shirt. I closed my eyes tightly. "Oh God!" I gagged. I could feel vomit creeping up my esophagus. I frantically opened the car door and threw up on the ground. My stomach churned like crazy. That happened over and over for a good five minutes. I was a fucking mess, but I knew I had to get the fuck out of there. I was still shaking so badly when I pulled out that I could hardly control the steering wheel. The car swung all over the road until I settled down. I had to pull over at least three times before I got myself together enough to drive a safe distance. The smell of Scotty's blood was not going to make my drive easy. "Pull yourself together, Melody. Pull yourself together," I chanted, giving myself a much-needed pep talk. I needed to get to some place where I could wash up and change.

I also knew that I needed to get out of Tidewater because everyone there knew me. I would have never pictured my life ending up like this. I was the wife of a fucking gentleman. How could this happen to me? All sorts of thoughts trampled through my mind. "Shit!" I cursed when I looked down at the gas gauge. I only had enough gas to get me to Richmond, Virginia. I quickly decided that Richmond was far enough away from Tidewater. It would have to fucking do. I drove straight to Richmond, where I found a Marriott Residence.

When I rushed up to the front desk, the clerk eyed me up and down suspiciously. I asked if I could just pay cash for the room and told the clerk I had misplaced my identification and that I had had a really rough night. She was hesitant, and it was not until I slipped her an extra hundred dollars for herself that she said she could bend the rules. As she found something for me, she kept looking at my clothes and asking me if I was okay. I gave her some cockamamie story about having nosebleeds since I was kid, blah, blah, blah.

When she slid the room key toward me, she leaned over and whispered, "I used to be in a domestic violence situation. There are a lot of places that can help you get away once and for all."

At first I started to tell her ass off but decided it was good that she had taken it upon herself to make up a story for me. So I just lowered my eyes like I was admitting she was right. "Thank you for that. I needed to hear it. Sometimes we believe we are the only ones going through it when it happens," I fabricated, flashing a weak smile.

"I know. But you are not alone, girlfriend," the clerk said, smiling supportively. I shook my head and rushed toward the elevators. That was a close call too. Those hotel clerks could blow the cover on the most well-thought-out crimes. All it took was one call of a suspicious person asking to check in without identification or a credit card. Whew. I was really glad that in that part of Richmond, money talked and bullshit walked.

Once I got into the room, I had a breakdown. Before the door could fully close, I began peeling out of the bloody clothes. I rushed into the bathroom and leaned over the sink. I splashed water on my face. I glanced in the mirror and realized how bad I looked from all of the crying I had been doing. No wonder the clerk thought I was a domestic violence victim. I put the clothes into the sink and ran cold water on them. I didn't have anything else with me, and I knew I would have to leave. Although the blood wouldn't come out completely, at least I wouldn't have to deal with the smell of it. I sat in a burning hot shower for hours, scrubbing myself to try to remove Scotty's blood, which had seeped into the skin on my arms and the tops of my feet.

As I let the hot water run over me, I kept seeing Scotty's bulging eyes staring up at me as the life drained out of his body. I closed my eyes and shook my head, trying to get the images out of my head. When I finally got out of the water, I paced the room for what seemed like hours. I paced until my legs damn near gave out. Finally, I collapsed onto the bed. I had to think of my next move. I needed to get back to the mailbox I had opened. My mind raced the entire night. I turned on the television, and there was nothing but bad news on or shows that were blood, guts, and gore. I couldn't stand it, so I turned the television off.

Each time I closed my eyes and tried to get even an hour of sleep, I would see the faces of the dead. It was too much. My brain was fried. Needless to say, I did not sleep a wink that night. The dead bodies were piling up: Richard, Christina, Paulette, and now Scotty. I couldn't help but feel like I was a fucking black widow or a bad omen. I lay still with my arm across my eyes, thinking everybody was dead now because I wanted to be rich. Don't get me wrong, I had planned some of it out. I thought I was entitled to everything that had come to me. I didn't feel sorry about Richard and his bitch being dead. I mean, the way he had treated me, there was no other type of punishment that would've been more fitting. They definitely got what was coming to them. That fucking Scotty . . . forget it. I definitely didn't give a fuck that his murderous ass was dead. I started to cry when my mind got to Paulette. She was the one person who was completely innocent in all of this. There was no fucking way on earth that Paulette should have ever suffered that fate. That was probably the only thing I would take back about the entire situation.

10

Two days later, I finally pulled myself together enough to leave Richmond. I returned to Tidewater. I couldn't stand to just leave and not see to it that Paulette had a proper burial. It took everything inside of me to go back. Especially to my mother's house. I knocked on her door tentatively. I waited a few minutes and she didn't answer. Just as I headed down my mother's porch steps, I heard the door open behind me. I stopped dead in my tracks. My heartbeat sped up and a cold sweat broke out all over my body.

"Melody?" my mother said, more like a question than a statement.

I closed my eyes and swallowed hard. I plastered a fake smile onto my face and turned around. "Hi, Diane. I . . . I . . . just came by because . . . ," I stammered.

"I know why you came. I mean, she was your baby sister," my mother said sadly.

I was glad she filled in that blank, because my

mind had gone completely numb at the sight of her. I hadn't seen my mother in years. I wasn't at all prepared for how she looked standing there. I took the sight of her all in. She looked old now, frail and helpless. She held a cane and leaned all of her weight on it like it was keeping her up. She looked so vulnerable. Nothing like the fire-breathing dragon I was used to as a kid. It was crazy to me how time could change things and people. Still, as much as I tried at that moment, I couldn't even find an ounce of sympathy for her. I immediately regretted coming to her house. I wanted so badly to turn and run, but it was too late. She was already expecting me to come inside and make nice with her. I sighed loudly.

"Come on in. I'm just here sorting out what I'm gonna do to bury my baby," my mother rasped.

I could tell she had lost that deep, booming voice I was used to. She had probably screamed and cried so loud when she'd found out about Paulette that her voice went hoarse. I slowly went back up the steps. Hearing her refer to Paulette as her baby would have probably torn me up at one time, but I was used to it. I was also aware that in her condition, without Paulette, my mother would have no one. There was no way I could ever stick around and take care of her ailing ass.

"Look, Diane, I didn't come here to stay and have tea and crumpets. I just wanted to pay Paulette back for what she had done for me. I was planning on giving her something, and I know deep in my heart she would've given you something," I rambled off rapidly. All the way over here, I had rehearsed the speech I was going to make.

"I know you never loved me. I am not ever going to forget that stuff. But Paulette did love me. No matter what you tried to do to drive a wedge between us, my little sister did love me," I croaked. I began crying. I was so mad at myself for losing it, but it was overwhelming.

"So just take this and make sure Paulette gets the burial she deserves. You can do whatever you want with the rest. That is the way Paulette would have wanted it," I said with finality. I placed the check down on the table. For the first time in years, I looked Diane in her eyes. She was crying buckets of tears. I could tell she might have finally been sorry for everything she had done to me. I turned and began walking away.

"Melody!" my mother called at my back. I stopped short for a minute and closed my eyes. I was trying to squeeze the tears back in.

"I always loved you. I only wanted what was best for you. I didn't always know how to deal with my feelings, but one thing always remained the same—I love you," my mother cried out.

I started walking again. This time I let the tears fall down my face. It was the first time in my entire life that I ever remembered my mother saying the words *I love you* to me. It was something I needed to hear, but after all of the turns my life had taken by then, it was just too little too late.

I slammed my mother's front door for the last time. The sound signaled the closing of a part of my life I would never open again. I exhaled and headed for the new life I had planned for myself. With three million dollars in the bank and no more worries, I felt vindicated in all aspects of my life. I felt free. Or so I thought.

As I drove out of the Tidewater area for the very last time, I smiled. "You are on your way, Melody. You did it, girl. You fucking did it!" I yelled out loud to myself. I pumped up the volume on the radio and sang along with Rihanna's "Man Down." It was crazy how that song was so relevant to my life right then. I headed back to Washington, D.C., to check the PO box I had opened for the purpose of receiving my documents. I parked the car and headed to the post office. Of course I had dark shades over my eyes; I felt like myself again thanks to a short shopping spree before I left Virginia. I had purchased a brand-new Louis Vuitton bag, a pair of oversized Gucci shades, and a couple of outfits, including a hot Nicole Miller dress. I didn't know where I was going to wear it when I bought it, but I just fell in love with it. I felt like I no longer had a care in the world.

I walked into the post office ready to receive my birth certificate so I could go and get a passport. That was my main priority. The money was in my hands; now all I needed to do was get the fuck out of Dodge. I planned on leaving the country, maybe going to live in Europe someplace. I had not yet decided.

There was nothing suspicious about the post office or the blocks surrounding it. Maybe it was just that I was so focused on getting the fuck out of there that I hadn't noticed what was staring me right in my face. I sauntered into the post office like I didn't have a fucking care in the world. It even took me about thirty seconds to fish the PO box key out of my huge purse. "Ugh, there you are," I said when I finally located that pesky little key. As I placed my PO box key into the lock, suddenly I heard rapid footsteps around me, and it quickly seemed like they were getting close to me. I turned around because the sound had grown loud like a herd of wild elephants trampling through the post office. I finally paused. I crinkled my face in confusion and turned to investigate the noise. When I whirled around, my eyebrows went from furrowed to high arches. I almost fainted when I was met with several guns in my face. "What the . . . ?" I gasped, mouth open wide. I dropped all of my mail and my jaw went slack. My shoulders slumped in surrender. I went to raise my hands to let them know I wasn't going to fight them, but as I went to move, I heard a bunch of barking voices coming at me from every direction. "Don't fucking move a muscle or you die! Keep your hands where they are! Don't try anything funny or you will be shot!"

I froze in place. I could feel my sphincter muscle about to let loose. My knees were trembling. There had to be about one hundred SWAT officers surrounding me as if I were public enemy number one.

"Melody Goldman, you are under arrest for

the murder of your husband, his lover, and your hired hit man," one of the officers huffed at me as I was roughly thrown to the floor.

I closed my eyes and shook my head. I couldn't figure out how they'd found out or found me.

"You're mistaken! I didn't do anything! I'm innocent!" I yelled as I was roughly handcuffed and dragged up from the floor. I was dragged outside, but this time I wasn't fighting or trying to get myself another disorderly conduct charge for fighting the police. A crowd had gathered outside of the post office. People were pointing and hushed murmurs spread through the ever-growing gaggle of onlookers. "I'm innocent," I yelled out. "This is some sort of mistake!" I screamed, looking right over at the crowd. This made the officers who held on to either side of my arms rush faster to get my ass into the back of the squad car. "Call the media! I am innocent!"

Right before my head was pushed down into the awaiting police car, I saw the female detective from the Tidewater police department. *What the fuck is she doing here? What the fuck is going on?* I thought. My eyes locked on hers. I looked at her strangely. She seemed to have a smile of satisfaction on her face. She whispered something to another detective in a suit. I didn't recognize him. She handed the guy a writing pad and then she started walking over toward me as I was forced into the car. By the time my ass hit the seat and I adjusted myself so that the handcuffs weren't stabbing me, the female detective was standing right at the door. She leaned down into the door with a fucking evil look covering her already manlike face.

"Well, well, well. If it isn't Mrs. Melody Goldman, widow of the late—or should I say the murdered—Mr. Richard Goldman," the detective remarked snidely.

I looked at her through squinted eyes. My nostrils flared. If I didn't have these fucking handcuffs on, I probably would've tried to rip that bitch to shreds. "Did you think the day we came to tell you the investigation was over that we really meant it? Tsk, tsk, tsk. We thought you'd be smarter than that. You had been so clever throughout the entire thing. You almost had us. We didn't find out about Lil Man until much later. I guess now that he's dead, you thought you were in the clear. I don't think so. May you rot in prison for the rest of your fucking life," that bitch-ass detective hissed in my face. She was so close she looked like she wanted to kiss me.

I hawked up a wad of spit and shot it in her face. "Fuck you, you jealous bitch!" I spat. It felt so good to do that shit.

"Ahh!" the detective cried, stumbling back, frantically wiping the spit from her face. The next thing I felt was a fist slam into the side of my head. That's when everything went black around me.

11

I sat in that fucking jail for an entire year. After my arrest, I had refused to speak to the police without an attorney. That was something Richard had taught me. Mark Blue, one of Richard's fiercest competitors, had agreed to represent me pro bono. I knew Mark was doing it for two reasons: for notoriety and because it would be the best way for him to finally have one up on Richard.

Mark and I spent hours going over my defense. I found out that the police were basing their case solely on a letter that Scotty had sent them and a card he'd given me right before Richard's memorial service. I never even realized I had dropped the card. Inside, Scotty had written: *I did you a favor. Now when you get that money, I want my cut.* There were a lot of ways that could be interpreted. Scotty never wrote, *I did what you asked me to do.* He wrote that he'd done me a favor, not that I had asked him to do it. The letter he sent to the police was vague in the same way. It said something like, *If I end up dead, it's because Melody Goldman set me up because I killed her husband.* Another dumb move. Still, Scotty could've gotten very detailed in his death declarations, but he hadn't.

Mark was very confident that he could introduce reasonable doubt to the jury. I wasn't so sure. One thing I was sure of was that they would never find the murder weapon. I had taken it apart and disposed of the pieces in several different places. The most important piece, the barrel, was left right in a plant pot on my mother's porch. They would never think to look there, and I knew it.

The trial seemed to drag on and on. I had grocery-sized bags under my eyes. My hair had suffered and my nails . . . forget about it. The weight loss was something I welcomed, since I had put on a bunch of pounds while I stayed with Paulette. Depression had made me eat like a pig.

"Goldman, jury is in!" the CO hollered.

I walked slowly over to the cell bars and waited to be cuffed and let out. I had a strange feeling in my stomach. I can't say that it was fear. I wasn't scared. I had been conditioning myself for a guilty verdict. I had made it up in my mind that I would probably never benefit from the insurance policy money, which, through litigation, had been decided they could not snatch back. A civil court judge had ruled that once they paid the money to me, it was mine. The responsibility was on the insurance company to withhold the money if they thought anything was suspicious. That was another way the detectives had fucked up. They had not coordinated with the insurance company in time. Ha! I guess it was in the cards for me to have that money. Maybe it was really karma for what Richard had done to me.

I walked into the courtroom, and cramps invaded my stomach like a rogue army. I stood next to Mark and the entire defense team he had assembled to work my case. Mark reached down and squeezed my hand. I gave him a weak squeeze back and cracked a weak smile. The jury came in, and I couldn't read their faces at all. My heart was hammering so hard against my chest that I felt like I'd faint right there on the spot.

The court officer announced the judge back in.

"Jury, have you reached a verdict?" the old, gray-haired judge asked perfunctorily. A tall black man stood up.

"Yes, Judge, we have," the man said loudly.

His voice immediately annoyed me. I guess he was the foreman. For some reason I had the urge to look around the courtroom.

The courtroom was pin-drop quiet, and packed to capacity. The jury foreman stood up, the rustle of his suit making everyone in the room feel tense. He cleared his throat. The judge asked the foreman if the jury had reached a verdict. The foreman nodded and unfolded a piece of paper. He opened his mouth and the words seemed to come out in slow motion. I closed my eyes. I said a silent prayer, although I knew I shouldn't be calling on God at a time like this.

"We the jury, in the case of the *Commonwealth of Virginia versus Melody Goldman,* find the defendant . . ."

I couldn't really hear. For some reason I was suddenly weak and my ears were ringing. Mark put his hand on my back to stabilize me.

". . . not guilty of the charge of first-degree murder in count one of the indictment."

A loud round of groans and moans filtered around the room. My eyes popped open in utter shock. I had been sure they were going to find me guilty.

"Order!" the judge shouted, banging his gavel. Silence came once again.

The foreman continued apprehensively. He could feel the evil eyes from the courtroom crowd bearing down on him. "We the jury also find the defendant not guilty of the charge of manslaughter in count two of the indictment," he finished up.

I almost jumped up and down. The courtroom erupted in pandemonium. There were screams and moans. Reporters were running out of the courtroom so they could be the first to break the news.

"Oh my God, Mark. We did it! You did it! I could never repay you!" I cried. Then I grabbed Mark in a long, tight embrace as relief settled on my shoulders like a cloak of comfort. I bounced up and down on my legs. I was overjoyed. I swiped away the happy tears from my face and mouthed, "Thank you," to the rest of my defense team.

"I told you all we needed to do was introduce the remote possibility of reasonable doubt," Mark whispered to me.

I was frantic inside. I didn't know what to do with myself.

I could hear the news reporters and tabloid media personalities yelling outside the courtroom doors. "Melody Goldman may have just gotten away with two murders! The verdict has shocked the nation!" they were all saying at once. I was ushered out of the courtroom on wobbly legs, shrouded by my team of attorneys. I had to go through the process of checking out. There would be no more jail for me. I was finally free! Finally vindicated! We had done it. I, Melody Goldman, was a free woman.

I was released to Mark and the others. We smiled and hugged again. "Now it's time to go celebrate your victory!" Mark exclaimed.

"You mean your victory," I said excitedly. It didn't matter who took responsibility for the victory. The fact was, I had gotten off scot-free.

Once we hit the courthouse doors, the throngs of reporters moved in for the kill. I quickly threw my hands up over my face. Mark pushed my head down and he threw his Brooks Brothers jacket over me. He had to lead me because all I could see were a bunch of feet.

"Ms. Goldman, how did you do it? How did you get away with murder?" the reporters screamed, all trying to drown each other out. I was just trying to get out of the building. "Stay down. Ignore them. Don't say a word," Mark was screaming in my ears.

I did just as he told me. I kept my head hung low, hiding my face with my arms. I couldn't help it, but I was smiling. I don't think anything felt as good as getting away with murder.

The Day of the Interview

"But did you know you'd be infamous?" Michelle blurted out, cutting in before I could say anything else.

Her words struck me like a gut punch. I grabbed the edges of the chair and gripped them tightly. I was more determined than ever to tell the story now. I opened my mouth . . .

"Melody? Melody? Are you all right?" Michelle Moyer was asking me. I exhaled and shook my head. "Melody, you seemed to be zoned out . . . in a trance," Michelle said, shaking my shoulders.

"I-I'm so sorry. I-I was just thinking. . . ." I stammered. I looked around and remembered that I was supposed to be giving an interview about how I beat the murder charges.

I didn't even realize that I had been flashing back to everything that had happened.

"Can I get a drink of water before we start taping again?" I asked, standing up.

"Sure. Get Mrs. Goldman some water," Michelle called out.

I drank the water down in one gulp. I closed my eyes and shook off my memories. I had rehearsed for days the story I was going to tell Michelle during the interview, yet as soon as I started to think about it, the truth had completely came to the forefront of my mind. There was no way I could tell the truth about what happened. That would always be buried in my mind.

"Okay, I'm ready," I said, smoothing down my skirt. I sat down in front of Michelle. The makeup people touched up my face and then Michelle's.

"Starting from the top," Michelle told her crew. This time I was going to give them what they were looking for. A television-special-worthy story of how I got caught between a gangsta and a gentleman and got away with murder and three million dollars. I had to smirk to myself. I guess the only truth that mattered was the one I told them.

"Well, first things first. My husband started off being the perfect gentleman," I began.

I lay on an exclusive, celebrity-only beach in St. Tropez with huge oyster shell shades covering my eyes. I wore a bright yellow Tory Burch bathing suit and a black floppy hat. Not to mention the golden tan I had that was customary of St. Tropez. When I had chosen the French Riviera, it turned out to be the best place in the world for me. I had a lot of lazy days and exciting nights. Ahh, the life. I picked up the *People* and *US* magazines I had purchased earlier that morning. I was like a starstruck teenager when I saw my face plastered on the cover of both magazines. I smiled so wide I probably looked like the Cheshire cat. I couldn't get rid of the smile if I tried. I had to say I was very proud of myself. It was a long, crazy road, but I, Melody Goldman, had finally taken her rightful place in the world as a fabulous celebrity.

I snickered as I read the stories. Some magazines were still repeating the exact story I had made up the day of my interview with *Date Time.* It was amazing how the media could take anything for fact. I guess telling the truth is just not that interesting. Next, I was expecting that big book deal. The publishing houses that loved the scandalous memoirs were already calling. I was thrilled; that would just be more money in my pocket. I had already been throwing some titles around in my head. "How about *I Need a Gangsta*?" I said to myself. "Or better yet, *A Gangsta Instead of a Gentleman.*" I busted out laughing at my own joke. I would pick a dumb-ass so-called gangsta any day. Those days I had spent with Scotty were probably the most exciting days of my life. Bored with reading about myself, I snapped my fingers at the boy who was serving the drinks. He was a fine hunk of French masculinity. He loved me because I always tipped well. Why not? I had it like that! The boy rushed over and brought me an icy mango daiquiri. He also handed me a small napkin that was folded in half.

"This note is for you, madam," the boy said in his heavy French accent.

"For me?" I asked, curious and confused. I tilted my glasses down on my nose and looked at the little folded square strangely. I unfolded it and read it. *I've been watching you. Can I get to know you?* I raised my head and looked around frantically. Who the hell was watching me?

"Who sent this note?" I asked the boy, a little concern in my voice. It was a little weird, and I was still quite paranoid about the possibility of people watching me.

"It came from the gentleman over there," the boy said, pointing to a man sitting on a bungalow chair. The man smiled when he saw me watching him. I eyed him from behind my shades. He was wearing a fedora, a button-down shirt, and some chinos. The man waved at me and flashed another big smile. I rolled my eyes and handed the note back to the boy.

"I am not interested, so take this back. And tell your friend over there that a gentleman is the last thing I need right now. I need a gangsta or nothing at all." I smirked. Then I pulled my shades back up over my eyes and continued to entertain myself with all of the stories about me. I, the fabulous Melody Goldman, was back in business and I would not take any more shit for another man from this day going forward! It's about me and no one else. Fuck 'em all!

Gentlemen Prefer Bullets

De'nesha Diamond

Prologue

BOOM!

Eight-year-old Elijah Hardwick's eyes flew open the second lightning lit up his small bedroom. By the time he pushed up onto his bony elbows, the room was pitch-black again. His heart hammered against his small rib cage as his eyes darted around. He hated thunderstorms—always had—but something in his gut told him that this one was different. Something was wrong.

Thunder rumbled overhead. The storm was far from over.

BOOM! BOOM!

Eli's head jerked toward his bedroom door. *Was that inside the house?*

He brushed off the top sheet and swung his legs over the side of the bed while his ears strained to pick up any usual sounds. But the silence was as loud as the occasional thunderclap, and he couldn't tell if his ears were playing tricks on him. At long last he stood and crept toward the door.

"Where are you going?" Ezekiel, Eli's twin brother, asked, sitting up on the top bunk.

"I heard something," Eli whispered, twisting the doorknob.

"Again?" Ezekiel groaned, dubious.

"For real this time."

"What did you hear?"

"I don't know. Something."

BOOM!

The twins jumped; shortly after, the windows rattled violently. Eli's hand flew over his heart while another flash of lightning blinded them temporarily. A second later, the sky opened up and rain pounded on the glass like a million glistening hammers.

Ezekiel laughed. "It's just a damn storm, Eli. Fuck. I swear you're scared of your own shadow. You better get back in bed before Mama beats the black off of you."

Eli frowned and resisted pointing out that his brother had jumped too. "That's *not* what I heard. It was something else—something *inside* the house."

"Yeah, yeah." His brother plopped back against the pillows, rolled over, and burrowed deeper beneath the blankets. "When you can't sit for a week, don't say that I didn't warn you."

Eli stood frozen for another second, wondering whether he should really go check things out. His mother had warned him repeatedly to keep his narrow butt in bed because he had a habit of coming up with excuses to get up in the middle of the night. He had used everything from there being monsters in their closet to being thirsty, hungry, wet, sick, or having a bad dream.

Bad dreams.

He had those often. Ever since his best friend Brandon had been gunned down right in front of him. One minute they were arguing over who was going to be on whose basketball team and the next firecrackers started popping off. Before he could understand what was happening, the left side of Brandon's head exploded open and warm blood and chunks of brain splattered across Eli's face. While he stood frozen in horror, his quick-thinking twin brother rushed over and tackled him to the ground. Since then, there hadn't been a single night when Eli hadn't relived that horrible moment. He truly believed that had it not been for Easy, he would be in a worm hotel just like Brandon was at that very moment.

Still, the nights of his mother lifting the sheet and telling him to climb in were over. His father made it clear that he didn't want her babying him anymore—and what his father said was law. Eli was afraid of his father, and even more afraid of the man he worked for—Mafia Don.

No one in the family talked about what his father did for Baltimore's notorious gangster, but with the nickname *Killa E*, it wasn't too hard to guess. Elliott Hardwick had a dangerous look about him. At six-five, with dark, brown skin and shoulders so wide they looked like they could carry the whole world, his father had a lot of niggas shittin' in their pants when they saw him comin'. And the few people who *weren't* scared were certainly scared of his huge customized Colt Commander and its bull barrel.

Eli wished that he was more like his father and brother, but it just didn't seem to be in him. No matter how hard he tried.

I'm not a baby. He glanced at the door. Had he really heard something, or was it just his imagination?

BOOM! BOOM!

"What was that?" Ezekiel popped back up in bed.

Eli's eyes bulged to the size of silver dollars. *Gunshots!* His hand flew off the doorknob as if it were a hot poker, and he quickly backed away.

Ezekiel bolted out of bed and rushed to the door. When it was clear where he was going, Eli jolted out of his fear and grabbed his brother's hand. "Wait. You can't go out there," he hissed. "We gotta hide."

"Hide? Are you crazy? We gotta go see what's up," Ezekiel snapped, swiping off his brother's hand.

Eli didn't miss the annoyance in his brother's voice. His twin was like their father: strong, decisive, and fearless. Despite the powerful love flowing between them, Easy never missed a chance to scold Eli for punking out all the time. It was Easy who rescued him from schoolyard bullies, neighborhood lil g's, and even a few ass whoopings he had coming his way at home. So it was no surprise when Easy jerked open the door and charged into the hallway's eerie darkness like a mini-superhero.

"Easy," Eli hissed. "Easy, come back here!"

BOOM!

"Easy," Eli mumbled, taking a trembling step backward. A sudden rush of acidic tears burned his eyes. "Easy, please come back."

Lightning flashed, giving all the toys in the room oddly shaped shadows. Eli was tempted to turn and dash under his bed, but then his mother screamed.

Eli jumped as a warm trickle of piss rolled down his legs. "Mama?" Tears sprang to his eyes while his bottom lip trembled. He still wanted to hide . . . but he also wanted to help his mother.

BOOM! BOOM!

Knees knocking, Eli sucked in a deep breath and then finally plunged into the darkness . . . and smacked into something hard—or rather *someone.*

"Where the fuck do you think you're going, lil nigga?" a deep, raspy voice demanded.

Before Eli could even think about responding, the mystery man's hand locked on to the front of his pajamas and jacked him up into the air. Piss rolled faster down his legs and dripped off of his toes.

"I asked you a fuckin' question," the man growled. His attempt to cover up his bad breath with gum wasn't working. In fact, the cloud of hot, spearmint funk singed Eli's nose hairs.

"I . . . I . . . ," Eli stammered, and then slammed his eyes shut. *Concentrate.* However, the stammering grew worse. "I . . . I . . . I . . . s-s-sorry."

"You're s-s-sorry?" the man mocked, and then

laughed at his imitation. "You don't even know what the fuck sorry is yet, you pissy lil nigga." He dropped Eli back down to the floor, where his small knees buckled and landed him in a pool of his own piss.

"Bring your ass on," Funky Breath said, grabbing Eli's arm and dragging him down the hallway. "I GOT THE OTHER ONE!"

"Good. Bring him down here," another ominous voice barked.

Eli flailed his arms about, hoping to grab hold of something—a table, a lamp, a railing, something. "N-no . . . p-p-please," he begged.

"Shut the fuck up!" The man slammed something hard against the back of Eli's head, plunging him into a darker blackness.

Easy didn't know who the four-man crew dressed head to toe in black was, and he didn't give a shit. He just wanted them out of his house—now! He jerked and twisted, hoping to break the nylon rope that was cutting into his small waist. To his right, both his mother and older sister, Erica, were tied to their own chairs, their mouths stuffed with dishrags and sealed with duct tape.

Seeing the fear on their faces only made Easy struggle that much harder to break free.

"Well, look at this lil nigga here," a man as big and wide as a brick building chuckled, and then scratched the side of his face with his Glock. "This muthafucka got heart."

"Is that right?" The leader, the only one defying the night's dress code to wear pristine white, turned away from the window just as another bolt of lightning brightened the room and revealed his sinister face.

Easy glared at the man, unafraid. If he could get loose, he'd prove how much he was like his father. His evil thoughts of revenge were interrupted when another dude joined them in the dark living room, dragging his twin behind him. Once in the center of the room, he stopped, reached down, and tossed Eli onto the couch as if he weighed nothing.

Ezekiel's heart stopped. The scene was close to an out-of-body experience. Eli's face so like his own, with blood rolling down the side.

His mother screamed, but the rag in her mouth reduced it to a muffled moan.

Fat tears rolled down Erica's face, despite her squeezing her eyes tight in prayer.

Ezekiel forced his gaze away from his brother's limp body and returned his glare to the leader. If only he could get loose. He tugged at the tight rope.

Lightning flashed as the leader strolled over to his mother, his eyes glittering like black diamonds. "Now. I'm only going to ask you one more time. If you don't answer my question or if you scream again, I'm going to order my man there to put a bullet in each one of these lil fuckers' foreheads. You feel me?"

His mother whimpered and then rolled her head around in silent agony.

"Good." With one swift jerk, the tape was wrenched off her face.

She recoiled from the sudden pain while the

rag sprang out of her mouth, but she didn't scream. She didn't dare.

"Where. The. Fuck. Is. He?"

"I don't know. I . . . I swear."

The leader shook his head, disappointed. "Shoot the girl."

"Wait!"

Big Brick Building swung his Glock in Erica's direction and squeezed off a shot before Easy even had the chance to blink.

Erica, and her chair, flew backward.

A scream ripped from his mother's chest, but it was knocked out of her when the man in white backhanded her with his own piece.

Easy rocked onto his bound feet and then charged, hunched in a ninety-degree angle. "Muthafucka!"

"What the fuck?"

Before Mr. White or his soldiers could react, Easy tackled the nigga like a crazed linebacker and knocked his ass to the floor. The man's gun flew out of his hand as Ezekiel's chair snapped in half.

"Easy, stop! Please," his mother begged, sobbing. "Please, don't hurt my baby!"

BOOM! BOOM!

Thunder rolled, as two bullets whizzed by Easy's head.

"Stop shooting, you dumb muthafuckas! You gonna hit me," the man roared.

"Sorry, Boss."

Easy's hands came free. Enraged, he landed one punch after another. However, his element of surprise was over, and this nigga punched him as if Easy were a grown-ass man and sent him reeling back across the room.

"Now shoot his ass," the leader commanded.

"No," his mother shouted, bouncing in her chair.

Big Man swung his gun toward Ezekiel, but before he could squeeze off a shot, Eli bolted up from the couch and flung himself toward the gunman, causing his shot to go wild and find a new mark—straight through the center of their mother's neck.

"MOM!" the twins shouted.

Both stared into their mother's wide, shocked eyes. She opened her mouth to say something, but admitted a wordless gasp before her head plopped sideways, her dead eyes staring at nothing.

"Fuuuuck." Big Man laughed. "Guess she can't tell us shit now."

Mr. White pulled himself up from the floor and retrieved his gat. "Don't matter. That grimy muthafucka's mug shot is gonna turn up sooner or later. We'll just finish these two lil niggas and roll the fuck up out of here." He took aim at the closest twin, who was still frozen in shock, and fired.

Eli jerked as the bullet entered his shoulder and spun him around.

"Noooo!" Ezekiel rushed forward, arms outstretched. But it was too late.

The next bullet slammed into Eli's chest like a heat-seeking missile, lifting him off his feet and slamming him into the coffee table, the glass top shattering into a million pieces.

Before Ezekiel could knock the gun from the man's hand, a bullet slammed into his shoulder from behind, spinning him around to receive his own missiles to the chest. While he propelled backward, the front door banged open.

"Y'all niggas want to get down?" his father thundered. "Then come on, muthafuckas." He took only a second to survey the scene before his own cannon pumped bullets. "Let's do this shit!"

Ezekiel crumpled to the floor with his chest on fire. However, his gaze didn't focus on the raging battle but instead searched out his twin among a sea of broken glass. Pain consumed him while his eyes searched for any sign of life.

Eli's eyes opened, blinked.

Ezekiel tried to smile, but the pain and heat in his chest made that impossible. *Everything is going to be all right,* he conveyed through his eyes. He and Eli always had a way of knowing what the other one was thinking. *We're going to get through this. I promise.*

Eli blinked as though he'd received the message and then stretched his arm out to try and touch his brother. They were a mere foot apart, but it may as well have been miles.

Ezekiel fought like hell to move his arm, but all he could manage was an inch at best. The pain was too much and darkness crept up fast.

Hang in there.

He closed his eyes but couldn't open them again.

* * *

Mafia Don didn't appreciate having to roll through B-more at three in the fucking morning. The sky was crying and bolts of lightning were threatening to crack open the earth every other minute. Usually he had his best niggas handling this type of shit, but after a rash of disloyal muthafuckas snitching like tricked-out bitches, he decided to handle this late-night creep personally.

"They are all dead, Boss." Teardrop shook his head outside the don's black-on-black bulletproof Navigator.

Mafia Don tilted down the rim of his sunglasses and leveled Teardrop with a deadly stare. "All?"

"All," Teardrop confirmed.

"Midnight?"

Teardrop shook his head. "He's not here. Maybe he didn't do the job in person."

"Since when have you ever known for Midnight to miss a slaughter?"

Teardrop didn't respond.

"Exactly." Mafia Don pushed up his shades and then powered up the window. He took a couple of seconds to digest the information. He pulled a cigar from inside his jacket, then took his time biting off the back and lighting up. The mighty Killa E dead?

"Where to, Boss?" his driver asked.

"Give me a minute." He reached for the handle and opened the back door.

"Wait, Boss." The driver bolted from behind the wheel and rushed around the car while opening an oversized umbrella to shield the don from the rain as he stepped out of the vehicle.

Teardrop knew better than to try and huddle underneath the shelter of the umbrella and instead fell back to trail behind, getting completely drenched in the process.

The moment he stepped into the Hardwicks' residence, Mafia Don assessed what resembled a battlefield. Blood and bodies lay everywhere.

"It looks like we have ourselves a modern-day Alamo."

"A what?" Teardrop asked.

Mafia Don rolled his eyes behind his shades and then ventured farther into the house. The shit was ugly. When he found the man he was searching for, Killa E, he stopped. "Damn."

Teardrop stepped up next to his boss and shook his head. "Looks like your boy went out Tony Montana style. Real fucking gangster."

Mafia Don forced his face to remain neutral. He'd known Killa E for a long-ass time, and it was too bad that things had to come down to this—to see his whole family go out like this. The hard truth was that in this street game, they were all dead men walking, pretending that they were two steps ahead of the devil.

Mafia Don shocked everyone when he bent a knee to close the eyes of a man who had been like a son to him. "Rest in peace, my nigga." When he started to rise, a movement caught his attention from the corner of his eye. The don's head jerked to his right, and the men around him tensed.

"What is it, Boss Man?" Teardrop asked, Glock at the ready.

"I thought you said that everybody was dead."

Teardrop hesitated as if the statement confused him. “They are.”

“Then you need to get your eyes fixed.” He stood and walked over to one of the twins’ blood-soaked bodies. When he checked for a pulse, the kid’s eyes sprang open.

“Holy shit,” Teardrop whispered.

Mafia Don cocked his head as his chest muscles tightened. “Hey, lil man. Don’t worry. Your godfather is here. I’m going to take good care of you.”

1

Twenty years later . . .

Darkness cloaked Elijah as he stepped away from the back of his black-on-black Escalade. Both he and his right-hand man, Omar, slapped in clips to their twin M16 Vipers and then rushed in low toward a dilapidated warehouse a good five hundred feet away.

Despite his towering six-foot-five height and muscular, broad frame, Eli had no trouble moving stealthily through the night.

Having cased the joint, he knew there were four Haitian niggas posted on the eastside.

Fifty feet out, the two enforcers screwed on their M4 upper can silencers to their lightweight weapons and took their targets out with two shots apiece.

They waited a full thirty seconds to see whether an army of niggas would rush to the fallen soldiers' sides, but the coast remained clear and Eli and Omar went back into stealth mode.

Adrenaline pumping, they entered the warehouse by the back door and interrupted a product delivery by blasting every nigga in sight with their weapons on full auto. Most went down, roaring in agony before they ever got the chance to reach for their own weapons let alone take aim.

Eli recognized one man struggling to make it toward a door with his left side chewed up with bullets. Eli eased off the trigger and gave Omar a signal to do the same.

"Where are you headed off to, Dutch?" Eli's deep baritone rumbled over the spacious warehouse.

Dutch dragged his tattered body across the concrete floor, leaving a wide swath of blood behind him.

Omar chuckled and then fired a few shots up at the ceiling.

Dutch's arm wobbled and nearly collapsed.

"Nigga, I know that you hear my man talkin' to you!" Omar followed up behind the injured man, sidestepping rivers of blood.

Eli detoured to the stacks of bricks and bundled cash on a large foldout table. He whipped out the rolled-up duffel bag that was tucked in the back of his jeans. In less than a minute, he had it all packed and was ready to roll.

When he looked up, Omar had Dutch's ass jacked up against the wall.

"Everybody knows that the don's reign is over. Finished. *Finito.*" Dutch laughed bravely, even though sweat poured down his face like Niagara Falls.

Omar swung his M16 back over his shoulder with a homemade strap, but then grabbed the

Glock he had tucked in the back of his jeans and jammed it beneath Dutch's chin. "You want to say that shit again, nigga?"

Fear polished Dutch's eyes. "C'mon, man. I ain't saying nothin' that every nigga on the street don't already know."

Omar's nose twitched at the alcoholic fumes rolling off the loose-lipped, begging-to-be-a-corpse paper gangster. As a small act of mercy, he rammed his knee straight into the nigga's groin.

Dutch tried to straighten back up but then wobbled on his legs for so long that he had to reach out and try to support himself with Omar's arm. "Aw, fuck, man. You done fuck my shit up."

Eli rolled his eyes.

"Lookie here, Dutch." Omar grabbed him by his soiled T-shirt and slammed him back against the wall, making sure that his head hit first. "You done hooked up with that dusty-headed immigrant Midnight. After all Mafia Don has done for you and your fam, nigga? Where's your fucking loyalty?"

With his eyes still rolling around in his head, Dutch tried to shake the shit off and take his pleading to Omar's boss behind him. "Eli, man. I ain't got no beef with y'all. This shit is just business. My customers are geeked up on that Haitian's product. Fo' real. I'm a fucking capitalist. Supply and demand. You know? I haven't been able to move the don's product like I used to. I got to give the people what they want. You can understand that shit, can't you?"

WHAP!

Dutch's head snapped back with the swing of Omar's Glock, and a tooth flew out of his mouth. When Dutch moved his head back into position, Omar rocked his shit in the opposite direction.

WHAP!

Dutch doubled over and threw up at least half a pint of blood and alcohol.

Omar jumped back, but the foul mixture splashed over his sneakers. "Nigga, do you know how much I dropped on these vintage Jordans?"

Dutch cowed. "Oh. I-I'm sorry. My bad."

Omar sucked in a long breath. "Eli, please tell me I can put a cap in this nigga's skull for disrespecting my shit. Please."

Behind them, Eli chuckled as he reached into his jacket and pulled out a cigar. He took his time, biting off the back and whipping out his gold lighter. Once the end glowed amber, he took a few tokes and then blew out a long, thick stream of smoke.

"Fuck, Eli. It's the fuckin' general principle of the shit, Boss." Omar slammed Dutch's head back against the wall and then smirked when the muthafucka's eyes rolled around in his head. "Ain't nobody gonna miss this nigga."

"Wait. Wait. I . . . I got six kids."

"Yeah? When was the last time you fuckin' seen them?"

Dutch stalled, thrown by the question.

"Just like I thought." Omar slammed Dutch's head again. "You tossing your seed in miscellaneous pussy don't make you a father, nigga. I swear. You and my old man. I—"

"Omar," Eli snapped, not wanting his boy to

turn this shit into an episode of *Dr. Phil.* "Focus, nigga. Focus."

"Oh, yeah. Right." Omar looked contrite for half a second and then cleared his throat. "Sorry, Boss Man." Omar slammed Dutch again. "Ain't you gonna thank the man for sparing your life for a few more seconds?"

Dutch's eyes had a hard time focusing, and now that his liquid courage was all over the concrete floor and Omar's shoes, he realized how fucked his situation was. "Um. Th-thanks, Eli. Y-you know I didn't mean no harm. You know I ain't shit. I got a serious drinking problem. I-I've been trying to beat it, but the shit got its hooks in me. I be saying shit and I don't even know what the fuck I be saying sometimes."

Disgust curdled in Eli's gut, but he kept his cool while his tone remained ominous. "Nigga, this ain't a goddamn intervention. I don't give a fuck about your personal problems. I want to get at that nigga Midnight. Where he at?"

Dutch's eyes widened. "I don't know. Why the fuck would I know?" He laughed, but the shit sounded off.

Omar shook his head. "This Pinocchio muthafucka is lying." He glanced over his shoulder at Eli. "Can you believe that shit? Right to our faces."

"That *is* fuckin' bold," Eli agreed gravely.

Dutch held his breath while more sweat rolled down the side of his head.

Eli usually enjoyed prolonging these damn sentences, but tonight was an important night and they had someplace they needed to be. "Waste his punk ass."

Omar's fluorescent smile stretched across his oil-black face. "With pleasure."

"Whoa. Whoa. Wait!" Dutch tried to squirm his way out of Omar's grip. "C'mon, Eli. No nigga knows where that crazy muthafucka stay at. You gotta believe me. That muthafucka's creep is so strong that you don't know he's on you until there's a cap in your ass or a foot on your neck. Him and his boys are like ghosts. They are everywhere and nowhere at the same time."

Eli remained unmoved.

Omar clicked off the safety.

"Please. Please. I'm telling you the truth. That Haitian muthafucka ain't playing by the same rules as everybody else. I swear that nigga made a deal with the devil or something. He's into some fucked-up shit. Everybody done heard about how he waged war with King Cobra and his boys on the west side last month. When niggas found their bodies, those muthafuckas had been gutted like fish. Real medieval shit. Now he done set his sights on Don Mafia's shit, and no disrespect to your gangster, but ain't nobody seeing how y'all gonna hold this nigga off."

The blood in Eli's veins heated as he finally strolled forward. "The devil is my muthafuckin' bitch. Baltimore has been bought and paid for by Mafia Don with blood and bullets. You feel me?"

Dutch cowered while Eli's brown eyes turned black. "I hear you, Eli. I swear. I told you—I . . . I don't know what the fuck I be sayin' sometimes. Forgive me, man. Please. Don't kill me. I got some information that maybe . . . maybe you'd like."

Eli puffed out a cloud of smoke in the drunkard's face and dared his ass to cough that shit back at him.

Dutch's face turned green, but he held the shit in.

"What sort of information?"

"All right. All right. I'll tell you and then you'll let me go and we'll just forget this night right here ever happened. I didn't see you and you didn't see me—all right?"

"That depends on the information."

"All right. All right. See those niggas over there?"

Eli glanced back over his shoulder. "Those *dead* muthafuckas? What about them?"

"They . . . they were just telling me how they needed to hurry with the deal because they had a flight to catch."

Omar twisted his face. "Nigga, we ain't interested in some dead niggas' traveling plans."

"Where were they going?" Eli asked, not ready to dismiss where this was headed.

"California," Dutch answered eagerly. "The tall nigga bragged that Midnight ordered a blackout on Mafia Don."

Eli ground his jaw but failed to understand the California connection. "The don doesn't have any people out on the West Coast." *Hell, he doesn't have any on the East Coast either.*

"According to them he does . . . a kid."

Eli's hardened gaze raked the tremblin' nigga's

face for any trace of deception. Then, without saying a word, he strolled off.

Dutch's scared gaze zoomed back to a grinning Omar. "Wait, Eli. We had a deal, man."

Eli kept walking.

Omar smiled.

"Wait. Wait. Omar, wait," Dutch begged as Omar gave Dutch one last hard shove up against the wall. When he released him, the cryin' nigga slid down the wall and plopped into his own puke. "Don't do this man. Please."

Omar took one look at his fucked-up sneakers and shook his head. "You fucked up my sneaks, nigga."

"Omar—"

POW!

Dutch's head exploded open. At last, the begging stopped.

"Sloppy muthafucka," Omar spat, and then rushed after his boy. It was party time.

2

On the eastside streets of B-more, Rick Ross's latest track blasted out of Club Platinum. Security around the place ran extra deep for Don Mafia's welcome-home party. After the don spent two years behind bars, his high-priced lawyers got the charges dropped, and everybody who ever thought they were somebody came to pay their respects.

Hoodrats and street hoes writhed around the joint with their tits and asses hanging out, thinking the shit was going to get them past the velvet rope faster. There was no point in trying to tell one from the other. They all wore the same uniform and wanted the same things: a good dick to ride, a nice buzz, and a couple of dollars—not necessarily in that order. Sprung and desperate niggas rode high on a few fat bumpers and flossed harder than what was necessary.

By the time Eli was sixteen, he had long stopped looking at such females as being anything more than a way to satisfy his primal urges. It didn't stop them from trying to sink their claws into him, each one thinking they had what it took to go from ho to wifey.

There were all wrong.

Eli didn't believe in getting tangled up in strings. Having a family was like Kryptonite to a real hustler. Once niggas knew what and who were your weaknesses, they could control you.

That much Eli learned from his father.

"Looks like we have a full house," Omar commented, cutting the engine while Eli finished transferring the money from the duffel bag to a steel case. When he finished, he shoved the bricks into a compartment in the floorboard, locked it, and then handcuffed himself to the case.

"Yo, man. Do you believe that shit Dutch was spittin' back there?" Omar asked.

"What? About the blackout?"

"Yeah."

Eli shrugged. "It's possible. But I don't know shit about no kid in Cali. You?"

"Humph. Mafia Don is a man with many secrets," Omar dismissed.

"That may be true, but I think in twenty years of him raising me like a son, I would've heard about him having his own flesh and blood."

"Humph." A smile twitched on Omar's lips. "If I didn't know better, I'd say that you sound a little jealous, my man."

"But you do know better," Eli answered evenly, and met Omar's gaze through the rearview mirror.

Omar's hands shot up in surrender. "You're right. You're right."

Eli sucked in a deep, calming breath and then opened the back door. "Let's roll."

"You got it, Boss."

"Yo, Eli, man. What's up?" a miscellaneous nigga hollered when Eli hopped out from the back of his whip and slid on his Luxuriator sunglasses.

All eyes zoomed toward Mafia Don's infamous godson.

Stone-faced, Eli remained ready in case niggas wanted to try him and take that trip out to the morgue. As Mafia Don's head enforcer, he was a one-man stimulus plan for the local funeral homes—and that shit hadn't quit when Mafia Don got locked down. Eli stepped up and did what he'd been groomed to do: run shit. Under his hawkish eyes, money rained like manna from heaven and niggas feasted.

But success bred jealousy—and jealousy bred enemies. Case in point, this Midnight muthafucka. Years ago, the nigga worked for Mafia Don, but not too many muthafuckas talked about the shit. Eventually niggas did talk, and Eli now had his suspicions about the Haitian gangsta being the one who ordered the blackout on Killa E. Every time Elijah thought about that night, he remembered the man dressed in all white who was mysteriously missing when all the bodies were counted.

The nigga dropped out of sight for a long time. Now his name was becoming legendary, and the product his ass pushed was crushing the competition. For Mafia Don's crew, what had been a feast was turning into a famine.

Plus the Haitian nigga rolled into town with enough soldiers and machinery to start yet another war in the Middle East. Though Eli and his crew held the line, the streets still ran red with blood.

Omar slammed the door behind Eli and then turned with his hand on his piece tucked inside his waist. He was as black as oil, and niggas usually joked that the only way to see him at night was when he smiled—but since he didn't do that shit too often, people never saw his ass coming.

"Chill out," Eli said, placing a hand on his boy's shoulders. "We're here to have a good time."

Grunting, Omar eased off his piece, but he looked far from relaxed. Every nigga, white and black, knew they were at war—and despite the party mode everyone was in tonight, they remained tense and ready for shit to jump off at any moment.

Eli strolled past the long line, and the mountain-sized bouncers at the door parted as if his name were Moses. Inside, the place was packed to capacity. Easing through the crowd, Eli clocked the hooker and hoes ratio at warp speed. Once business was handled, he wouldn't mind releasing some stress, preferably with a thick redbone.

"Heeey, Eli," women cooed with big, greedy smiles.

Nodding, he tossed out winks to the beauties

and the chicken heads as he made his way to VIP.

"Well, well, well." Mafia Don pulled his head out from between Shemeka's new pair of double-F breasts to flash a toothy smile. "Look who decided to finally show up at my party."

To his left, Teardrop eased on a matching smile.

Mafia Don slapped Shemeka on the ass. "Leave us so that the men can talk some business."

Shemeka pouted but popped out of his lap like a toasted Pop-Tart.

Before strolling off, Shemeka's big chocolaty eyes performed a slow drag down Eli. When her lips twitched in silent invitation, Eli ignored it.

"Sit on down here, my boy." The don reached out for the bottle of Hennessy XO sitting in the center of the table as the waitress arrived and set down two more glasses.

"Make it just the one," Mafia Don said.

Omar took the hint and melted away from the table.

Eli took a seat.

"All is well?"

"Of course." Eli removed a silver key from his pocket, unlocked the handcuffs from his wrist, and slid the case under the table.

"Body count?"

"A few."

"Three?"

"A few more than that."

The Don waited him out.

"About twenty or so."

"Ho. Ho, my boy. Just you and Omar?"

Teardrop shook his head, impressed. "We need to start calling your ass the Terminator."

Eli shrugged. "All in a day's work."

"You could've taken a few more guys with you," Mafia Don said, but his smile remained stretched wide.

"It was more important that they remained here with you."

"Still don't think that the party was such a good idea?" He smirked.

"It's a bit risky."

"These days breathing is considered a high-risk game." He huffed out a breath and poured Eli a drink. "We work hard and we have to play hard—you know what I'm saying?"

"I hear you." He just didn't agree.

Mafia Don pressed his point. "A king is always safest in his castle—and the east side is my throne. I'm not about to let some crazy nigga chase me off it. If Midnight wants to roll over here and blast, we blast. But in the meantime, I'm going to celebrate with my people. You feel me?"

Eli bobbed his head and kept his real thoughts to himself. For his trouble he received another dismissive wave.

"You worry too much."

"No. It's just that a lot of things have changed since you've been gone."

"The street game has been the same since they invented asphalt: only the strongest survive. It's going to take a lot more than some nigga with breast milk on his breath to get me out of the game."

"That's what King Cobra said before Midnight relieved him of his head," Eli said, easing off his shades and meeting his godfather's gaze with sincerity.

The don's face hardened. "Don't tell me that you've traded your dick in for a pussy while I was gone too."

Eli's eyes narrowed. Had it been any other nigga who'd said that shit to him, he would've blasted a hole in the center of his fucking forehead. "I'm just informing you the new realities out here. Midnight ain't no joke, he's got a military mind—and he's ruthless with his shit."

"Yeah, yeah, I done heard about his methods. Decapitation, disembowelment—I get it." The don shifted in his chair as he took another healthy gulp of his drink. For the first time in twenty years, Eli thought he saw a crack in his godfather's bravado. Midnight *did* worry him.

"There's a new word out on the street," the don said, refilling his glass. "Have you heard?"

Eli blinked. Had he already heard about the ordered blackout?

"A snitch." Anger stiffened Mafia Don's jawline. "Can you believe that shit? It's one thing for the nigga to try and get at me with guns blazing. It's a whole 'nother thing to try and label my ass a snitch. I done caught more than a few niggas looking at me sideways tonight."

"Who?" Eli barked, glancing around and reaching for his piece.

"Too many to muthafuckin' count," he spat. "I didn't cut any fuckin' deal to roll up out of that shit hole. But with King Cobra out of the picture and Whitlock, Bell, and Graham recently locked up, this muthafucka puttin' unnecessary questions in ignorant minds. *That* shit is what worries me."

Teardrop kept bouncing his head like he was listening to a preacher on Sunday morning.

Truth be told, it worried Eli too—especially since he was a little hazy on how the trafficking charges disappeared. However, he learned a long time ago to not ask too many fuckin' questions. He sat up straighter and reached for his drink. Once he chugged half of it down, he figured that it was time to drop this latest bombshell. "Look, Don. There's something else you should know."

"Aww, shit. Can it keep?" The don stretched back in his chair and pulled out one of his favorite cigars. "Talking about this muthafucka is already affecting my mood."

"It may be nothing."

"Do you think it's nothing?"

Eli hesitated and then shook his head.

"Then let's hear it."

"Midnight ordered a blackout."

"Give me a muthafuckin' break." He laughed and then glanced over at his boy.

Teardrop grinned, but he clearly took the news more seriously.

Eli nodded until his godfather's laughter died out.

"Humph." Don tilted up his drink again, growing angrier. "Somebody needs to get me that bold muthafucka's head on a platter." He slammed his glass down on the table and then ignored it when it shattered in his hand. "I don't care if we have to look under every brick in this city. I want that son of a bitch found!"

"Believe me, I'm working on that shit."

"Not fast enough," Mafia Don snapped.

The waitress rushed over and attempted to clean up the glass.

"LEAVE IT!"

She scrambled away as fast as she came.

Jaw clenched, Eli mentally counted to ten before he spoke again. "Look. Midnight is barking up the wrong tree on this shit. Dutch said those niggas at the drop-off tonight were heading out to California. Clearly somebody fed . . ."

Mafia Don's walnut complexion paled six shades.

Mafia Don is a man with many secrets. Eli allowed Omar's words to float through his mind while his godfather struggled to compose himself. Teardrop didn't look too good either.

"How in the fuck?" Mafia Don spat, and glared over at Teardrop.

He shook his head, looking equally dumbfounded.

Despite the questions racing through Eli's mind, he held his tongue and waited until his godfather decided whether to volunteer any information.

"You're going to California," Mafia Don announced matter-of-factly.

Eli's expression remained stony. "Yes, sir."

"No bullshitting. I want you on the first flight out to L.A."

Without missing a beat, Eli reached into his

jacket and whipped out his cell phone and looked up flights online.

The don glanced over at Teardrop. "Give us some privacy."

"You got it, Boss." Teardrop hopped out of his seat and melted into the crowd.

Once they were alone, Mafia Don reached for the Hennessy in the center of the table with his bleeding hand and chugged from the bottle.

After assessing a time he needed to be at the airport, Eli returned his phone to his inside pocket and waited.

Mafia Don got straight to the point. "I have a daughter."

Eli hid his shock. At his silence, his godfather continued. "Don't take it personally that I kept it from you all these years. I only tell muthafuckas my business on a need-to-know basis. You feel me?"

Eli bobbed his head.

"*Now* you need to know," the don said. "And I need for you to go out there and protect my little girl. She doesn't have nothing to do with this street shit. Her mother . . ." His voice choked off, and he snatched up his drink again for another chug. "Her mother, Angel, took off after an ambush attempt over on Lombard. Shit. If it wasn't for your father, Beecher and his niggas would've taken me out that night. Probably woulda been ruling all this shit on the east side."

Eli's lips hiked upward into a proud smile. Hardly a day went by that someone didn't tell him how much of a street superhero his father had been back in the day. He'd snatched a lot of niggas out of the jaws of death but blasted a whole lot more.

"Anyway, Angel and I survived the ambush. I took some lead, but my girl got shook and took off out west. She didn't tell me about my daughter until her second birthday. And that was only because I popped up unannounced. Shit got dicey and complicated real fast, but in the end we continued on in our separate ways. It was probably for the best. A few years later, she married some slick-talking lawyer and tried to pretend my ass never existed."

Mafia Don glanced off thoughtfully.

Eli waited through the silence, which included another chug of Hennessy and the don pulling out two cigars. "Smoke?"

"Sure." Eli accepted the fat cigar and bit off the back.

"I'm telling you all this because your presence may not exactly be welcomed when you get out there."

"Is that right?" Eli said, leaning forward to accept the offered flame for his cigar. After a few tokes, he eased back with thick billows of smoke coiling between them.

"Yeah. Just because things didn't work out between me and Angel doesn't mean that I shirk my responsibilities. I mean . . . I'm a man. I take care of mine. You feel me?"

"I hear what you're saying."

"We didn't talk much, but she never turned down the money." He grunted. "At the same time, she kept me away from my kid." Mafia Don reached into his jacket again. This time, he pulled out a picture from his wallet and slid it across the table. "That's my little girl. Named her Blake."

Your government name.

"I hated it at first, for a girl, but it kind of grew on me."

Eli glanced down, but then his brows sprang up.

"She's quite the looker, ain't she?" the don baited.

Eli's gaze took in a breathtaking redbone with seductive green eyes and a Playboy smile. His chest tightened up when he also took in baby girl's perfect Coke bottle frame.

Mafia Don snatched the picture back. "Show the proper respect, nigga. That's my lil girl you're drooling over."

Chuckling off his embarrassment, Eli tried to clean up the damage. "Nah. It's nothing like that. I'm just surprised, that's all."

"What? That I can have a daughter this beautiful?" The don looked back down at the photo while another smile hugged his lips. "She's the spitting image of her mother." He sighed. "God rest her soul."

"She passed away?"

"Yeah. A couple of years back—about a week before I got busted."

Eli remembered his godfather taking a trip out to the West Coast back then. He was really hush-hush about it.

"Car accident," Mafia Don said. "Took out her and her husband. Muthafucka was drunk at the time and got T-boned at an intersection. I went out for the funeral. Thought I could be a shoulder for my lil girl—even thought that it would be a chance for us to establish a real relationship. Turns out, she inherited her mother's stubbornness and temper." He sighed. "Last time I talked to her, she yelled that she never wanted to see or hear from me again. So . . . don't expect a red carpet to be rolled out for you when you get there."

"Thanks for the heads-up." Eli digested the information. "How many niggas know about her?"

"Counting you and Teardrop? Two."

Eli's lips twitched. "Then how?"

"I don't know but I ain't gonna sleep on this shit. You get out there and you protect my lil girl whether she wants you to or not."

"Done," Eli said simply.

"And another thing." The don took a long toke off his cigar. "Keep your dick in your pants."

The men's eyes locked.

"I love you like a son, but she ain't for you. Got it?"

"Got it."

3

Two weeks later . . .

Who in the fuck is this muthafucka? Blake's gaze shot back up to the rearview mirror of her Jaguar convertible as she eyeballed the black Mercedes GL550 stalking behind her off Wilshire. Mercedes were a dime a dozen in Beverly Hills, but it was the blacked-out windows that caught her attention first thing that morning. Still she dismissed it. Maybe it was some celebrity or overpaid professional athlete who was getting their rocks off riding behind the illegal tint. The second time she spotted the vehicle, she dismissed it as being a coincidence. Then she spotted it a third time.

And now a fourth time.

Her mind flew through a list of potential shady characters she'd worked with in the past. The entertainment business had its share of dangerous and unscrupulous people, and she had crossed a few of them to take B. Scott Management firm to the top. A few illegal recordings and a couple of compromising photos had opened quite a few doors that would've otherwise been closed to her. Recently, one door blasted open when a certain studio head, Ajet Austin, with conservative family values had been recorded freebasing and fucking a snaggletoothed crack-head who went by the street name Juicy.

So what that Blake hired and paid Juicy for the lurid and graphic video. So what that she blackmailed the scum for $2 million and then forced his studio to hire a few of her clients for major features. Hardball was the only game played in this industry—and she was a champion at the game. Besides, only idiots and fools believed in luck—and she was neither. She believed in hustlin' and creating the illusion of luck. Don't pimp the player, pimp the game, right?

Blake smiled, but then her gaze drifted back to the tag rolling three cars back. *Austin.* Clearly he trusted her about as much as she trusted him to fulfill her end of their bargain. But he'd soon find out that she didn't intimidate easily. Blake opened the glove compartment and removed the pink handled .38 Special and slipped it into her tote sitting in the passenger seat.

"Ms. Scott, are you still there?" her annoying, perky new assistant, Perri, chirped through the Bluetooth clipped onto her ear.

"Um . . . yeah. I'm still here," Blake said, jerking her gaze back to the road in front of her and immediately slamming on her brakes. A blue Bentley was stopped at a red light. "Fuck!"

Tires screeched as her hand locked in a death grip on the steering wheel. She slowed the momentum down enough so that when she tapped the back bumper, her airbag didn't deploy. However, the Bentley's driver still jumped out from behind the wheel. "What the hell, lady?"

"Shit. Shit. Shit." Blake snatched off her sunglasses, shifted her car into park, and killed the engine.

"Ms. Scott? Is everything all right?" Perri's high-pitched voice penetrated.

"Does it sound like everything is all right?" Blake snapped, climbing out of her vehicle. "Call Mr. Braddock and tell him that I'm running late for our meeting, but I'll be there as soon as I can."

"Yes, ma'am. What happened?"

"Nothing I can't handle. Just make the call." The mysterious Mercedes slowed as it rolled past the fender bender.

She used the opportunity to try and peer into the vehicle, but the driver jammed the accelerator and zoomed off down Wilshire—but not before her photographic memory got a good look at the license plate.

"Gotcha, muthafucka."

Did this chick just make me? Eli expelled a thick cloud of smoke from the corner of his mouth while his black gaze sliced back up toward the rearview. Despite the growing distance, he had no trouble at all making out the dangerous curves of Blake Scott's Coke-bottle frame. Hell, he hadn't been able to take his eyes off of it for the past two weeks. When he had headed out to the West Coast, he knew the don's daughter was attractive, but the cute fatherly picture in his godfather's pocket didn't do justice to the real thing.

Kissing six feet, Blake Scott was one hell of a tall drink of water, with mesmerizing D-cups and an ass shaped like an upside-down question mark. She was the total package with cinnamon-kissed skin and haunting green eyes. He'd sat and watched her hypnotize every man she came in contact with. No doubt she'd get out of this little fender bender without the cops being called.

Elijah pulled over in front of Saks Fifth Avenue and then shifted his surveillance from the rearview to the side mirror. He was taking a calculated risk that the minor accident was what it appeared to be and that the muthafucka riding in the quarter-million-dollar car wasn't one of Midnight's henchmen ready to open fire the moment Blake stepped out of her car.

With one hand on the steering wheel and the other on the chrome Colt in his lap, Eli sat on edge, praying that his hunch was correct. He didn't mind playing babysitter, but this shit was damn near impossible to do on the DL. However, the Don was clear that he didn't want to scare his daughter or intrude on her life. Eli was only to step in if there was a clear and direct threat. After all, they were operating on the word of a dead street hustler.

As he predicted, Blake charmed her way out of having the cops called to the scene, and she even gave the driver an extra thrill by slowly sliding his number in between her breasts.

Eli laughed. Blake definitely knew her power over men. He didn't know what he'd expected when he arrived, but in the weeks he'd been tailing the voluptuous businesswoman, he'd surmised that Daddy's little girl didn't fall too far from the tree. Sure, the hustle was in a different field, but the hustle was still the hustle. From his wiretaps, he surmised the beauty had a list of enemies as long as her father's. But she handled her shit with a smile and a roll of her hips.

The Bentley and the Jag started up again, and a minute later, Ms. Scott blazed past him at a clip that was a good twenty over the speed limit.

Eli pulled off from the curb and rushed to catch up. A couple of minutes later, he parked outside of Spargo and watched Blake race inside. There was no stopping the erotic thoughts that flashed in his mind as her ass jiggled and her tits bounced as she made her way inside.

"Stop it, man. That's the boss's daughter," he voiced aloud in order to break his trance. Problem was that at this point, it wasn't working. He had never seen or met anyone like her. She stacked her own paper, kept herself up, and owned a multimillion-dollar crib in Denzel Washington's neighborhood. Apparently all earned by her own hustle. What nigga wouldn't be impressed by that shit?

In fact, more than a couple of nights, he had fantasized about kicking in her bedroom door and mussing up her perfect hair and funking up her silk sheets. She may look like an angel but something told him that baby girl knew how to put it down in the bedroom.

"Get your mind out of the gutter," he warned again. But that shit was easier said than done.

His "California Love" ringtone interrupted his private conversation with himself, and he pulled out his phone and recognized Omar's number. "Holla at me."

"Yo, nigga. You still out there enjoying your fuckin' vacation?"

Eli smirked. "It's hardly a vacation."

"Nigga, if you ain't dodging bullets, your ass is in fucking paradise right now."

"Streets still hot?" he asked, missing the action like a dope fiend.

"The muthafuckas are on fire. We lost ten soldiers last night at a swap over off riverside. Fuck. I took one piece of lead to the hip and had another graze the side of my head."

"Shit, man. Are you all right?" he asked, concerned. Resentment for being placed on babysitting duty set in.

"Yeah, man. I'm all right. But I tell you what—that nigga Midnight is putting a serious hurtin' on our operation, man. I can't wait for your ass to get back here. You have any idea when the hell that's going to be?"

"No clue." Eli expelled a long breath and then looked at his watch. *How long is she going to be up in this bitch?* It was damn near going on two hours.

"All I know is that we could've used your Terminator ass last night. I swear, some of our younger niggas learned how to shoot on a damn Xbox or some shit."

"That bad?"

"Worse."

Eli's gut looped into knots. "Yeah. Maybe I'll give the don a call. I think Dutch played our asses on this one."

"Doesn't surprise me. That nigga and the truth mixed like oil and vinegar."

Eli chuckled as he glanced at his watch. He jaw-jacked with Omar for another thirty minutes before he started getting anxious again. "Yo, man. Let me holler at you later. I need to go check on my package. Keep me posted on what's going on out there. Hopefully I'll see you soon."

"Sure. That or we can switch places. I know I wouldn't mind sitting on my ass doing nothing for a little while."

Instantly, Eli didn't like the idea of his boy peeping out his girl—well, not *his* girl technically. He shook his head in the hopes of untangling his confusing thoughts. "Later, man." He disconnected the call and then hopped out of his vehicle.

The sun was setting and the dinner crowd was milling toward the door. Eli sported a pair of seven-hundred-dollar jeans, a crisp white shirt, and a pair of aviator glasses. As he glanced around, the hostess asked whether he had reservations. He gave her a distracted shake of his head while his gaze took a second lap around the spacious restaurant.

Where in the hell is she?

"There's a forty-five-minute wait," she told him, smiling. "What's your last name?"

"Um, Mitchell," he lied with the first name that came to his head. "Can you tell me where your bathrooms are?"

The hostess pointed to the back of the restaurant. When he strolled off in its direction, his gaze took its third lap. *She's not here.* Eli's chest muscles tightened. *Where in the hell did she go?*

Instead of hitting the men's room, Eli burst into the women's' room and caused a minor riot. "Sorry, ladies. Excuse me."

"What in the hell are you doing in here?" one woman demanded.

He ignored her as he bent over to check the bottom of the stalls for the expensive blue pumps he'd seen Blake sashay around town in all day.

No such luck.

"What the fuck?"

"Hey, asshole. Get out of here," an indignant middle-aged white woman yelled.

Without a word, he rushed back out as the restaurant's manager closed in. He held up his hands and flashed his best smile to preempt the dude from going off. "Sorry, man, but you didn't happen to see a tall African American woman, stacked wearing a light blue dress, did you?"

For a moment the man looked confused. "Sir, there have been some complaints, and I'm going to have to ask you to leave."

"Yeah, okay. I just need to know whether—"

"Sir—"

"Goddammit, ANSWER ME!"

The manager jumped at Eli's thunderous roar. "I . . . um . . . no. I haven't seen—"

"Fuck it." Eli shoved the man out of the way and stormed back toward the door. One look at his hardened face and muthafuckas scrambled out of his way. *Where the fuck could she have gone?* He rushed over to the parking lot and found the spot where Blake's Jag had been parked now occupied by an Aston Martin.

"What the fuck?" He spun around. Was he completely losing his shit? Maybe she slipped out while he was searching the ladies' bathroom. That had to be the only explanation.

Eli turned and raced back to the Mercedes he had parked across the street. Chances were she had either returned to her office or was headed home. "Goddammit." Now he had to roll around town, trying to play catch-up. If something happened to this chick because of this fuckup, Mafia Don would have his head.

He jerked open the door and hopped in behind the wheel, but before he had the chance to start the car up, he heard the click of a gun a second before cold steel was pressed against the back of his head.

"Who the fuck are you, asshole?"

4

Blake's heart skipped a couple of beats when she finally took in the sheer size of this man. In a lot of ways, it felt as if she were pressing her .38 up against the back of a mountain. When their gazes crashed in the rearview mirror, danger charged every atom in the SUV and made every hair on her body stand at attention. It also could've had something to do with dude being fine as hell. There was also a sudden thumping in between her legs that she was strugglin' like hell to ignore.

"I don't have all night," she hissed, pressing the barrel harder against his skull. "Who sent you? Why are you following me around?"

Dude didn't speak, but his glittering black gaze told her that he didn't appreciate her ass getting the drop on him. Maybe the shit had never happened before.

Blake thought of the plan after her business meeting. She hid out in Spargo and called her assistant to catch a ride down. She made Perri wait despite her string of questions, hoping the man tailing her would eventually go into the restaurant to check out what was taking her so long. When he did exactly what she expected, she forced her assistant to take her car while she broke into dude's backseat and waited.

Now they were at a checkmate.

"Don't fuck with me," she hissed when it was clear he wasn't inclined to answer her questions. "I'm not afraid to use this."

Still unfazed, he remained mute.

Blake whipped the gun from his head, fired a muffled shot into the glove compartment, and then returned the weapon to his skull. "Try me if you want to."

Finally a smile crept onto the corners of his lips, and his onyx gaze twinkled with amusement. "Like father like daughter."

The simple phrase sent a shock wave through her entire system. "What the fuck are you talking about? My father is dead."

"I'm not talking about the one your mama had you calling *Daddy.*"

"That mutha—"

"Ah, ah, ah. That's no way for a lady to talk."

"What?" *Who in the hell is this muthafucka?* Blake twisted her face as if the man had crawled out from under a rock. "I don't *fucking* believe you. I don't have anything to do with that . . . criminal."

"Said the woman with the gun pointed to my head."

"I have every goddamn right since you're the one stalking my ass."

"And a fine ass it is," he said with his smirk growing. "Now do you mind moving that shit from my head before you have an accident?"

"Trust me. If I fire at you, it won't be an accident." She narrowed her gaze, but it only tickled his ass more. For a fleeting moment, she wanted to pull the trigger just so she could wipe that annoying smirk off his face.

"Why in the hell would he send you to follow me?"

His smile disappeared. Instead of feeling satisfaction, her heart skipped a beat. "What it is? Spit it out already."

"Mafia Don sent me because he believes that your life is in danger."

"Mafia Don," she chuckled, and then eased the gun from his head, but it remained pointed at him. "Look, I don't want anything to do with any of that street bullshit. I have my own life, and I can take care of myself."

"Clearly."

"I got the drop on you, didn't I?"

His jaw twitched before he said, "It will never happen again."

Blake smiled. "You're almost cute when you pout."

There was another twitch in his jaw before he growled, "Blake, I'm only here for your protection."

"It's Ms. Scott to you, and I don't want or need your so-called protection. So run your gangster ass back to dear ol' Daddy and tell him that." She pulled out her cell and texted her assistant. "If not, if I ever spot you in my rearview again, the shit won't end so amicable. You feel me?"

Perri pulled her Jag up next to his dark-tinted GL550.

"It was nice chatting with you." She clicked on the safety and then reached for the door.

"You don't understand the situation," he said.

Blake rolled her eyes, pretending that the nigga's voice wasn't like warm honey rolling over her body. "Please. You can miss me with all that ghetto drama. I don't know and I don't want to know. So get ghost." She hopped out of the backseat and crammed her piece into her purse before slamming the door. As she walked around the front of the SUV, she could feel the driver's dark gaze follow the seductive roll of her hips. Hell, he better. It took her years to perfect her walk.

She opened her driver's side door, and Perri climbed over into the passenger seat.

"Is everything all right?" Perri asked, still sounding chipper but looking confused.

"Everything is perfect," she lied, sliding on her shades, shifting the car into drive, and jamming her heavy foot onto the accelerator.

Perri clutched the dashboard while her eyes nearly bugged out of her head. "Um, Ms. Scott, maybe you should slow down."

"Buckle your seat belt," Blake said flatly while her mind raced. What the hell was her gangsta daddy thinking sending a nigga like that out here to stalk her every move? When his ass showed up at her mother and stepfather's funeral, she thought she made it clear that she wasn't interested in anything he had to offer.

She might deal in some dirt in her own industry, but she didn't want to have anything to do with a man who dealt poison on the street. Now, she'd blaze some trees from time to time, but that hard shit? Blake shook her head. She lost her stepbrother to that game. Coke, crack, heroine, Jayson didn't care as long as he could smoke, snort, or inject the shit; he was always down to take a flight.

Drugs destroyed their once-close-knit family. The lies, the stealing, the constant run-ins with the law. Her teenage years were hell and were punctuated with Jayson's death on his nineteenth birthday.

It was dealers like her biological father who fed her brother's addictions. How her mother ever hooked up with a muthafucka like Mafia Don was beyond her.

"Ms. Scott, are you crying?" Perri asked.

"What? No. Don't be ridiculous," she spat, and swiped the moisture from her face. They flew the rest of the way in silence.

Once they returned to her business office off Santa Monica Boulevard, Perri bolted out of the car and looked ready to kiss the ground.

"If you don't need me for anything else, I think I'm going to head home."

"Fine. Whatever." Blake climbed out of the car and headed toward her building. She still had a long list of shit she needed to take care of before she called it a day. But once she was nestled behind her desk, her mind refused to focus on work.

Damn. She didn't need this shit. She glanced at the phone, not so she could return any of the two dozen messages waiting for her but to contemplate placing a call out to the East Coast.

I don't want to talk to him.

But if she didn't, she knew damn well that sexy-ass Goliath would ignore her outburst and become her new shadow. "Fuck. Let's just get this shit over with." Blake grabbed her purse again and dug for the card Mafia Don had given her at the burial.

She couldn't find it. Hell, it was probably in some landfill by now. "I gotta get out of here," she announced, bouncing back onto her feet. There was no way she was going to be able to get any work done until she could find that number and give her father a piece of her mind.

Storming back out of the office and into the parking deck, Blake's mind tumbled over other possibilities where she could have placed Mafia's Don's phone number. When she was halfway to her parking space, the sound of a gunning engine and screeching tires forced her attention back to her surroundings. By that time, a black Range Rover was barreling toward her at lightning speed.

Wide-eyed, her brain frizzed out and she had mere seconds before impact.

Then out of nowhere, a muscular body flew toward her from the right while pumping a large gun that looked like a cannon.

POW! POW! POW!

Blake and her Terminator-sized protector kissed concrete while the speeding vehicle swerved again. The putrid smell of burnt rubber singed Blake's nose. When she jerked her head away from the bed of muscles that was this man's chest, it was just in time to see the SUV crash head-on into a pillar of cement.

BAM!

The impact nearly blew out what was left of her eardrums. Still, she was unable to process what had just happened.

"Are you all right?" that deep honey voice rumbled from above her.

Shit. She had no idea whether she was all right. But the brother wasn't about to wait while she performed a six-point inspection on herself. He jumped back onto his feet with his gun still cocked and aimed at the smoking Range Rover. He offered only one hand for her to use as an anchor to stand. That was when she felt the pain in her legs, ass, and back.

But all thoughts of complaining about it were put on the back burner when a second set of tires screeched into the parking deck.

"You got to be fucking kidding me," she hissed.

"Let's go. Let's go. MOVE!" His one hand now locked on to her arm as he forced her to start running.

"Wait! What's going on?" she cried, running the best she could with one heel on and one lost somewhere and clutching her purse for dear life.

"I told you earlier," he barked. His long legs carried them across the deck in Olympic speed.

"Who are these guys?" She raced along and drilled for answers at the same time.

"The people you claim not to need protection from!"

They reached the stairwell and jerked open the metal door. From there they plunged down the staircase at an even faster clip. Two flights down, she was tempted to end this madness by stopping and yanking her arm back before he pulled the muthafucka out of its socket. Hell, she didn't know this brother any better than the ones trying to mow her ass down. However, a door banging open above them told her to keep her mouth shut and to keep moving.

"Get that bitch!" a man barked.

Me? They're trying to kill me? Why?

Blake got a second wind or some shit because she finally kicked off that one shoe and took off past this bulky muthafucka who was blocking her way. On the bottom floor, she bolted out the metal door and took off running toward the main street.

"Blake, wait up!"

Shit. That brother could eat her dust. She had to get the fuck out of there.

When she dashed out into the busy intersection, cars honked and screeched, trying to avoid hitting her. It was a miracle they didn't given how dark it was.

"BLAKE!"

She kept hoofing it. However, her illusions of getting away from this gangsta gladiator were dashed the moment her foot reached the curb on the other side of the street and she was jerked straight into the air as if she weighed nothing.

"If you want to stay alive, you need to stick with me," the man growled, practically tucking her under his arm.

"Let go of me!" She clawed at his steel-like arm, but it was useless.

"Calm the fuck down," he yelled, running.

Once again her protests were cut short when a shot rang out and something hot grazed the side of her head. "Shit. Shit. Shit." This couldn't be happening. But it was. Nothing brought it home more than when more bullets started whizzing around.

POW! POW! POW!

"Shit. Shit. Shit."

"You said that already."

Blake wrenched her neck around to level him with an incredulous glare. "What, are you fucking with me?"

Instead of answering, her real live action hero turned with his cannon and started pumping bullets at the niggas chasing them.

One of the men hollered out before falling. He didn't quite touch the ground before a speeding car slammed into him and launched his body a good ten feet into the air.

Blake watched the shit like it was some type of 3-D film. Suddenly, he made a hard right and rushed into a shopping center lot.

"Help me find an open door on one of these cars," he said, releasing her.

"What?" She wobbled around on her shaky feet. But when another round of bullets slammed into a Lexus that she was standing in front of, she got moving again.

As luck would have it, the doors to the first vehicle her bodyguard tried opened. "Come on, come on. Hop in," he ordered.

She didn't hesitate and before she was even fully in the seat, he had the engine roaring to life. Great. Now she was involved in some Bonnie and Clyde bullshit. "Where are we going?"

"Does it fuckin' matter?" he snapped, shifting the car into reverse and jamming his foot on the accelerator almost at the same time. However, the moment he peeled off, a new series of bullets punched the front windshield.

"Fuck. Goddamn it," Blake screamed. Would this nightmare ever end?

In response, her driver continued to gun straight toward the muthafucka who was trying to empty his entire clip into the car.

"What the fuck are you doing?" she yelled, diving onto the floorboard.

"Saving your hardheaded ass. What does it look like?" he said, sounding calm as a muthafucka.

Next there was a thump and a man hollering out in pain.

Blake climbed up from the floor in time to see the dude through the back window as he fell back to earth again. Mouth wide open, she cut her gaze toward her maniac driver.

"You're welcome." His black eyes met hers as he swerved onto the main street.

The last thing she was going to do was thank his ass. "Who in the fuck are you?"

5

Eli smiled—not because he found their situation amusing but because he wanted to alleviate some of the fear that was plastered all over her face. "I told you. I work for your father."

"What does my father have to do with this shit that's going down right now?"

"Look. Let me just get you to a safe place and we'll talk," he countered, jerking the steering wheel to the left.

A series of loud horns blared, but Eli kept his foot jammed to the floor.

"You'll take me home is what the fuck you're going to do. Then I don't want to see you or these crazy muthafuckas chasing you ever again."

He cut her a look. "C'mon. By now you've been able to put two and two together and know that I'm not the one they're after."

Her wide eyes resembled globes of green fire. "Why the hell do they want to kill me? I don't know these bastards."

Elijah didn't want to have this conversation

like this. She was angry and scared and clearly prone to hysterics—three characteristics he'd rather not deal with. "I *said* that we'll talk later."

Awkwardly, Blake jerked open her purse and dug for her .38. In no time, she had the cold steel pressed against the side of his head.

"What—You're going to shoot me while I'm driving?" He laughed. "You really do have a wire loose."

She clicked off the safety.

"Well, baby girl, you do what you have to do. Until then, I'll do what I have to do."

"You're not leaving me with a whole lot of choices. For all I know, you're taking me somewhere so you can rape me and hack me into a million little pieces."

"Yeah. Because that makes a hell of a lot of sense." He laughed. "I'm saving you so I can kill you." Eli rolled his eyes.

Blake's face heated with embarrassment while she warred with herself on what she should do.

His patience wore thin. "Either shoot me or move that damn gun from my head. The last thing either of us wants is for you to have a muthafuckin' accident." As if speaking prophecy, Eli clipped a curb and Blake was thrown against the dashboard. Her arm went wild as she squeezed the trigger.

POW!

The back window exploded.

Eli ducked and then cut an angry glare at her. "What the fuck? Are you crazy?" He reached over and snatched the gun out of her hand. "Gimme that shit."

"I'm . . . I'm sorry," Blake stammered.

Eli clicked the safety back on and ground his teeth together. "Sorry?" he thundered while tightening his grip on the steering wheel. His ears were still ringing. What he wouldn't give to replace the wheel with her long, beautiful neck.

"Well, excuuuuuse me if I'm a little rattled right now. I'm not used to having gangsters from Baltimore stalking, manhandling, and now shooting at me. Take a look around. This is Beverly Hills, not an episode of *The Wire.*"

He rolled his eyes.

"You know what? Fuck you!" she yelled, clawing her way back up from the floorboard. "Why don't you pull the fuck over and let me out?"

"Why? Did you just remember that you have a Superwoman cape flying out your ass and bullets can't harm you?"

"No. I'm violently allergic to arrogant assholes."

He smirked. "Well, pop a pill, baby girl. I'm not going anywhere."

His slick smile made Blake's heart flutter. Before she could process her reaction, her protector's GQ smile melted away and ripples of pain replaced it. "What is it? What's wrong?"

He released one hand from the steering wheel and clutched at his side. "Nothing."

Blake's gaze swept downward, but she couldn't see through his black T-shirt. "Liar!" She reached across the seats and jerked up his shirt. Her hand was instantly soaked with blood. However, she couldn't get a good look at his wound before the dude shoved her back into the passenger seat. "Hey!"

"It's nothing," he snapped. "It's just a scratch."

Blake glanced down at her red hand and then back up at him. "We need to get you to a hospital."

"Nah. Nah. It's cool."

Twisting her face, she tried to evaluate whether he was serious.

He was.

"Look," she started, "if you're hurt—"

"No," he barked, but then upon seeing her shocked face, he tried to soften the blow. "Really. I'm fine. Besides, hospitals ask too many questions."

And they will probably call the cops.

He glanced into the rearview mirror and was satisfied that they had evaded whoever it was who had been chasing them because he started to ease off the accelerator. "We have to dump this car," he said.

"What? But you have to get me home."

"Chances are the po-po will pull us over long before we get anywhere near your side of town. I might be wrong, but I think the bullet holes may stand out." He turned onto the next street, where a long string of restaurants lay ahead. "Bingo."

Blake looked at him like he was crazy, but this time she kept her mouth shut.

A couple of seconds later, he pulled into an Italian restaurant's crowded parking lot.

"This is stupid," she mumbled under her breath.

"Just make sure that you grab all your shit," he told her. He glanced over her shoulder to her gun lying on the seat. "I'll get it," he said, physically thrusting her away from the door.

Blake rolled her eyes while he grabbed her weapon and purse. He shoved it all into her hands and then tucked the gun into the waist of his jeans. "What? You don't trust me?"

"I don't trust anyone."

Climbing out of the car, they caught curious gazes from guests heading into the restaurant.

Blake fluttered on a fake smile, tugged on her ripped dress, and hand-ironed her tousled hair. However, her self-appointed protector gave them all a *mind-your-own-fuckin' business* glare.

"C'mon," he said, yanking her arm.

Blake tried to jerk free, but with his steel grip, it wasn't happening. "I could scream," she warned.

"And I can knock you out and sling you over my shoulder," he retorted in the same fake syrupy-sweet voice she'd used.

"You wouldn't dare."

His answer was a deadly glare that sent goose bumps marching down her spine. He would dare . . . and probably would enjoy it.

"Fine," she said. "Where are we going?"

"Somewhere safe."

"Like?"

"We'll figure something out," he said, still dragging her along.

"No. Hell no. That doesn't work for me." She tried to dig her heels in but was reminded that she was now barefoot. "Stop. Or I swear I will scream rape at the top of my voice."

Growling under his breath, he snatched around and faced her. "What is it now?"

"I want your word that you'll take me home," she said.

"That's probably not the safest place for you right now. If these clowns are bold enough to come at you at your job, I'm sure they'll try your house next."

"Then what the fuck are you here for? If you're going to protect me, protect me. But I'm not going to turn my life upside down and start hiding out in shady hotels for the rest of my life. No fucking way." She glared up at the towering gangster, but in truth, she was just seconds away from bursting into tears.

He sucked in a deep breath, and Blake sensed that there was a small window to reason with him.

"Look, I have a top-of-the-line security system there. There's no way they—whoever the hell 'they' are—will be able to get past it."

"I got past it."

Blake's confidence collapsed. "You did? When?"

"That's not important right now." He sucked in a deep breath but appeared to be mulling over her request.

Even this pissed Blake off. Somehow she found enough strength to break his steel grip. "Fuck it. I'm going home. You can shoot me if you want to." She turned and marched. She didn't know what the fuck he was going to do next, and she was past caring. "I don't know you, and I'm tired of this whole fucking situation."

"Trust me. You're safer with me," he warned.

"Says you." She kept marching.

Stalemate.

A series of muscles twitched along Eli's jawline before he tossed up his hands and marched behind her. "All right. I'll take you home."

Blake jumped at the sound of his deep voice rumbling behind her, and when she swiveled around, she rammed into a brick wall of hard muscles. She stumbled backward, but he caught her before she fell to the ground.

Fuck. Was he built out of iron and steel? Blake swallowed and resisted the temptation to feel him up.

"Now, if you're finished with your temper tantrum, we need to get off this fuckin' street." He went to grab her arm again, but she jerked it out of reach.

He closed his eyes as if praying for patience. When he opened them again, his black orbs seared into her, but when he spoke, it was in a tone dripping with saccharin. "After you," he said, gesturing like a gentleman for her to walk in front of him.

Blake's lips twitched at the small victory. "Thank you."

Twenty minutes later, they arrived to her estate via a car service Blake kept on her cell phone speed dial. Since their little blowup, she and her protector hardly exchanged more than a handful of words. It didn't mean that her mind wasn't racing with new questions.

After entering her security passcode, she turned toward her unwelcome guest. The man's

Goliath frame swallowed up space like it wasn't shit, and there was such a dangerous vibe radiating from him that she found herself questioning her sanity in allowing him in her house. With her .38 tucked in *his* waist, she had no other choice but to trust that he was who he said he was.

And who is that exactly? She frowned when she realized she hadn't even asked him one of the most important questions. "What did you say your name was again?"

"I didn't," he stated as his eyes roamed about the foyer.

Blake's hands balled at her sides. "Don't you think you should tell me?"

His dark eyes zoomed back to her, causing her heart to stumble over a couple of beats. "Elijah. Friends call me Eli."

"And what do your enemies call you?"

"Who said I had enemies? I'm a pussycat." He winked.

"Uh-huh." Her gaze drifted downward to the slow, steady drip of blood hitting her marble floor.

"Shit!" Blake rushed over to him. "You're fuckin' up my floor."

Eli looked down and then allowed her to propel him to a half-bathroom on the bottom floor. "Pop a squat," she told him while she made a beeline toward the medicine cabinet.

Eli lowered the lid on the toilet and sat down.

"Take off your shirt," she commanded.

Ignoring the pain, he whipped off the shirt and then watched as Blake pulled out everything in the cabinet. "Do you know what you're doing?"

"Why? Do you want to go to the hospital now?"

"I didn't say that."

"Then pipe down and let me do what I have to do." She doused some gauze dressing with peroxide and went to work on his bleeding left side. "Huh. It's looks like it went in and out," she said, referring to the small hole.

"Disappointed?"

She glanced up into his amused face. "Just because I'm not happy about this new situation doesn't mean that I want you dead."

"Good to know."

Blake forced herself to concentrate on the task at hand, but it was difficult to pretend that she wasn't feeling this brothah. Hell, he was simply too fine with his chiseled six-pack, V-cut hips, and a tapestry of tattoos. Her heart and clit thumped in the same wild beat. She was even afraid that if he looked close enough, he'd see her hand and legs were trembling.

"Do you want me to do this?"

Fuck. He has noticed.

"I got it," she said, avoiding his gaze.

Eli's sexy lips expanded while he watched her.

Blake suspected that she looked as nervous as a cat in a room full of Rottweilers. She half wished that he'd say something slick again so she could hide her attraction behind a fake wall of anger, but he failed or refused to accommodate her. At the feel of his gaze slowly roaming over her, she sped up the process.

"You're getting a little rough there, aren't you?"

"I'm just trying to finish," she said tersely before slapping on an adhesive bandage. "There. That should hold you for a while."

He glanced at her handiwork and then nodded. "Thanks."

She shrugged as she stepped back. "Don't mention it." This time when he stood, she noticed old bullet scars. "Looks like you're no stranger to getting shot."

Eli glanced down at the keloids on his shoulder and chest. "Got them when I was eight."

Her brows jumped. "A little young to be gangbanging, isn't it?"

"You can say that."

Blake waited for him to say more. She sensed that he wanted to, but only dead air hung between them. When he reached for his shirt, Blake grabbed hold of it first. "I'll toss this into the wash. After that you can start this whole crazy story from the beginning."

6

An hour later, Blake interrupted Elijah's story for the millionth time. "What the hell is a blackout?"

Huffing out a long breath, he wrestled with his straining patience. He understood her need to know why her life had been tossed upside down, but it grew harder to remember his place in the story while trying to keep his dick from stretching down his leg while he did so. He found that last part frustratingly difficult.

Bossy—yes.

Attitude—off the fucking charts.

None of that shit had nothing to do with the fact that he wanted to toss her back on the over-pillowed chaise she was sitting on and fuck her damn brains out. He didn't normally go for the uptight, bougie type, but then again, Blake Scott did exhibit some gangsta touches that appealed to him. And what the hell was the name of that sweet perfume she had on? *Come Eat Me*? Fuck if that wasn't exactly what he wanted to do right now. On cue, Eli's stomach churned and his mouth watered at the thought of some Grade A pussy.

She's Mafia Don's daughter, he reasoned with himself. *And you're like a son to him. So hooking up would be like some fucking weird incest thing.* As soon as that jacked-up rationale crossed his mind, the devil on his right shoulder reminded him that there was no shared DNA coursing through their veins. Like a son was not the same thing as actually being a son. That was a major fucking loophole as far as his dick was concerned right now.

"Hello?" Blake waved a hand in front of his face. "What the fuck? Are you going to tell me what the hell a blackout is or not?" she demanded.

"It's when a hit has been ordered on someone's whole family."

Her already large green eyes grew wider. "What?"

He held up his hands in an attempt to calm her down.

It didn't work.

Instead, she launched onto her feet and shouted louder, "WHAT?"

Eli stood and towered over her. "I know that all of this is coming at you fast and heavy. Just take a couple of deep breaths—"

"FUCK YOU!"

"Or not." He shrugged. "Though screaming and shouting isn't going to change anything. What's done is done."

"That's easy for you to say. Nobody is trying to kill *your* whole fucking family!"

A memory clip of Eli's sister, mother, and twin brother and father getting smoked flashed in his head.

"What the hell am I talking about?" she asked, smacking her forehead. "The only fucking family I have left is some ghetto wannabe mafia boss on the East Coast who got me into this situation in the first place."

She's fucking beautiful when she's mad.

"C'mon. He's your old man. You can't seriously believe that he wanted any of this shit to come down on you."

"How in the fuck should I know? I don't even know the man."

"And who's fault is that?" he asked.

"Excuuuuuse you?" Blake folded her arms and swiveled her neck. "What the fuck do you know?"

Eli's lips twitched while his dick did a slow creep back down his leg. "Correct me if I'm wrong, but a few years back Mafia Don did roll out here and reach out."

"Yeah. At my parents' funeral." She paused while her eyes narrowed. "He didn't get them killed, too, did he?"

"No." Eli thought about it. "At least, I don't think so."

She gasped.

Quickly he shifted back into damage control. "No. No. No. I'm sure he didn't."

"You know what? I don't want to hear any

more of this shit. I want *you* and your boss out of my life!"

"I'm sorry, but that's not going to happen—especially now that we know Midnight's threat is real."

"For how long?" she erupted.

Eli shrugged his big shoulders. "For however long it takes."

A look of sheer horror covered her face. "That is unacceptable!"

He laughed. "This isn't a contract negotiation. You can't pay me off or blackmail me."

Blake unfolded her arms to jam her fist onto her hips. "And what the fuck is that supposed to mean?"

Eli kept his stony features blank. "It means whatever you think it means."

Blake's fiery green eyes narrowed, while a cute wrinkle lined her forehead. "Just how long have you been following me around?"

"Long enough to know that you and your father aren't as different as you like to pretend." He lowered back into his chair and stretched out his long legs.

"You gotta be fucking kidding me. The last time I checked, playing hardball with a bunch of Hollywood studio heads isn't the same as selling poison to the young and the weak-minded." Her gaze raked him again—this time with a hell of a lot more contempt. "Something I imagine you know a whole lot about yourself."

He smiled. "I know a whole lot about a lot of things." Eli took his time allowing his gaze to roll over her Coke-bottle curves, and he reflectively bit his bottom lip.

"Stop that," Blake snapped.

"Stop what?"

"Stop looking at me as if you're mentally fucking me."

One of his groomed brows rose toward the center of his forehead. "Familiar with that look, are you?"

"Go fuck yourself," she hissed, turning and marching toward her kitchen.

Eli climbed back up onto his feet and followed.

Opening the refrigerator, Blake grabbed a beer and turned around, only to jump two feet at seeing him standing so close to her bumper. "Goddamn. Are you going to follow me if I have to take a piss too?"

"Only if you're into that kind of thing."

"What? No. Gross." She popped the top off her beer bottle and then downed half the contents in one chug.

"Feel better?" he asked.

"That will happen only when this whole nightmare is over and you and Daddy Dearest are out of my life."

Eli bounced his shoulders with indifference. "I'm not so bad. I have a way of growing on people."

"Yeah. Under the nails like fungus."

He threw his head back and laughed. "Damn. Is that your bougie way of telling me to fuck off?"

"Oh. I haven't made that shit clear yet? Fuck off!"

"Baby girl, you're directing your anger at the wrong person. I wasn't the one trying to shoot that beautiful head of yours off your shoulders. If Midnight—"

"Midnight?" She rolled her eyes. "What fucking kind of name is that anyway?"

"You know, I'll make a note to ask him just before I put a bullet in the center of his forehead."

"Oh. You will do that for little old me?" She batted her eyelashes.

"I just so happen to have a few scores to settle with him myself," he informed her.

She sucked in a few more angry breaths, but she still looked pissed as shit.

"You know," he said, stepping closer, "I could use a beer myself."

Blake's neck swiveled. "Clearly your ass got me confused with Hazel the maid." She stormed off.

Eli chuckled and grabbed himself a beer out of the fridge. When he returned to the living room, it was to see Blake dialing on her cordless. "Who are you calling?"

"The police."

"What the fuck?" In two quick strides, Eli crossed the room, snatched the phone out of her hand, and tossed it against the wall.

"Hey! What the hell is your problem?"

"What the fuck is your problem? You can't call the police."

"The hell I can't. You said yourself that a crazy muthafucka put a hit out on me."

"And what the fuck do you think the boys in blue are going to do for you?"

"How about arrest that crazy muthafucka?"

Eli shook his head. "It don't work that way, baby girl."

"Will you *stop* calling me that? I'm not your fucking baby girl."

"Take a laxative and chill out," he yelled. "I've told you that I'm not the fucking enemy. I'm here to make sure that you keep sucking air. But you're crazy if you think the po-po are going to do anything more than hand your ass a fuckin' report, especially on some street shit. I'm the best chance you got to stay alive, and if you took two seconds to calm down, you'd recognize that."

Blake glared.

Eli took it as a sign that they were headed in the right direction. "Good. Glad you're finally listening to reason." He turned up his beer and emptied the entire bottle. "Now where am I sleeping tonight?"

She opened her mouth and he held up a finger. "And don't say outside."

Blake snapped her jaw shut.

Eli rocked his head back and laughed. "You know, baby girl, I think we're going to get along just fine."

7

Blake stormed into her bedroom and slammed the door. When the loud bang didn't immediately alleviate her anger, she opened it back up and slammed it again. She would have gone for a third time, but it occurred to her that her antics were probably tickling the shit out of the big Goliath downstairs. This shit couldn't be happening, but one look down at her scrapes and bruises told her that this nightmare was real.

"Okay. There's got to be some other way to settle this shit." She plopped down onto the edge of the bed. She was a smart woman. Surely she could figure something out. But how does one go about talking someone out of killing them? Offer them money? Hell, she'd met her father. She understood why someone would want to eighty-six his ass. What kind of medieval shit was it to order a hit on a muthafucka's whole family?

Her mama was right to get away from Mafia Don. Blake's gaze shot over to the black-and-white picture of her mother sitting on the nightstand. Her heart muscles wheezed painfully. There had never been a stronger or more beautiful woman. Sure. Her mother had made her share of mistakes—her brief time with Mafia Don was a testament to that—but after relocating to California, she got her shit together and put herself through nursing school. After that, she found a real man who was willing to put a ring on it and not just put a baby on her.

When Blake was thirteen, her mother opened up and told her the truth about Mafia Don. The drugs, the women, the violence—from the jump Blake didn't want anything to do with the man. He was just a sperm donor as far as she was concerned. Over time, she did develop a natural curiosity about the man. He sounded more like urban legend than a real character.

Then came her brother's issues and once again Blake despised men like Mafia Don. No, he didn't deal drugs to her brother, but it was niggas like him who did.

Now she had a glorified drug dealer in her house, playing bodyguard.

So what he was the finest thing she'd seen in a long-ass time. The man was dangerous. He killed two people like it was something on his to-do list. Blake's stomach churned, and the next thing she knew, she was on her feet and racing for the adjoining bathroom. She barely got the lid up on the toilet before she was spewing her guts. There wasn't much before she was dry-heaving and suffering stomach cramps.

When she finally lifted her head, she jumped when a cool, wet towel was pressed against it.

"Shhh. Calm down," Eli said. His black gaze was riddled with concern. The way he could so easily flip the script from being a gangster to a gentleman threw her. "It's all right. You just had a bit of a shock tonight," he said.

Shock was an understatement.

Eli smiled, and as a result her ass melted on the stone floor. "What are you doing in here?" she asked.

"You took care of me downstairs. Figure that I should return the favor." His hand drifted down the right side of her face and cupped her cheek. For a full minute they shared an electrifying charge that stole their breaths.

Blake quivered and a second later her clit exploded with an instant orgasm. First time that shit had ever happened to her . . . with her clothes still on.

Oh, this nigga is dangerous.

And then Blake went back to throwing up.

Eli went back to playing nurse. "Shhh. Shhh. It's all right."

After a while, her stomach settled down, though having his hands still touching her kept her temperature sky-high. "I'm all right," she croaked, shoving his hands away and forcing herself back to her feet, but her legs had turned to Jell-O. Judging by the thick, rubber band smile stretching across his lips, he knew his effect on her. "I appreciated you trying to help, but next time, knock before you barge in here."

Eli unfolded his large frame and hovered above her. Even if someone planted an AK-47 to the back of her head, Blake wouldn't have been able to stop her eyes from roaming over the brothah's chiseled body. Not only was he fine as fuck, but he smelled good too.

Too good.

"Sorry. I didn't mean to overstep my bounds," he said, not looking sorry at all.

Blake nodded, but he wasn't making any attempt to leave. Worse, there was a strong part of her that didn't want him to leave—at least not until after he ripped her clothes off and fucked her until she qualified for disability benefits. "Do you mind?" she snapped.

Those sexy-ass lips stretched wider. "Not at all." Eli backed away. "But if you need anything—"

"You'll be downstairs on the couch," she finished for him, not bothering to offer him one of the other eight bedrooms in the house.

"You got it." He winked, then turned and strolled off.

Blake's gaze dropped down the gangster's broad back and settled on his nice ass. What she wouldn't give to grip that mutha—

What the fuck am I doing? She shook her head as if that was going to somehow force common sense back into her brain.

It didn't.

She still had images of him ripping her clothes off and pounding her pussy like it stole money from him.

At the door, Eli flashed a final smile over his shoulder and headed out.

It wasn't until then that Blake realized she hadn't been breathing. When she sucked in a breath, her weak lungs threatened to collapse. She unrooted her feet and then rushed to slam the door behind him. This time, she heard his laughter from the other side. "Asshole."

A chuckling Eli took his time strolling through the house. He was aware of the sexual tension humming between them, and if it hadn't been for his loyalty to her father, he would be waist-deep in pussy right now. Instead, he roamed through her large mansion, checking rooms and windows. Her much-bragged-about security system was some simple bullshit from a local alarm company. A nigga worth a pinch of salt on the street could bust into this muthafucka with his eyes closed.

First thing in the morning, he would have to see about upgrading her shit. An hour later, he had a list of all the things that needed to be changed or updated if he was truly going to make this bodyguard thing work.

The one question that looped through his mind was the same one that Blake asked earlier: "How long is this job going to last?"

Surely the don didn't expect him to stay out in Cali forever. Surely the crew was closing in on Midnight and bringing his reign to an end.

If not, his position as number two would be at

great risk in the organization. After all, who in their crew would respect a glorified babysitter?

Eli mulled the question over in his head and then reached for his cell phone.

The don picked up on the second ring. "Eli?"

"Yeah. It's me."

"Is there a problem?" Mafia Don asked. "Is my baby girl all right?"

Eli wasn't used to hearing such worry and concern in his boss's voice. But again, he never had to worry about his daughter on such a level. "Yeah. Everything is cool. We had a little bit of trouble today, but it was nothing that I couldn't handle."

"So the threat is real?" he huffed.

"I'm afraid so." Eli drew a deep toke from his cigar before dropping more news. "My cover has been blown. Couldn't be helped."

"Damn." The don exhaled a long breath. "I imagine that she's not taking that shit too well."

"A little cursing, a little yelling, but all in all I think she sees the value of my sticking around."

"Oh yeah? Did she, um, say anything about me?"

Eli hesitated.

"Never mind," Mafia Don said sourly. "I don't think I want to hear it. Just . . . keep her safe. That's the most important thing I need you to do right now."

"Hey, you know that you can rely on me. Always."

"Good. Good." He expelled another breath, and Eli could hear some tension leave him.

"How is progress going on that nigga Midnight?"

"Muthafucka still floating around this town like a goddamn ghost. This now-you-see-him-and-now-you-don't bullshit is rocking my nerves. But trust and believe I'm going to murk this nigga myself."

"Yeah?"

"Hell yeah. This fucking city ain't big enough for the two of us."

8

Blake woke with a massive headache. In fact, it was so bad that at first she was convinced that she was suffering from a hangover—but she couldn't remember drinking anything. Groggily, she lifted her head off the pillow and was stunned to see that she was wearing the same clothes she'd worn the day before.

"What the fuck?" Slowly, yesterday's and last night's event came back to her.

Elijah Hardwick.

The shooting.

Mafia Don.

The blackout.

"Fuck, fuck, fuck." Blake plopped her head back down onto her pillow and pounded the mattress with her fist. Why couldn't this shit have been just a bad dream?

Knock. Knock. Knock.

Blake's head shot back up as the doorknob turned. She exhaled in relief when she remembered that she had the good sense to lock the door last night.

"Blake?" Eli's sexy baritone melted through the door.

"What do you want?" she snapped, making sure that he couldn't miss her irritation.

He had the nerve to chuckle. "I wanted to see if you were interested in breakfast?"

Blake's stomach growled at the mere mention of food—so loud, in fact, she didn't have any doubts that he heard the bastard out in the hallway.

"Come on. I make a mean Spanish omelet," he coaxed.

Rolling her eyes, Blake climbed out of bed and crept toward the door. "Toast?"

"If you'd like," he said.

She cracked open the door and experienced a jolt to her system at seeing him standing there, bare-chested with his peek-a-boo V-cut hips above his black jeans. Blake forced herself to stop staring. "Coffee?" she croaked.

"Already percolating."

She nodded. "I'll be right down."

His smile expanded. "Can't wait."

Blake shut the door before she actually started drooling. The man had that kind of effect on her, which was insane, considering that she couldn't stand his ass. She rushed and submerged herself into a hot shower, hoping the pelting, hot water would take the edge off her growing horniness.

No such luck.

As a poor substitute, she reached for the baby

oil and proceeded to rub one out. She closed her eyes and imagined Eli's thuggishly fine body hovering above hers. No doubt, a man with his incredible shoe size was working with a pipe that could hit her three G-spots at the same time.

Blake tossed her head back as she pictured grabbing hold of Eli's muscled ass as he thrust his thick shaft into her tight walls. A soft moan slipped past her lips as her fingers eased in and out of her pussy. Surely, a brothah like him talked shit when he was putting in work.

"*You love this dick, baby girl?*"

"Yes," she panted aloud.

"*Whose pussy is this?*"

"It's yours, baby."

Blake's fingers quickened their pace while a scorching heat swept across her body.

"I'm coming," she announced, feeling the first orgasmic quake hit her knees. "I'm . . . I'm . . ." At long last her mouth sagged open in a soundless scream. When her clit detonated, her entire body rattled like 7.0 earthquake. The tremors were so powerful that she had to reach out and brace herself against the tiled wall with her free hand until her body's honey finished gushing down the drain.

However, the minute Blake entered the kitchen and Eli turned to hand her a piping-hot cup of coffee, she was right back where she started with her titties and clit aching for his touch.

"Cream and sugar?"

Blake was creaming all right. "No. Black is fine."

Eli's lips hitched upward.

Her eyes narrowed. His ass was too damn cocky.

"Breakfast is ready," he said, picking up her plate and handing it to her.

Blake's stomach roared like a lion about to feast on wildebeest.

"Damn, girl. Maybe I should hook you up with one of those T-bones you got in the freezer too."

Blake snatched her plate. "That won't be necessary."

"You sure?" He lifted his thick brows while his gaze roamed over her thick frame. "You don't have to be all sidity around me. I like a woman with a healthy appetite."

"I'll file that under useless information," she said, rolling her eyes and shuffling toward the dining room table.

Eli laughed as he grabbed his plate and followed her to the table. "You know, just because we started off on the wrong foot doesn't mean that we have to stay there. After all, we're going to be spending a lot of time together."

"That's up for debate," Blake mumbled.

"Actually, it's not," he countered. "Your father made that shit clear to me last night."

"You talked to my father last night?"

Eli bobbed his head while he cut into his omelet. "Had to give him a progress report."

"And what did he say?" she demanded.

"Nothing much. He was relieved that you survived our ordeal yesterday." He cocked his head. "Would you like to talk to him?"

She fixed her mouth to say no, but she hesitated.

Eli lowered his fork and reached into his jeans pocket to retrieve his cell phone.

"No. I don't have shit to say to that man," she finally snapped, and then shoveled eggs into her mouth. During the ensuing silence, Blake made sure to avoid meeting Eli's intense gaze. It was hard, considering the tears in the back of her eyes felt like battery acid.

"Look. I'm not going to pretend to understand the beef between you two, but—"

"Good. Then drop it," she said, shoving in even more eggs. When she thought that she was about to gag, she went for the coffee, hoping that it would help wash it and her pride all down.

Eli kept his lips zipped while she ate like a pig. Eventually, the silence grew to be too much.

"*What*?" Blake tossed her fork down, but the loud clanking only agitated her more.

Eli remained as cool as a cucumber as one of his perfectly groomed brows lifted to the middle of his forehead.

Blake felt silly for overreacting. "Just . . . stop staring at me."

"Why?"

She blinked. "What do you mean, why? Because it makes me uncomfortable."

Eli shrugged. "Can't be helped. I like looking at beautiful things." He took a sip of his coffee while she blushed a hundred different shades of red. "Besides, aren't you used to men staring at you?"

When Blake's mouth remained opened for too long, Eli chuckled again.

"I'm so glad that I amuse you."

"You're something else. I'll give you that. Part bougie, part gangsta. I'm surprised that some unlucky bastard hasn't snatched you up and pumped you full of babies."

Blake's face twisted. "How appealing."

"Don't front. You know you want that shit. It's what all women want."

"What kind of sexist bullshit is that?"

"I'm just spitting the truth, baby girl." At seeing her embarrassment purpling into anger, Eli held up his hand in an attempt to cut off the pending explosion. "Before you start lying and calling me everything but a child of God, maybe you need to check yourself and ask whether your bullshit job can keep those cold silk sheets you got on your bed upstairs warm at night? Does running around this fake-ass town pretending to have balls like the big boys really satisfy you?" He glanced around. "This is a big house you got . . . too bad it's empty."

"Fuck you." Blake shoved her plate and knocked over Eli's coffee, making him jump up.

"Goddamn it," he roared. "What the hell is your problem?"

"You're my fucking problem," she snapped, hopping up too. "You don't know me, so don't act like you do."

Eli's lips curled. "Did I hit a nerve?"

With lightning-fast reflexes, Blake sent her hand flying across his stonelike face.

He didn't flinch.

Blake struggled like hell not to howl from the pain exploding in her hand.

"I'm going to take that as a yes," he said, smiling.

Blake's eyes narrowed. "And what about you? I don't see a ring on your finger. Is this babysitting job pulling you from a little lady back home? Or maybe I should ask how many baby mamas you got running around *the projects*?"

"Why? You want a baby by me?" His lips kicked up a couple of notches while he stepped closer. "Something like that could be arranged."

The moment he invaded her personal space, she scrambled backward.

At her frightened look, Eli's laughter rumbled throughout the house. "Calm down, baby girl. You talk a good game, but it's clear that you can't handle a real nigga."

She wanted to tell him that she could handle anything he tossed her way, but common sense told her that she needed to be careful calling his bluff. Instead, she raised her chin and tossed out, "I'm *not* your baby girl."

Eli stretched out his large hand and cupped her right cheek.

Blake flinched but held her ground.

"No. Not yet."

What the hell does that mean? She waited for her brain to squeeze out another smart-ass remark, but instead only static sizzled between her ears. "I'm going to get dressed before I end up throwing up that greasy omelet you made."

He laughed as she backed away. "Running scared?"

"Keep dreaming." She marched away with her heart hammering in her ears.

Eli kept laughing while he watched those thick hips of hers sashay away. He didn't know why he got such a kick out of fucking with her head, but he did.

As much shit as she talked, she couldn't handle what she dished out.

Eli returned to the living room and checked out the morning local news to see whether there was any mention of last night's shooting.

Nothing.

Honestly, he didn't know whether that was a good thing or not. An hour later, he glanced at his watch. Two hours later, he glanced up at the ceiling. *How long does it take for her to get ready?* Unfolding himself out of the leather sofa, he headed over to the staircase and marched up. "Yo, Blake. What time you tryna make it in?"

No answer.

Eli reached her bedroom door and, remembering her outburst last night, politely knocked. "Blake?"

Knock. Knock. Knock.

"What? You're not talking to me now?"

No answer.

"All right. All right. I'm sorry. I didn't mean to hurt your little feelings." He exhaled and rolled his eyes. "But didn't your mama ever tell you not to dish it out if you can't take it?" He chuckled at putting in his last jab.

When there was still no response, he expelled another long breath and knocked again.

"Blake? Don't you think this silent treatment is childish?"

No answer.

He tried the door.

Locked.

"C'mon. You gotta be shitting me," he said, feeling his patience draw near an end. "Blake, open the door." He waited and told himself to count to ten. He reached three before he started hammering and banging on it. "Enough with the fucking games," Eli snapped. "Open the door."

No answer.

Alarm bells fired off in his head. "Goddamn it!" Eli rammed his shoulder into the door. The hinges gave way like they were made out of plastic, but what shocked him more was finding Blake's bedroom empty. "Fuck!"

9

"Fuck that muthafucka," Blake hissed under her breath as she peeked over at the side view mirror of her candy-apple-red Aston Martin DB9. That arrogant ass had another thing coming if he thought she was just going to lie down and let him and her shady-ass daddy hijack her life.

Fine. Her life is in danger. Now that she knew the 411 and the type of characters she was dealing with, *she* would handle it.

"A security company?" a stunned Perri echoed back over the phone. "Is everything all right?"

"Everything is cool. Just get ahold of that company we hired for Ahmed last year when he went out on tour. They did a good job."

"Are you kidding? Those guys were a part of Ahmed's crew when he ran with the Crips back in the day. Ahmed was hit with twenty-odd lawsuits during that tour. They broke more arms and rib cages than we could keep count."

"But they did their jobs, right?"

Perri paused. "Are you sure that everything is all right?"

"Fine. Everything is fine. Just find a number and get me in contact with those guys. Call Ahmed if you have to."

"All right. I'm all over it."

Blake disconnected the call and zipped over to the Paramount lot to put out a bush fire between one of her clients, Wendell Faison, and A-list director Thomas Dash. The hardest part of her job was dealing with actors and their overinflated egos. And Wendell Faison's ego was growing out of control.

"Where is he?" Blake asked one of Wendell's flunkies as she hopped out of the car.

"He's in his trailer," the short man said, scrambling to keep up. "The director is over there, too, threatening to fire Wendell if he doesn't come out."

"And?"

He shrugged his pencil-thin shoulders. "He ain't feelin' it."

Actors. She rolled her eyes. "After all the shit I went through to get him on this picture, he's bringing his ass out."

"Good luck," he said.

"Luck ain't got shit to do with it." Her Prada heels stabbed the concrete as she quickened her pace. Sure enough, the director and a team of men were crowded outside the door.

"Blake, thank God you're here!" Dash tossed up his hands. "Your boy is costing me a fortune."

"I'm on it," she promised, rushing up to the door and hammering away.

Dash complained, "If it were up to me, I would've fired his ass a long time ago, but the studio won't let me. They're actin' like his name is Denzel Washington or some shit. I'm caught between a rock and a hard place."

"I know. I know." Blake attacked the door again. "Wendell, open up!"

Dash leaned over and hissed, "I don't know what kind of bullshit you pulled to get this two-bit actor on this project, but I'll be damned if I'll let you sink my career along with it."

"It's not going to come down to that," she snapped.

"You're damn right it's not. I still got a name in this town, and if I get fucked on this, you better believe I'm going to return the favor."

Their eyes locked at the clear threat, but unlike her hardheaded client, she knew better than to piss off a four-time Oscar director—not without some kind of insurance policy. "Give me five minutes."

After another round of silent eye combat, Dash bobbed his head and stormed away. His team followed behind him, leaving her and Wendell's flunky to share an *oh, fuck* look. Drawing a deep breath, Blake turned toward the trailer door and pounded that mutherfucka like the damn police. "Wendell, open this goddamn door before I torch the muthafucka with you in it!"

At the sound of heavy footsteps approaching the door, she eased up.

"Are you alone?" Wendell asked.

Is this negro high? Blake glanced at her watch. *Shit. It's not even nine o'clock yet.* "It's just me and—"

"Gerald," his short flunky answered.

The moment the lock disengaged, she threw open the door and stormed into a thick marijuana haze. "Have you lost your damn mind?" She shoved him back from the door.

"Ow," he whined like a bitch as he stumbled backward.

She was not in the mood. "Do you have any idea what the fuck I went through to get your ass on this picture? Now you're holed up in this fuckin' trailer costing the studio more money than you've ever seen in your damn lifetime actin' like some scared bitch."

"I know. I know." He twisted up his face and tugged on his robe.

"You fuckin' *know*—so what's the problem?" She jabbed her hands onto her hips as a way to prevent them from flying across his jaw.

"I . . . don't know if I can do this. Kissing on niggas and shit." He shook his head. "What if muthafuckas start thinking my ass is really gay and I get typecast?"

"Please tell me that you're fuckin' with me." Blake twisted around. Was Ashton Kutcher about to pop out and say that her ass is being punked? She glanced around to check for cameras.

Wendell picked up a blunt from an ashtray and toked on it before answering, "Nah. I wouldn't joke about no shit like this." He blew out a long, steady stream of smoke while his eyes drifted low. "Look, I already got a bunch of niggas from my old crew clownin' about my ass being in some black *Brokeback Mountain* shit. How am I supposed to hold my head up after that shit?"

"Let's get some shit straight." She marched over and snatched the blunt out of his hand. "It's called *acting* for a reason. You came to me moaning and groaning about how your last agent couldn't even get you an audition for this picture. So now that I've pulled some strings and put you on *without* an audition, you want to pull a big *fuck you* on me and blow my shit up. Do I have that right?"

"Nah. It's nothing like that," he weaseled.

"Yes, muthafucka, it is." Blake got up in his face. "You're fuckin' with my rep now, and I can't have that shit. You wanted into the big leagues. I got you in. Now quit your bitchin' and get your ass out on that set. You're going to kiss, fuck, or do whoever or whatever the hell Dash wants you to."

Wendell opened his mouth, and Blake slapped her hand over it before he said word one. "If you so much as *think* about fuckin' this shit up, I'll hire someone to shove a hamster up your ass and then drop you off in front of a string of paparazzi at Cedars-Sinai. You feel me?"

Wendell's eyes bugged.

"Don't. Test. Me," she warned, smashing the blunt out on his chest.

Wendell winced, but he kept his mouth shut.

"Good. I'm glad that we understand each other." Blake straightened up and hand-ironed her black trousers and crop blouse. "You have two minutes." She turned and stalked toward the door. "Don't make me come back on this set," she said, and bolted out. *Ungrateful muthafucka.*

Blake spent the rest of her morning putting out fires all over town. She didn't mind so much since it made her feel like she was back in control of her life. It didn't stop her from checking the rearview for Eli's fine ass every two seconds. Skipping out on him this morning didn't mean that she had seen the last of him—nothing about him said that he was the kind of brothah to give up easily.

I can still go to the police.

"And tell them what?" she argued with herself. That story Eli laid on her last night sounded dubious at best. All she had were street names of characters who lived in another state. No. She was going to handle this shit herself. Blake placed another call to the office.

"B. Scott Management," Perri answered.

"Did you call Ahmed?" she asked.

"I, uh, just hung up with him."

"And?"

"Bad news. Apparently the man who was head of his security last year was killed a couple of months ago. Ahmed said it was all over the news."

Blake rolled her eyes. "Great. Just great."

"Would you like for me to find, er, a more *legit* security firm?"

"I don't know," she hedged. If she was dealing with street thugs, shouldn't she get people who knew the game? Instantly, her mind skipped to Eli again. Not only did the brothah take down niggas like the Terminator, but he also looked damn fine doing it.

"Ms. Scott?" Perri chirped.

"I'll call you back." Blake disconnected the line and swore under her breath.

Riiiing. Riiiing.

She glanced down at her cell's caller ID.

UNKNOWN.

Eli.

She didn't know how she knew. She just had a sneaking suspicion that it was him ready to cuss her ass out. Her fingers itched to accept the call. If she did, she would be giving up control—and she wasn't ready to accept her father's henchman into her life *indefinitely.*

Blake shook her head and allowed the call to go to voice mail. If she had to, she'd check into Hotel Bel-Air and hide out until this whole thing blew over.

Over the next few hours, she submerged herself back into her work. Wheeling and dealing with studio top dogs ate away the day. By the time night descended, she'd almost forgotten about her *gangster* problem.

"I want that video," Ajet Austin stressed from across the dinner table.

"That's not possible." Blake took the last bite of her salad. Had she known that he was going to spend the whole meeting begging her for the tape, she would've canceled.

"This is unacceptable," he said, mopping the sweat from his forehead. "I've already kept my end of the bargain. I've put *six* of your clients in top film productions. How much longer are you going to hold that video over my head?"

"It's called insurance," she reminded him.

Ajet slammed his fist onto the table, causing the dinnerware to jump.

"And that's my cue," she told him, dabbing the corners of her mouth. However, when Blake went to stand up, Ajet's hand struck out like a snake and latched around her wrist. "Wait! Don't go."

She glanced down at his grip and waited for him to remove it.

"Please," he added, and then slowly released her.

Holding her temper in check, Blake shifted her gaze back to him. She couldn't help but get off on the way he squirmed in his seat. She remembered when she first got into the business and applied for a position at his studio. The jerk-off had taken one look at her and gotten up and locked his office door. Muthafucka thought that every bitch was desperate enough to suck his pasty-ass, needle-thin cock in order to get through the door.

He thought wrong. Now look at his cryin' ass.

"Sorry, sweetheart, but we're going to play this game until I get good and tired," Blake informed him, and watched as a rainbow of color rushed across his face. She knew if she was just dealing with Ajet and his greedy Hollywood ambitions, he would have told her to kiss his ass a long time ago, but Ajet's older brother had political aspirations. Some people even speculated that he had what it took to make it all the way to the White House. All of that would be shot to hell if he had a brother who loved snorting smack off ten-dollar hoes.

"C'mon. Smile," she told him. "This is the *beginning* of a beautiful relationship."

More sweat beaded across Ajet's forehead while his left eye twitched.

"I don't like this shit," he grumbled.

"Too damn bad." She glanced at her watch again. "You got this? I got somewhere else I got to be."

"But we're not finished talking."

Rolling her eyes, she reached into her clutch and then tossed down a stack of twenties. "I hate to eat and run, but we've covered everything." She turned and, again, Ajet grabbed her hand.

"I'm not finished talking to you, *goddammit*!"

Every head in the restaurant turned toward them.

Somehow she managed to keep her smile intact while she calmly told Ajet, "Unhand me."

Sweating like a pig, he lowered his voice. "I need guarantees. That . . . that as long as I play ball, no one—absolutely no one—will ever see that shit."

"I've already given you my word."

"Your word?" He laughed.

"Take it or leave it."

"And what if something happens to you?"

The hairs on the back of her neck jumped to attention. "What the hell is that supposed to mean?"

"N-nothing," he stammered. "I'm just asking. Is there a law against me asking a question now?"

Blake held her tongue while her mind raced with a new possibility. How desperate was this man to get his hands on that video? "Let's just say that you better hope that nothing ever happens to me or that lil recording will go viral faster than you nuttin' on that crackhead's titties."

Ajet's jaw tightened into a hard line.

She flung his hand off of her as the puzzles inside her head clicked together. "Fucking asshole." Blake stormed out of the restaurant before she did something that was going to land her behind bars. Blazing out the front doors, she now had no doubt in her mind that last night's attempt on her life had nothing to do with her father's bullshit and *everything* to do with her own.

If it hadn't been for Eli, the shit probably would've worked too. Fuck. That meant that she really was indebted to her father.

She was so preoccupied rearranging the puzzle pieces inside her head that she didn't hear Ajet come up from behind her to swing his big-ass arm around her neck.

After the initial shock, she used one hand to try and break his hold and shoved the other hand into her purse for her piece—but it was gone. Eli never gave her weapon back.

"Fuck you and your damn word," Ajet hissed, tightening his grip.

Plan B.

Blake used both arms to try and break his grip

while simultaneously jumping up and bringing her sharp heels down onto his toes.

"Awwww!"

Despite Ajet's howl of pain, his hold remained locked across her neck. Her lungs burned inside her chest while the pressure inside her head built. Any second now she was going to fuckin' pass out, and God only knew what that asshole's plans were after that.

No. I can't die out here like this.

She kept scraping at his arm, getting nowhere. When darkness crept around her peripheral, a familiar baritone rumbled from somewhere out of the night.

"Let her go."

Ajet and Blake froze until Eli's voice returned, even more menacing. "Don't make me repeat myself."

At long last, the pressure against her windpipe loosened and she was able to slip away. She choked on her first sip of air and stumbled against the trunk of her car.

"Please . . . don't shoot," Ajet begged.

She turned and saw this big-eyed muthafucka with his hand up and trembling like a leaf. "Please, Blake. Tell him."

"Tell him what—that you *didn't* just try to kill me?"

Eli clicked off the safety.

"What?" Ajet tried laughing the shit off. "We were talking. We were just having a simple misunderstanding . . . that's all."

Blake straightened up, but with one hand still

pressed against her sore neck. "I know you don't think my ass is about to save you."

"I wasn't . . . I wasn't going to kill you or nothing. I swear. I just maybe . . . wanted to scare you a lil bit." Tears raced down his face while he blew a few snot bubbles. "I don't want to die. Please. Don't kill me."

She couldn't believe this shit. Her gaze shifted to Eli. The murderous look on the brothah's face caused her heart to skip a beat. However, when his inky black eyes shifted to her, the last thing Blake felt was danger.

"Are you all right?" Eli asked in a velvet tone that fucked with her already-weak legs.

"I'm cool," she lied.

He nodded and then returned his attention to where his huge cannon was planted at the back of Ajet's head. "Want me to waste this muthafucka?"

Ajet dropped to his knees and burst into tears. "Please, please don't. I'm sorry. It'll never happen again. I'll do whatever you want. Just please . . . please, don't kill me."

Blake had never seen no shit like this before. "How do I know that you won't hire some more goons to come after me like you did last night?"

Elijah's face twisted.

"I won't. I swear."

And there it was. This muthafucka just confessed.

"You son of a bitch!" She rushed his ass and gave him a good two-piece that rocked his head around his shoulders. Instead of taking the shit like a man, this spoiled mama's boy curled into a fetal position—but that didn't stop Blake from trying to stomp his ass into the ground. "Fuck you, muthafucka. Fuck! You!"

Ajet whimpered and cried while trying to dodge her spiked heel.

She went at his ass with everything she had. After a good two-minute workout, Eli grabbed her by the waist and dragged her away.

"Okay. That's enough."

"No! That muthafucka tried to kill me! Twice!"

"I know. I know," Eli growled. "We'll take care of his ass at another time. Right now we gotta bounce."

"What? No. We—"

"Look around," he hissed. "We got an audience."

Her gaze shot around, and sure enough, couples were staring at the scene with their mouths open.

"He attacked me!" Blake shouted with the need to set things straight. "Tell them, asshole!" She delivered a kick that burst open his nose.

"I'm sorry. I'm sorry!" Ajet cried.

"C'mon. You've made your point. Let's go."

"Fuck that. I want that muthafucka dead. You hear me? Shoot him!"

Shaking his head, Eli picked her up as if she weighed nothing.

"No. Goddammit. Shoot him!" When Eli ignored her, she searched his waist for a gun. He had to have one tucked there somewhere. She didn't get close before she was shoved into the passenger seat of the car. "How fuckin' dare—"

He slammed the door in her face. By the time she got over her shock, Eli was dropping into the seat behind the wheel.

"What the fuck do you think you're doing?"

"What does it look like?" he asked, tossing over her purse and then jamming the key into the ignition. "I'm getting us out of here before someone calls the police."

"Let them!"

The car's engine roared to life.

"When are you going to learn that the police aren't your friends?"

"You mean that they're not *your* friends. What? Is your picture plastered all over some Most Wanted poster? Is that it?"

Eli shifted the car into reverse. "Ah. There's a brain in that beautiful head of yours after all. I was beginning to worry."

"Fuck you."

"But that *mouth.*" He shook his head, shifted into drive, and then rammed his foot down on the accelerator, leaving Ajet to choke on their smoke as they peeled out.

10

"You need me," Eli boasted, cutting a look over at her. "Admit it."

"Humph!" Blake rolled her eyes and ground her teeth into a fine powder. The car was charged with so much anger, lust, and resentment that she was percolating in her seat. It was the second time in twenty-four hours that the dangerous stranger had saved her life, and she was not used to being indebted to anyone.

"Pride is a tough bitch going down," he added, reading her thoughts like an open library book.

"Speaking from experience?"

"Always." His full lips curled into that cocky smile that had her stomach twisting like crazy. She squirmed in her seat while trying to focus her attention on anything other than him. That shit wasn't easy. Elijah Hardwick was *all* man. There's so much testosterone rolling off him that her clit was as hard as a dick, and she was ready to bust a nut at any given moment.

"How's your neck?"

Until now, she hadn't realized she was still rubbing it. "It's fine."

Eli laughed. "You really are a bad liar." He pulled over to the side of the road and hit the interior light. "Let me take a look."

Alarm bells went off in her head. She didn't know if she could handle his ass touching her. She might do something she'd regret—like jump his fucking bones and ride that damn anaconda she saw stretching down his leg until she blacked the fuck out. As his hands approached, she shrank back like a bitch.

Elijah's face twisted, but then a second later his cocky smile glided wider. "What? You're going to act like a big baby now? A few minutes ago you were demanding that I put a bullet in someone's head in front of witnesses."

"Yeah. And you couldn't do me that simple favor," she pouted.

His black gaze locked onto her. "There's a right way to do things and there's a wrong way."

The look he gave her was both deadly and sexy. She didn't even have to check her panties to know that they were completely soaked.

"Tell you what," Eli said, leaning toward her and flooding her senses with his scent. "If you *really* want me to erase that muthafucka, just say the word and that white nigga won't see the sun. I promise you."

Her breath tripped up in her lungs while two things hit her at once: one, she had never ordered anyone to be killed before, and two, if Ajet was out of the picture, her leverage at the studio would go up in smoke. It was one thing to be pissed but was a whole 'nother thing to bite the hand that fed you.

Eli cocked his head. "Well? What's it gonna be, baby girl?"

"I'm thinking. I'm thinking."

"Scared to take your gangster training wheels off?"

"I'm not scared," she lied defensively. His sexy lips twitched again, and she wanted to smack the smile off his face—either that or fuck his brains out. Blake was having a hard time deciding which.

"Uh-huh. Just what I thought."

"Whatever." Blake rolled her eyes with attitude to try and cover the fact that she punked out on ordering her first hit.

Still laughing, Eli crooked a finger at her. "C'mon. Let me take a look at your neck."

"Why? Are you a doctor now?"

He laughed. "You don't believe in cuttin' a nigga a break, do you?"

"Not if I can help it."

"Let me guess. Some nigga done you dirty and now the rest of us muthafuckas got to pay for it?"

"Get the hell on with that shit," she said, cutting her eyes away and folding her arms underneath her breasts.

Eli's laughter filled the entire car. "I swear, all you females are the same."

"No. The. Fuck. You. Didn't." She rolled her eyes up and down his frame.

"Look. I keep it one hundred at all times. If you can't handle the truth, then it's best not to come around me." He shut off the light. "Personally, I don't have time for bitter bitches. Life is too fuckin' short."

"Bitter?" Her head damn near snapped off her neck. "How come every time a woman roadblocks a nigga's weak-ass game, she gotta be bitter? Did you ever think that maybe *you're* the problem?"

Eli laughed. "I hear you talkin', baby girl, but you ain't saying shit."

"Whatever."

"Does that mean that you're *not* going to tell me who old dude was? Did he cheat on you?"

"It's none of your damn business," she snapped, and then realized that she'd walked right into his trap.

"I knew it."

"Fuck you."

"If you weren't the boss's daughter . . ."

While the sentence hung in the air, some really freaky, nasty shit floated across her head. "Wait. Come with it. If I wasn't Mafia Don's daughter . . . what?"

"Nothing." His lips twitched again.

"And I'm supposed to be the bad liar?" She rolled her eyes. "Who would have thought that a big nigga like you is actually afraid of—"

"Ain't nobody said shit about my ass being afraid of no damn body," Eli growled with an intensity that scared her. "Elijah Hardwick ain't afraid of no man. You feel me?"

"Right. Because you do everything my father tells you to do." She folded her arms. "I'm confused. Does that make you his boy, his bitch, what?" Judging by his body language, her words were like lighting a bundle of dynamite.

"I've never hit a woman before." His eyes glistened dangerously. "Don't be the first."

Blake's heart stopped beating.

His dark eyes looked like bottomless black holes.

She struggled to swallow the knot in her throat. "Whatever."

A few long seconds passed before Eli nodded and eased back into his seat, but there was still a tension between them that a chainsaw couldn't slice through. "It's about respect," he qualified. "And more than anything, I respect Mafia Don—for shit you can't even wrap your bougie mind around. I owe that man my life—and for that I agreed to come out here to La-La Land to babysit your ungrateful ass."

"Ungrateful?"

"Call me crazy, but I don't think it's too much to expect a lil more gratitude from someone whose life constantly needs saving—from her own shit as well as from her father's."

If she kept grinding her teeth, she was going to need dentures before the week was out.

His right brow lifted. "Well?"

"Well what?"

Eli shook his head. "Whatever, baby girl. You do you." He eased the car back onto the road and headed out to her crib. The whole time, he did this sexy gangsta lean with one hand on the steering wheel that caused her to keep checking him out from the corner of her eyes.

Blake pretended like she didn't give a damn what the fuck he was doing or thinking. But the truth was, she was aware of every breath his ass took. If her clit was a dick, it would be sticking straight up—Lord knew it was hard and thumping against her panties.

By the time they rolled back up to her place, she was angry *and* horny.

"We need to talk," Eli announced, following her into the house.

The last thing she wanted to do was talk. "Later. I'm not in the mood." Blake kept marching toward the staircase. She needed to put as much distance between them as possible. However, she didn't get so much as a foot on the staircase before her arm was almost wrenched out of its socket and she was jammed up against the wall.

"Who in the fuck do you think you're talking to?"

Eli mean-mugged her so hard that she wondered who was supposed to protect her from *his* ass.

"You really think that I'm some punk muthafucka you can pop the fuck off to, don't you?"

"I . . . I . . ."

"Well, let me correct you on a few thangs, baby girl. That ain't how this shit here is going to go down. I'm a fuckin' man, and I'm going to be respected as such."

"Or what?" The words were out of her mouth before she had a chance to stop them.

A black cloud blanketed his face before the nigga wrapped one arm around her waist, picked her up, and marched with her tucked under his arm toward the living room. When it finally registered that she was staring at the floor and at his feet, she kicked and screamed, "Are you crazy? Put me down!"

"Not until we get that mouth of yours under control," Eli growled.

"Fuck you! Get out of my house!" Blake pounded on his steel thigh but hurt her hands in the process. Next thing she knew, Eli dropped down onto her couch and stretched her across his lap. She still didn't get what he was up to until that first *whack* across her ass.

Blake screamed as though a blowtorch had been lit under her—mainly because that's exactly what the fuck it felt like.

WHACK!

"What the fuck are you doing? STOP!" She thrashed around, trying to scramble off his lap, but it was like being locked down by steel bars. Her ass wasn't going anywhere.

Whack!

Shit. My entire ass is on fire. "Stop!"

"Apologize."

"Fuck you!"

Whack!

"*Aaargh!*" Her eyes burned as water poured out of them, fucking up her vision.

"I said, apologize." *WHACK!*

"Let me go! Let. Me—"

Whack!

The pain was now radiating up her back and down her legs. *I can't take any more of this shit.*

She had never had a spanking in her entire life. The shit was beyond humiliating.

Whack!

"All right!" Blake panted like she had run around the world in sixty seconds. She wasn't going to be able to sit down for a week.

"All right, what?" Eli growled behind her.

She hesitated as her brain scrambled for another way out of this shit.

"A hard head makes a sore ass." He lifted his hand again.

"All right. I'm sorry," she barked as her pride shattered into a million pieces across his lap—but he didn't let her go.

"Are you going to control that smart mouth of yours?" he asked.

What choice do I have? "Y-yes."

"Is that a promise?"

She heard the amusement in his voice, and her humiliation expanded until her face was as hot and sore as her ass.

"I can't hear you," he teased, lifting his hand again.

"Yes, dammit!"

With a loud chuckle, he released her. She scrambled so fast that she lost her balance and tumbled onto the floor, causing the pain in her ass to explode.

Eli's head rocked back with laughter.

"I'm so glad this shit amuses you," Blake spat, struggling to get up.

"Would it make you feel any better if I told you that spanking you hurts me more than it hurts you?" He jutted out his hand as an offer to help her up.

She ignored it and climbed up from the floor on her own.

He shrugged with a big ol' smile. "Suit yourself." He stood. "Now that we've come to an understanding about your attitude, let's address some of the other issues. For example, no more Houdini bullshit. If I have to chase you around town again, tryna figure out how to sit will be the last thing on your mind. You feel me?"

Blake was too angry to speak, so she nodded.

"Good." He puffed out his chest, entirely too pleased with himself. "From here on out, think of me as your shadow. Where you go, I go. Understand?"

She nodded again.

Elijah laughed at her forced humbleness. "Call me crazy, but I think that you're growing on me."

11

It looked like tearing Ms. Thang's ass up was just what the doctor ordered. For the past thirty days, things churned like butter. While Blake wheeled and dealed with the big shakers in town, Elijah played bodyguard in the background though clearly he made a lot of her Armani-clad business partners nervous, but so far nobody tried to flex since he left Ajet Austin choking on exhaust fumes.

It's a good thing, Eli guessed. Few niggas would complain of having to follow Blake's fine ass around town, but he wasn't the ordinary nigga. He could see himself getting used to the West Coast's laid-back style. And he sure wouldn't mind making some of the long green he saw floating around Beverly Hills.

True, he was used to being in the eye of the storm and fighting his way out. It kept the mind active and the reflexes sharp. But seeing how things rolled out here, he could be open to changing shit up one day.

Life without gangbanging. What would that shit be like?

Today, they were back on a movie set where a client was acting like a stone-cold bitch. He had lost count of how many times they had been out there to see this muthafucka. Don't get it twisted—he wouldn't want to be slobbering on some nigga on camera either, but all the whining was working his nerves.

"Nigga, just quit if you don't want to do this shit," Elijah blurted out after Blake spent another hour yelling and threatening this muthafucka.

Wendell's eyes bugged out as he shot a look over at him.

"Don't pay him any attention," Blake said, giving Eli the *shut-the-fuck-up* look. "Nobody is quitting anything. Wendell here is going to stop bitching and stack this paper."

Elijah rolled his eyes but checked his commentary. Good thing, too, because Blake really let him have it when they returned to the car.

"What the fuck do you think you were doing back there?" she raged as they slid into the backseat of the car of the day: a white Maybach 62.

"Looked like you needed some help." He shrugged.

Her head nearly rotated off her shoulders. "Did I ask you for help?"

"Nah. But it seemed like the gentlemanly thing to do."

"And what the fuck do you know about being a gentleman?"

Drawing a deep breath, he thought about that for a moment. "Not much."

"Exactly." She crossed her arms beneath her chest and then dragged her sexy green eyes over him from head to toe.

After clocking a full minute, he asked, "What?"

"Award season is coming up."

Now she was talking Greek. "And?"

"And"—her gaze performed another drag—"I can't have you following behind me looking like . . . that."

Eli glanced down at his shit. "What's wrong with the way I'm dressed?" He couldn't help but be defensive.

Blake's groomed brows inched up to the middle of her forehead. "You're kidding me, right?"

He took another look. Black jeans, black T-shirt, and unscuffed black and gold Jordans. "You trippin'." He waved her off. "My shit is tight."

"Yeah, if you're thinking about rollin' into the Source Awards. But since we're going to be attending real red-carpet events, you're going to have to come more correct than Hood Vogue."

Eli shook his head. "If you think that I'm going to let you dress me up in some monkey suit, you can miss me with that shit."

Blake leveled him with that familiar sexy look that got his dick hard. "Look. I didn't hire you for this job, and up until now I haven't said shit about you rollin' behind me lookin' like you're on some prison-work program. But this shit is important to me. It's my job and I'm not about to let you or anybody else fuck this shit up."

"I hear you talking, but . . ." He shook his head.

"I'm not asking," she said, her face purpling. "I'll call Mafia Don if I have to."

It was the first time she'd made that threat. Eli did a double take to see if her ass was serious.

She was.

It was not in him to give into a woman's demands. Shit. If you let a woman put a chain on you, she'd tug that muthafucka every chance she got. "The don is *your* father . . . not mine."

Blake reached into her purse and whipped out her cell phone.

"I don't care if you call him." He shrugged, determined to call her bluff. She hadn't called her father the entire time he'd been out here, so he doubted she'd do that shit now.

"Give me the number," she demanded.

Still not believing her, Eli gave her the number by heart.

Blake made a dramatic show of dialing. "I'm calling," she warned.

"Uh-huh."

"It's ringing."

This time, he eased back against the seat and folded his arms. *She's bullshittin'. Gotta be.*

"Um, yes. Is this . . . Blake Archer?"

The cockiness eased off his face at the use of Mafia Don's government name.

"Yes . . . yes. It's me." She cut a look at him before launching into the reason behind her call.

On the one hand, he was impressed; on the other, the chick was making it sound like he was one of her diva-trippin' clients whose ass wasn't being pampered the right way before doing his job.

"He wants to talk to you," Blake said, smiling and handing over the phone.

Grumbling, Eli reached for the phone but not before grumbling, "Tattletale."

Blake stuck her tongue out at him while her father barked in his ear on whether there was some kind of problem. An hour later, his ass was standing in a fitting room in Giorgio Armani's on Rodeo.

"I can't believe I'm doing this shit," he mumbled.

"Are you going to stand in there all day, or are you going to come out here so I can take a look at you?" Blake barked from the other side of the door.

It was all he could do to keep his eyes from rolling to the back of his head. Next thing he knew, Blake banged on the door like B-more police. "What? Damn. I know how to dress myself."

"Says you," she snapped back. "Now c'mon and let me take a look."

Elijah knew that the only way to shut her up was to walk his ass out there, but it was hard as a muthafucka not to straight buck on her ass. Before he could do anything, Blake banged on the door again.

"C'mon. I ain't got all day!" *Bang! Bang!*

About to lose his fuckin' mind, he whipped

around and damn near snatched the door off its hinges. "Damn, baby girl. Slow your roll!" He waited for her to blast off with some smart-ass remark but then finally noticed that she was looking like she was stuck on stupid, staring him down. "What?" He glanced down at his slate-gray suit to see if he left his fly open or some shit.

"N-nothing," she sputtered. "You look . . . good."

Eli's brows leaped up his forehead. He knew his ass couldn't have heard her giving him a compliment.

"*Good* is an understatement," the saleswoman said from across the room before picking up a complimentary flute of champagne and downing that shit herself. "Are you two . . . together?" she asked with hope shining in her eyes.

Given that her ass looked at Eli as if she thought he was going to rob the place when they first rolled up in here, her sudden shift in interest was funny as hell.

Blake turned on the girl. "I like your nerve. Why don't you pull that blue suit I asked you for ten minutes ago?"

The woman jumped as if Blake had fired her .38 at her head. "I'll get that for you right away," she said, and then shuffled off.

He returned his attention to Blake. "You're being a little hard on her, don't you think?"

"Why? By asking her to do her damn job?"

Eli smirked because her eyes hadn't stopped raping his ass since he snatched open the door.

"What?" Blake challenged him.

"Nothing." He laughed.

Blake caught an attitude. "It ain't nothing. You got something to say, so spit it out."

He trapped her gaze, propped a hand up against the door frame, and leaned into her personal space. "Maybe I should be asking *you* that question."

Her attitude vanished. Seeing him close in on her, he knew her ass was about to bolt two seconds before she tried. He trapped her between the door frame and his chest by propping his other hand up on the other side of her head.

"What are you doin'?" she asked, alarmed.

"Nothing. I'm just talking to you." Her favorite Cartier scent tickled his nose. If he closed his eyes, he'd swear that he was lying in a field of lilies. He knew because every night, he fell asleep with that same fragrance drifting throughout the house. "What's the matter? I'm not making you uncomfortable, am I?"

Tickled as shit, he watched her tremble while she shook her head.

"You're lying again."

"Am not." Blake doubled down, puffing up her chest and brushing those luscious titties against his chest. Fuck. Now his stomach knotted up. And damn. Did they turn the heat up in that muthafucka?

"I got that . . . suit." The saleswoman rushed back to the dressing area. "I'll just hang it up . . . right over here," she said, and then backpedaled.

While the saleswoman was doing all of that,

Blake and Eli didn't take their eyes off each other.

"What would you do if I kissed you right now?"

"What?" Blake blinked.

"You heard me." He inched even closer but resisted the urge to place his hands where he *really* wanted to put them. "I want to kiss you."

"Well . . . you . . . can't."

He didn't like that answer. "Why not?"

Blake backed farther into the wall. "Because . . . because . . ."

She was adorable when she tried to lie her way out of shit. "If I didn't know any better, I'd say that you're scared of me."

"What?" She rolled her eyes. "Don't be ridiculous. I'm never scared."

"I hear you talking." He leaned in until their mouths were inches apart. "But you ain't saying nothing." It looked like there was a rock bobbing in the center of her throat. "Yeah. You're scared."

"Am not," she protested weakly.

"Oh yeah?" Eli ran his finger down the center of her white blouse. "Prove it. Kiss me." There was a long silence while Blake's green eyes lowered to his thick lips. He ran his tongue over them LL-style and waited.

Two seconds later, she leaned forward and he went for his.

Now, he'd had his fair share of ladies, and very little surprised his ass, but the minute his lips landed on baby girl, his head was blown.

Shit started spinning, and he swore his damn blood was on fire. A kiss wasn't enough. He had to have her. *Now.*

Blake's ass must have been feeling the same way because when he picked her up and slammed her up against the wall inside the changing room, she didn't do anything but moan. He kicked the changing room door closed, but he couldn't say whether the muthafucka stayed closed. He didn't give a fuck.

Skirt around her waist, panties jacked to the side, he didn't waste time whipping his shit out and plunging into her wet pussy. However, the surprises kept coming when he found her shit tighter than a muthafuckin' drum. Her ass wasn't no virgin, but not too many muthafuckas had been up in her shit.

"Fuuuuuck," he panted, twisting his head from her sweet mouth and burying it into the crook of her neck.

"What's the matter, baby?" she cooed, and then nipped at his ear.

He tried to answer but could hardly breathe.

Am I about to fuckin' come? He slowed this shit down before he ended up being a one-minute side note. Ladies saw that shit and they thought your ass had never had no good pussy before. The more he tried to get in control, the tighter her pussy got. He slammed his eyes closed and counted muthafuckin' sheep in his head.

Even that shit didn't work.

"Your breathing sounds funny," she said, chuckling and rotating her hips.

"Whoa. Whoa. Give me a minute," he said, barely able to keep the cork from popping off the champagne bottle.

"A minute?" she asked. "What? You can't keep up, baby boy?" Her hips sped up.

His mouth dropped open and there was a tremor in his left foot. Still, he couldn't let her clown him. "I . . . I got this," he lied.

"Oh you do, do you?" Blake worked her shit in a figure eight.

Eli's eyes rolled around in the back of his head. He took his hands off her ass and braced his weight against the wall—but her legs were in a kung fu grip around his waist, and she was fuckin' him like the muthafuckin' rent was due in the morning.

"You like this good pussy?" she asked.

"Oh. God. Yes."

"You ain't never had no shit like this before, have you?"

Normally, it was in his DNA to trash talk back, but damn. Fucking, breathing, and talking were too much to handle at the moment.

Blake laughed. "Ah. You ain't got shit to say now, huh, gangsta? You thought *baby girl* was scared of the dick?"

He shook his head while her hips and pussy put his shit in a choke hold.

Knock. Knock.

"Hey! What are you guys doing in there?" a high-pitched voice shrieked from the other side of the door. "This is a place of business!"

"Just . . . just a minute," Blake panted.

It was the first time he noticed her breathing was getting a little choppy too. Feeling his own swagger creep back, he gripped her ass again, locked in at a good angle, and pounded that sweet monkey with every fucking thing his ass had.

"Oooooh shiiiit," Blake howled, digging her nails into his back.

Knock! Knock! Knock!

"Stop it! Stop it, I say," the woman yelled.

Blake and Eli were lost in their own world. Her head dented the wall, her ass slapped against his balls, and the way she looked at him had him fallin' in love.

"Aaaaargh!" Elijah's nut exploded with the force of an AK-47. Meanwhile, Blake's tight, sticky walls convulsed while she called on God like a church elder possessed with the Holy Ghost.

"Oh, Eli. Eli."

He loved how his name sounded falling off her lips. When she finally nutted up, her mouth dropped into a perfect circle, and her eyes fluttered like she was in the middle of a seizure.

Knock! Knock! Knock!

Panting, Blake and Eli looked at each other through new eyes. Honest to goodness, he believed he was staring at his rib.

Knock! Knock! Knock!

Smiling, Blake unhooked her legs from around his waist, rolled her skirt back down, and hand-ironed her hair.

Eli's honey-glazed dick still hung out of his

pants when she jerked the door open to the stunned saleswoman and her manager.

"We'll take the suits," she said calmly, and produced a black credit card from somewhere. "No need to box them up." With that, she closed the door in their faces.

12

Blake was fuckin' a-dick-ted to Elijah. She didn't even know how the shit happened. One minute they were working on getting their whole bodyguard situation down and the next they were fuckin' like rabbits ten times a day. Well, maybe not ten, but it sure in the hell felt like it. It was bad enough they got their freak on in the changing rooms in Giorgio Armani two weeks ago, but since then it had been in the back of restaurants, movie trailers, her office, every room in the house, the swimming pool—you name it, their asses fucked all over it. Whenever Eli gave her that *look,* her panties melted off. The man's dick game was so strong that he could probably cure a bitch of scoliosis.

Every time she came off one of her fuck highs, she went back to asking herself what the hell she was doing. The brother might have been fine as hell and could tear up some pussy, but it didn't change the fact that he worked for her father. That meant her ass couldn't trust him. Fucking with one eye open had never been one of her strong suits. With her eyes closed, she felt shit that she didn't have no business feeling.

Tonight was the Screen Actors Guild Awards, and she had a trio of award parties at which she had to put in face time. Award season was in and of itself nerve-racking. Blake was worried about Elijah being able to blend in. Sure, he turned into GQ material in a suit, but he still sounded hood. His cocky I-don't-give-a-fuck attitude rolled off of him like water off a duck's back.

Everything is going to be just fine. No matter how many times she told herself that in the mirror, it did nothing for the ball of anxiety rolling around in her belly.

"Are you ready to go?"

Blake whipped around from her mirror and saw Elijah's fine ass darkening her doorway. It took everything she had to keep her mouth from hitting the floor. Dark, chiseled features, mountainous shoulders, broad chest, and trim waist—shit, her ass was dizzy and she hadn't even reached the big rodeo dick he knew how to sling around.

"You know better than to look at me like that, baby girl," he warned, waving a finger. "You going to start something that gonna make you late for these parties."

"I don't know what you're talking about," she lied before whipping back around to take a final look at her reflection in the bathroom's vanity mirror. While Blake pretended to rethink the teardrop diamond earrings, Elijah performed his sexy pimp stroll up behind her until she could feel his iron-hard dick pressed up against her ass. Her smile was instant while her clit thumped against her silk thong.

"If I were you, I wouldn't change a thing." He rolled his large hands over her hips and pulled her back so that now his cock was sandwiched between her cheeks.

She closed her eyes and tried to get a hold of herself, but all she felt was her stomach fluttering, her titties tingling, and her knees knocking.

"You look stunning," he said, lowering his pillow-soft lips to the side of her Cartier-scented neck.

Her knees finally dipped, and she practically sat on his dick. From that second on, her mind scrambled over excuses to back out of tonight's events.

"What do you say to my peeling you out of this dress and we have our own party up in here? Hmm?"

That shit was so fuckin' tempting. Right then, she didn't give a damn who sent his ass there or how much trouble it would eventually bring; she wanted him. Seriously, this was how he made her feel every time he touched her.

"Say the word, baby girl." His teeth skimmed her neck, causing her to soak her undies.

Her eyes fluttered open for a few seconds, and she caught a snapshot of them in the mirror. Her heart almost stopped. They looked so damn good together. Blake couldn't have dreamed up a better specimen of a man. One moment he looked like the hardest gangsta patrolling the hood, and in the next he threw on an Armani suit and could pass for an Oxford gentleman.

While she stalled on her answer, she heard the tiny zipper on the back of her red Dior dress slide downward. "Eli," she whispered.

"Shhh." His warm breath rolled across her collarbone. "I'll be careful not to mess you up"—Eli glanced up and met her gaze in the mirror—"too badly."

Her heart and clit pounded in double time.

"We shouldn't . . ."

His lips moved to the back of her neck and started down her spine.

"Oooh." Another zipper zoomed down before her thong string was moved to the side. "Eli, baby."

"Shhhh," he whispered again, and then spread her ass cheeks. Before she could process another word, the thick mushroom head of his cock slid through her wet trenches.

"Aw, damn, baby," he growled as he sank deeper.

Before she knew it, Blake had a firm grip on the bathroom's marble countertop, preparing for the ride of her life.

Elijah, as usual, didn't disappoint. As soon as she glazed his cock all the way to the balls, he worked his daddy-long stroke on her. Nothing in her entire life had ever felt that good. If he asked her for the deed to her house or the passwords to all her bank accounts, she couldn't definitively say her ass wouldn't give it to him. That shit was crazy. She knew in her heart that didn't make a damn bit of sense, but that was the way the shit was.

After a few minutes, her mind spun so fast she knocked over hairspray and perfume bottles. That shit was okay too—just as long as he kept stroking her to where they needed to go.

Her moans and his growls bounced around the bathroom's walls to the point where it sounded like there was a whole group of people in there fucking. Add on the long strokes shortening to quick, rapid fires and her ass slapping against his balls and thighs, it sounded like an audience was applauding their performance.

In no time at all, she hurled toward an orgasm that had her speaking in tongues. Two seconds later, Elijah roared like a lion and she could feel his hot seed explode.

Blake didn't know how long they stood there. Him clinging to the back of her and her death gripping the countertop, but at long last Elijah offered, "Let me help clean you up."

She said nothing when he slid out of her pussy and turned to retrieve a few hand towels from the linen closet. She remained mute even when he soaped up one towel, set her on the counter, and proceeded to clean her. It might have something to do with the fact that he was looking in her face and watching for her reaction.

After a couple washes and rinses, she thought he was about to pick her up and zip her back into her dress, but instead he rolled her thong completely off, hooked her legs over his shoulders, and then moved his face in for some blackberry pie dessert. The instant his silky tongue glided in beneath her clit, her eyes closed and every ounce of air seeped out of her lungs.

Blake's head fell back and banged against the mirror. She couldn't care less if she fucked up the hair bun that had taken her over an hour to create. All that mattered in the world was how delicious his tongue felt twirling around inside her pussy. In no time at all, she slid her hand down in between her legs and then locked them behind Eli's head. She wanted to bathe him with her juices.

Licking and slurping, Elijah wasted no time popping off orgasm two, three, *and* four. When he removed his glistening lips, every muscle in her body had liquidized. He could pour her ass into a glass and finish her off.

"That was delicious," he boasted, puffing out his chest.

"I don't know what the fuck I'm going to do with you," she said, shaking her head, but she knew the muthafucka wasn't working right.

Eli smiled. "Well, I could take you to the bed and finish having my way with you."

As tempting as that shit sounded, reality seeped back into her brain and she knew she had to get back to her job. "Can't," Blake whined, poking out her bottom lip. "I have to work."

His sexy lips curled into a smile. "Gotta admire a woman dedicated to stacking her paper." He climbed off the floor, cleaned her up again, and then zipped her back into the dress.

* * *

An hour later, Blake and Elijah climbed out of the rented limousine and entered Warner Bro's after party. Elijah was never more than two feet from her side while she did her thing to inflate egos and make impossible promises. The only hitch that kept throwing her off was how many people assumed that she and her GQ bodyguard were an item. Somewhere between the first party and the second one, she stopped correcting them.

"You two look good together," Perri whispered, easing up to her side.

Blake gave her the *don't-be-ridiculous* look, but Perri ignored it. When Elijah had started coming around the office, Perri had tiptoed around the place with her purse always clutched under her arm.

"You can't fool me. I know a thug when I see one," Perri kept saying. But tonight, her assistant looked at Eli with new eyes. "Talk about a diamond in the rough," Perri said, sneaking another look. "Now I see why you've been giving up the panties."

"What?"

Perri rolled her eyes. "Honey, everyone on our office floor has been complaining about the noise you two keep up in your office, the conference room, the kitchen . . . and the men's *bathroom.*" She shook her head. "You might want to invest in a ball and gag. You're definitely a screamer."

Blake's mouth dropped open and her entire face burned with embarrassment.

Perri elbowed her. "Don't be embarrassed.

Besides Denzel's wife, you're one of the luckiest women here." She winked and then strolled off.

Eli moved up next to her. "What was all that about?"

"N-nothing." Blake shook off the conversation and downed the rest of her champagne. *The whole floor has heard us?* So much for keeping shit professional.

At the third party, she just went through the motions. More air kisses, fake laughter, and empty congratulations. What surprised her was when people engaged Elijah into conversation. Suddenly his ass sounded like a Harvard alumni with a double major in economics and political science. He effortlessly stopped dropping all his Gs and kept all his subject and verb agreements on point.

Who is this brother?

In the deepest throes of her admiration, Blake stopped watching where she was going and bumped into Ajet Austin.

"Should have known that our worlds would collide sooner or later," he said with all the warmth of a Popsicle.

Blake smiled. "Aw. Don't tell me that you're still sore about that tiny little incident a while back?"

His brows climbed to the middle of his forehead. "Little?"

"Well, considering you tried to kill me, I think a simple ass-whooping is getting off easy."

Elijah stepped forward and slid a protective arm around her waist. "Problem?"

Ajet's face turned every shade of red imaginable. "N-no. There's no problem. We were just . . ."

"Talking," she filled in for him. "Ajet was telling me that he has a good part for one of my clients in his studio's next picture. Weren't you, Ajet?"

His gums bumped wordlessly for a few seconds—until Eli cocked his head and mean-mugged him.

"Yes! Actually, I was just thinking that we could have Jasmin Tyler come in for an audition."

"Audition?" Blake twisted her face. "I don't think an audition is necessary. She's perfect for the lead."

"The lead?" Ajet's face purpled.

"I believe that's what the lady said," Elijah pressed, and then took a threatening step forward.

"You got it." Ajet's hands shot up. "The lead it is. I, um, will have someone fax over an offer on Monday." He backed away and then turned and raced off.

She threw a look at Eli, and his plump lips spread into a smile.

"Nice guy," he joked.

Blake cracked up.

13

An hour later, they were back at her place, and Eli was unzipping her dress before she could even get the key into the door. "I thought that we would never get out of there," he complained while nibbling on her shoulder.

"What? You don't like hobnobbing with the rich and famous?" Blake tossed her keys and clutch onto the foyer table. A second later, her dress slid off her shoulders and hit the marble floor.

"The only thing I like doing is *you.*"

"Is that right?"

Elijah wrapped his arms around her, and she hopped up and locked her legs around him and kissed him feverishly while he climbed the steps. It felt like they had been doing this since the dawn of time. He'd become the very air that she breathed.

Blake's mother was probably rolling around in her grave. Nothing good could come from anything having to do with Mafia Don, but there she was, walking a tightrope in Louboutin heels.

She sighed when her body was pressed into her Egyptian cotton and gold threaded sheets. Next, Blake squirmed with anticipation while she watched him rip out of his suit in a time that would have made an Olympian proud.

You're in love with this man.

The realization stunned her, and she immediately told herself that she was being foolish. But the minute their lips and bodies connected, the truth was undeniable.

His touch burned and soothed her in places that most people would be ashamed or embarrassed to mention. But she found herself wanting and needing to do everything that pleased him.

Stationary, on top, reverse cowgirl, they did it all, and an hour later their skin was glossy with sweat and the sheets were musky. Blake lacked the strength to pop up for a quick shower and instead curled under his arm and snuggled.

"How you feelin', baby girl?"

"Ah, the gangsta returns." She chuckled.

"What do you mean?" He laughed.

She inched closer. "C'mon. Tonight, you were all suave and proper—and speaking the King's English."

"Aw. Surprised that a brother like me can just flip the script, huh?"

"Something like that." She made lazy circles across his chest before asking the question that she'd been dying to ask. "Did you really get these bullet wounds when you were eight years old?" The energy in the room shifted, and she wished that she could take the question back.

"Yes."

She sensed that he didn't want to talk about it, but her curiosity got the best of her. "What happened?"

A long pause filled the room, but she waited him out.

"A blackout," he said solemnly.

Shock raced down her spine. When their eyes connected again, she saw so much pain in his eyes. Blake brushed her fingers across his lips.

He grabbed hold of her hands and kissed her fingertips.

"It's all right. It was a long time ago."

But it wasn't all right. "Who?"

He hesitated. "Midnight."

The surprises kept coming. "The same Midnight that my father thinks will come after me?"

Elijah nodded.

"But . . . why?"

"To this day, I'm still not really sure. The streets have a lot of conflicting theories, none that I've ever been able to nail down. My father had a lot of enemies."

"Was your father . . . ?"

"A gangster?" he supplied.

She bobbed her head.

Elijah shrugged. "He was a man who provided for his family the best way he knew how. Does that answer your question?"

Another brother fighting against the Man.

"Don't do that," he warned.

"Do what?"

"That judgmental thing that you always do.

You didn't know my father, or my mother, sister, or twin brother."

She swallowed a huge knot in the center of her throat. "Are they all . . . ?"

"Dead?" He nodded. "I'm supposed to be dead too. If it hadn't been for Mafia Don, I probably would be. He showed up that night and plucked me out of the carnage."

Tears swelled and then leaked down her face. Elijah gave her a small smile and then wiped them away with the pads of his fingers. "So you can see how when a blackout was ordered on the don's family, he found a willing protector in me."

What the hell am I supposed to say to that? "I'm sorry."

"For what?"

She didn't know. It was the only thing that came to mind. "I'm sorry that you even had to go through something like that. I can't imagine . . ." She shook her head. "I guess I'm glad that my father did this for you."

"You think that maybe you've misjudged him?"

Blake hesitated, not sure if she could go that far with it.

Elijah laughed at her struggle. "That's all right. Rome wasn't built in a day."

"You really think I should allow him into my life?"

"It's not about what I think."

She couldn't help but wonder if she was being too hard on Mafia Don. But then all her mother's warnings about the man rang in her head, and she couldn't allow herself to go there.

Eli kissed the top of her head. For the first time in her life, an invisible cloak of protection wrapped around her. Nothing and no one could harm her.

She wished that had always been the case.

"Whatchu thinkin' so hard about?" Elijah asked minutes later, pressing another kiss against the side of her head.

"Nothing."

"Liar."

Blake laughed and lightly punched his chest. "Stop that."

"Stop what? Reading you like a book? I can't help it when you make it so easy for me."

"Please. If it was so easy, I wouldn't be where I am today."

"And where is that exactly?"

She watched while he rolled one finger down the curve of her hip, amazed at how her skin tingled in its wake.

"Baby?"

"Hmm?" She had gotten distracted. "Oh. I . . . um . . . well, you know, I run my own agency in one of the most competitive markets there is, and I make damn good money."

"And that's what you call success?"

Her head jerked up to meet his probing gaze. "Damn right it is. I've proven that I don't need to depend on a man to put a good roof over my head or a car in the driveway, and I don't have to beg for an allowance—only to be stuck on stupid when a younger bitch comes along and snatches everything from up under me."

"Ah. The independent woman's anthem." Eli chuckled and rolled his eyes.

"Call it what the fuck you want, but don't act like you don't see that shit happening every day. Men take, take, take, and the minute they get our asses to rely on them, they're out the damn door. Then we're standing there like Boo-Boo the Fool with our youth gone and stretch marks all over the place, and turning tricks and calling it dating just to get by."

"Damn."

"You can front all you want, but you probably got four or five baby mamas your damn self."

"All right. Now you're just playing yourself. I don't have any crumb-snatchers running around out there."

"Uh-huh."

"I'm serious. You got the wrong player if you think that shit. I don't get down like that."

"Says the man who has used a condom with me maybe two times during all our hookups," she charged back.

Eli nodded. "You're right. And don't think there hasn't been a day I don't ask myself what in the hell I'm doin'."

Blake frowned. "You want me to believe that I'm the first woman you've never used protection with?"

"That's exactly what I'm saying." He reached down and brushed a strand of hair from her face. His touch was so gentle and caring that for a moment, she believed his ass.

"What makes me so special?" she tested. As

she waited for his answer, she became aware that she held her breath.

After his eyes roamed over her face, a small smile eased across his lips. "So far, I think, just about everything."

The tears that sprang to her eyes caught her off guard.

Elijah curled toward her, tilted up her head, and laid a kiss on her that erased all fear and doubt from her mind. When he entered her yet again, it was like a homecoming to their souls. She didn't know any other way to describe it. All she knew was that they were no longer fucking but *making love.*

It was the first time in her entire life.

14

BOOM!

Elijah's eyes sprang open in the dead of night.

For a few seconds, he strained his ears to verify that his mind wasn't playing tricks on him. He didn't hear anything, but that disturbing feeling that twisted in his gut wouldn't go away.

Lightning lit up the bedroom, and then the next second everything plunged back into darkness. His heart hammered as his eyes darted around. Something was wrong.

Glancing to his left, Blake was tucked neatly under his arm and was doing that soft snoring that made her adorable.

BOOM! BOOM!

She didn't move.

He kissed her upturned nose and eased his arm from beneath her. She moaned, but he climbed out of bed and grabbed his gat from the nightstand without waking her.

As he eased toward the door, he snatched up his drawers. Nobody liked banging with their dick swinging. However, when his hand landed on the knob, Blake popped up from the tangled sheets.

"Where are you going?" she whispered, alarmed.

He placed a finger against his lips and alerted her to keep her voice down. "I heard something."

"What?" She scrambled out of bed. "Is someone in the house?"

"Shhh. I'm not sure." He held up his gun so she could see that he was going to check things out.

"Well, what did you hear?"

"I don't know. Something."

BOOM!

Eli jumped at the sudden clap of thunder. Shortly after, the large windows rattled violently. The next flash of lightning blinded him temporarily. A second later, the sky opened and rain pounded on the glass like a million hammers.

Déjà vu.

"Are you sure that it's not just the storm?" she asked, grabbing her .38 out of the opposite nightstand drawer.

BOOM! BOOM!

"No. It was inside the house."

"Then I'm coming with you."

He wanted to tell her that the shit wasn't necessary, but the truth of the matter was that he didn't know what waited on the other side of the door. All he could do was hope that she knew how to handle her gun better than what she'd demonstrated in the car a couple of months back.

Before he knew it, she'd slipped on a robe and took the other side of the door. They looked like a black Bonnie and Clyde.

Lightning flashed and he swore he saw his eight-year-old twin brother, Easy, standing next to Blake.

"Are you sure you don't want to hide?" he asked him.

He blinked and shook the vision from his head.

"Are you all right?"

When he opened his eyes, Blake was frowning at him. "I'm fine," he said. Pushing that shit to the side, he turned back toward the door and pulled it open. He ducked his head out for a quick look before sliding out into the hallway.

BOOM! BOOM!

"Where do you think you're goin', lil nigga?" a deep, raspy voice echoed so loud from his past that he jerked his head around and expected to see that muthafucka who slaughtered his family.

But no one was there.

"Eli." Blake grabbed his free hand and rattled him back to reality. "What the hell is wrong with you?"

"Nothing," he blurted.

Concentrate on what the fuck you're doing. He

nodded to the command in his head and then continued his creep down the hallway.

Blake wasn't so quick to follow, but eventually she caught up.

When they reached the top of the staircase, something shattered against the floor downstairs.

Blake gasped, and at his stern look, she slapped a hand over her mouth. But had the damage been done?

They remained as still as statues as they strained their ears to pick up the tiniest of sounds. Finally they hear, "Muthafucka, look where the hell you're going," a man's voice reprimanded.

"Sorry, Omar. Damn."

Omar? Talk about a muthafuckin' sucker punch. Every ounce of air fled his lungs. Somehow he shook off the shock.

Blake leaned over and whispered in his ear, "There's a hidden staircase in the upstairs study."

Eli perked at the news and then allowed her to lead the way. It was perfect because if they went down the main staircase, it would be too easy to pick them off. They made it to the study without incident. Blake pulled open a bookcase that revealed an iron staircase.

He gave her a questioning look asking why she hadn't shown this hidden treasure before. Her answer was a shrug. After that, they rushed down the staircase as quietly as they could. At the bottom, the door slid open in the living room—right behind three men cloaked in black.

Without hesitation, Eli aimed at the man pulling up the rear and fired. The nigga's head exploded like a watermelon. Then all hell broke loose.

More muthafuckas rushed in from the French doors, and suddenly bullets were being sprayed everywhere.

Blake and Eli spilled into the room, taking cover and returning fire. Any doubts he had about baby girl holding her own went out the window. She picked off one nigga like a sharpshooter taking wings off a fly and consequently saved his ass while he concentrated on another nigga. He counted three more muthafuckas rushing into the house and wondered if a whole army had surrounded the place.

Between the lightning and the gunfire, Eli's heart hammered. *Concentrate.* He redoubled his efforts to block out the loud thunderstorm, but to his horror he noticed a tremor in his gun hand.

Still shooting, he was ever mindful that this clip was about to run out of bullets.

One bold nigga sprang over the couch and grabbed Blake, knocking the gun from her hand. Her scream pierced the night.

He swung his piece around in time to see the nigga jam the barrel of his gun up against her right temple.

Eli's whole fuckin' world stopped.

"Let me go, muthafucka!" Blake yelled, kicking and screaming.

Suddenly, he was that scared eight-year-old, afraid of what was about to come next.

The terror in Blake's eyes destroyed him. He leveled his gun on the nigga holding her hostage, but any thought of pulling the trigger was erased when something hard whacked him on the back of the head and pitched him into darkness.

15

My God, he's not moving!

Blake was no longer concerned about her own welfare, though she should have been since the rope was cutting into her skin. With a rag stuffed halfway down her throat, her screams were reduced to muted moans. She was only aware of the tears streaming down her face because her vision was blurred and she could hardly make out shit.

"If I were you, I wouldn't be worried about him," a voice said, stepping out of the darkness. In one hand, he held a machete and in the other hand a gun. "You're the one who's not going to see the next sunrise."

Hatred like she had never known raged through her veins. She tried to break free. What Blake wouldn't give to be able to scratch this smug bastard's eyes out. Strolling up in her house, dressed head to toe in white like his ass was headed to a P. Diddy party.

Across from her, two goons finished tying Elijah down into a chair and then proceeded to smack him in the face until he finally awoke.

"Wake up, muthafucka," the man who was clearly the leader said in a thick island accent. *Haitian?*

Eli groaned a couple of times, but then his eyes snapped open and immediately took in their new fucked-up situation.

BOOM! BOOM!

The thunder was still doing a number outside, giving this whole scene an even more ominous feel.

Blake didn't know what was about to happen next. Her heart refused to acknowledge what her brain screamed was to be the end.

When Elijah's gaze zoomed over her, she experienced a ripple of relief. Then dread coursed up her spine and rendered her numb.

"You muthafucka!" Elijah jerked and screamed.

"It's no use," another man said, moving to stand next to the brother in white.

"You're not going anywhere."

"Omar, I can't believe that you jumped ship. Where the fuck is your loyalty?"

Omar's thick rubber-band lips widened until they reached each ear. "Don't start with that bullshit. I'm about my muthafuckin' paper. I'm backin' the strongest gorilla in the jungle. Mafia Don's reign is a wrap. I know it. He knows it. And every nigga on the street knows it. Besides, the muthafucka is a snitch. His ass cut a deal with the feds and gave up Whitlock, Bell, and Graham. It was the only way his ass walked on those charges. If you weren't so blinded by his bullshit, you'd see the truth too."

Eli bucked against his ropes. He'd love nothing more than to get Omar's oily neck between his fingers.

"It's time for new management. Time to jump on the train or get run the fuck over. You should listen to my man Midnight here."

Your man? Elijah's gut twisted.

As if stepping out of his nightmare, Midnight, dressed head to toe in white, stepped forward just as another clap of thunder boomed and the house lit up.

Elijah tensed as his past and present collided in the Twilight Zone.

"So . . . we meet again, Elijah."

BOOM! BOOM!

Midnight's sinister face had gotten uglier over time. "I have to admit that I kept my eyes on you throughout the years. Impressive. Mafia Don has turned you into quite the soldier. Although a misguided one."

Eli's gaze narrowed. "You killed my family."

Blake watched the whole scene with bulging eyes.

Smiling, Midnight didn't even flinch at the charge. "I've killed a lot of people. It's all in a day's work. You know a little something about that, don't you?"

Elijah rocketed to his feet at a right angle and charged. However, he didn't get more than a couple of feet before Midnight's goons tackled him back and delivered a few hard blows across his chiseled jaw for his effort.

With each right and left hook, Blake jumped in her chair and screamed for them to stop. It was useless.

When the men stepped back, Elijah's expression was as hard and mean as ever. Twin streams of blood flowed from the corners of his mouth.

Midnight continued. "I'm here to offer you not only the chance to join my team, but also give you the gift of clarity."

"Keep your damn gifts," Eli barked. "Just let *her* go."

Omar shook his head while his new boss tsked under his breath. "Now, you know that I can't do that. She's the don's daughter," Midnight said.

"She doesn't have anything to do with this street war. You know that, Midnight."

Blake swallowed. Her gaze raked her future murderer. Besides being ugly as fuck, he didn't look half as intimidating as her man. *Her man?* When in the hell did she start thinking of Elijah as her man?

"Rules are rules," Midnight said nonchalantly.

"I thought you made your own rules," Eli challenged.

Midnight cocked his head and then glanced back at Blake.

BOOM! BOOM!

The quick flash of light gave Blake a better view of Midnight's sinister face. The man wasn't just ugly—he was pure evil.

"Let me guess," Midnight said. "The don's

old faithful soldier here is fucking his daughter." Midnight laughed. "Classic."

Omar joined in. "Looks like you're in no position to preach to nobody about loyalty."

Midnight studied Eli. "Well, I can't say that I blame you. Mafia Don and his old hooker girlfriend made quite a little princess here." He strolled over to Blake and ran his fingers down the side of her face. "Hell, I wouldn't mind having a go with her before putting a bullet in the center of her pretty head."

Blake jumped and twisted away, but the evil muthafucka laughed.

"Yeah. I bet she's a fuckin' pistol on her back."

BOOM! BOOM!

"Leave her alone," Elijah warned.

Midnight turned and faced him. "Or what?"

"Or I'll kill you," Elijah said evenly.

If he hadn't been tied down to that chair at the moment, then maybe everyone would've believed him. As it was, Midnight threw his head back yet again and laughed. "Now that's a magic trick I wouldn't mind seeing." Still, he lowered his hand from Blake's face and moved back over to Eli. "Back to my offer. I'm sorry that you have only a couple of minutes to think this over. Situation couldn't have been helped, you understand?"

Elijah glared.

"Join me," Midnight said flatly. "I can use a man like you in my organization. Smart, resourceful, and, most of all, powerful. A lot of niggas on

Mafia Don's crew would come over if they knew that you switched teams."

"You must be snorting your own product if you think that I would *ever* work for you."

"Now, now. Wait a second. You might want to think this shit over a little bit. I mean, after all, I don't see the difference between you working for the man who carried out an order versus the man who made the order in the first place."

That statement confused Elijah *and* Blake.

"Awww." Midnight waved a finger. "The truth will set you free. Besides," Midnight shrugged, "I'm better than your current alternative."

"And what's that?" Eli asked.

"You die." Midnight shrugged. "Wouldn't you rather be *in* the game instead of buried six feet beneath it?"

"Fuck you."

"You're hurt." Midnight nodded. "I can understand that. Truly. But if you think about it, I'm offering a great opportunity here."

The men stared each other down.

"Not convinced. All right. I have to admit, I would've been disappointed if you switched sides that easily." He walked up behind Omar. "You're not like your friend here—he just follows the money. You got to wonder if a nigga like that could ever *truly* have your back."

Omar frowned.

"I mean, who's to say that the second another nigga offered his ass fifty cents more than you're paying him that he won't look for a soft spot to plunge his knife into your back."

"Heeeey!"

Before Omar could turn around, Midnight swung the machete and with one fell swoop lopped Omar's head clean off.

Blake screamed with everything she had as blood shot everywhere.

Midnight and his one lone goon stood over Omar's headless body. "Silly rabbit. Tricks are for kids."

Elijah forced himself not to react.

Midnight smiled as he returned his attention to Eli. "You, on the other hand, Mr. Hardwick, your loyalties lie in the fact that you think Mafia Don saved your life."

"He did save me," Eli said evenly.

Midnight's laughter deepened. "You know, I didn't start off in this business a self-made man. Like you, I had someone who taught me the ropes. I went from a lookout boy to locking down corners to becoming a true soldier—just like you."

"I'm nothing like you."

"Oh, we're more alike than you'll ever know. My teacher was a man named Killa E—a strong militant muthafucka who became a threat to the very man he pledged his life to serve."

Elijah's face changed up.

"Then one day, Killa E's boss realized that his men were more loyal to his second in command than to him. Some real Caesar and Brutus shit. You get where I'm going with this?"

Elijah shook his head. "You're lying."

"Am I?" Midnight cocked his head. "Why would I do that?"

At the next flash of lightning, Blake swore she saw tears glistening in Elijah's eyes.

"Now where was I? Oh yeah. What was the big boss supposed to do? If he killed his beloved right-hand man, he risked a mutiny among his street soldiers. But"—Midnight waved a finger in front of Elijah's face—"if the don set it up to look like a rival crew ordered the blackout, he could throw off suspicion. And who better to use than someone Killa E trained personally?"

Midnight pressed a hand against his chest. "Now, I'll admit that I've always been an ambitious muthafucka, so when the opportunity to leapfrog over the number-two man presented itself, I jumped at the chance. Only that wormy muthafucka double-crossed my ass, too, and put it in the streets that I acted alone. Niggas chased me out of my own hometown. Headed back to my mother's native home for a while until I was able to get back into the game on my own terms. You feel me? I made my own connections, raised my own army, and now I won't rest until Mafia Don is dethroned. As far as Mafia Don saving your scrawny ass, all I can think is that the muthafucka has a sick sense of humor."

Blake couldn't tell whether Elijah was buying the man's story, but the shit sounded exactly like the kind of games her mother warned her that her father loved to play.

After a long silence, Elijah shook his head again. "You're lying."

"Deep down, you know I'm telling you the truth."

BOOM! BOOM!

"He wouldn't. He couldn't . . ."

Midnight glanced at his watch as if Eli's struggle bored him. "So what do you say? You want to help me knock that conniving mutha-fucka off his throne?"

The truth had finally come home to roost.

"Even if I believed you," Eli said, shaking his head, "there's still no way I could work for you. *Ever.*"

BOOM! BOOM!

"Too bad." Midnight swung his gun toward Blake and fired.

16

"No!"

Blake and the chair she was sitting on flew backward.

With Hulk-like strength, Elijah tore out of his ropes and charged Midnight like a Mack truck. He was so fast that Midnight didn't have the chance to turn back around and fire. His side nigga squeezed off a couple of rounds. One missed. The other one nailed his shoulder.

It was no more than a bee sting.

He jabbed an elbow into Midnight's fat lips and snatched his gat. He took another bee sting a couple inches beneath the other one. Eli returned fire and a hole opened up between the nigga's eyes before he dropped like a stone on top of the headless Omar.

BOOM! BOOM!

Eli turned his wrath on Midnight and met the man's sinister glare with one of his own. Instead of shoving the nigga's gat down his throat, he tossed it aside but reached for the dropped machete inches to his right.

Midnight attempted to scramble up, but given Elijah's mountainous size, it was a futile effort.

BOOM! BOOM!

The flashing lights illuminated the twenty-five-inch blade.

Fear registered in the Haitian's black eyes, but he thrust up his chin to meet his fate with defiance. "Do it," he ordered as if it was a dare.

"With pleasure," Eli growled, and then relieved the gangster of his head. But once he started swinging, he couldn't stop. Like an enraged butcher, he hacked off every body part he could until he was covered in the man's warm blood.

BOOM! BOOM!

More lightning flashed, allowing him to see the entire carnage in the house. Across the room, he saw eight-year-old Easy, smiling. Slowly, the image faded and the house fell silent. Elijah knew from that moment on that he would never fear another storm.

Rising to his feet, he turned toward Blake. Not sure whether he was walking or floating, Eli snatched the ropes from around her and pulled her limp body into his arms. She looked like a broken mannequin that he didn't know how to put back together again. How was it that he could always take out the meanest gangsta patrolling the street but fail to protect the ones he loved?

"Blake, baby. I'm so sorry." He brushed her

bloody hair back and stared down at her angelic face. Before Eli knew it, he was crying and praying for her green eyes to open. But he doubted that God even knew who he was.

Two weeks later, Elijah returned to the hard streets of Baltimore a different man. The cleanup he had to do in California wasn't the easiest shit he had ever done, but it was necessary.

There were going to be a lot of questions, especially since he'd refused to return any of Mafia Don's calls or text messages since that stormy night. What he had to say needed to be said in person.

"Mafia Don will see you now," Teardrop said, strolling out of the boss's office and eyeing Eli wearily.

Elijah understood. The don had suffered a lot of defectors while Eli was playing bodyguard to his daughter. However, he was careful to keep his face blank as he stood, adjusted his brand-new Armani suit, and headed into the office.

The moment he walked in, Mafia Don looked up from his polished mahogany desk with a smile that was too wide for his face. "Eli! Long time no see." He stood and looked him over. "Look at you. California agrees with you. You clean up well."

Eli smiled, knowing that the shit wasn't reaching his eyes.

Mafia Don glanced to Teardrop behind Eli. He sensed the older gangsta was shaking his head. "You didn't bring Blake with you?"

"I'm afraid she was unable to make it."

"So you left her in California? Alone? What about . . . ?" Fear seized the don's face. "She's not . . ." The don drew in a shaky breath. "Please don't tell me that Midnight . . . ?"

Elijah didn't respond.

Mafia Don dropped back down into his chair like a stone. "She's dead, isn't she?"

Eli met his gaze head-on. "I failed you."

Mafia Don's hardened features cracked. "She's gone." He let the full force of that hit him. After a minute, he added, "I thought that we would eventually . . ." He glanced back up. "Teardrop, give us a few."

"You got it, Boss."

Elijah remained standing as he listened to Teardrop walk toward the door. After it clicked closed, Mafia Don offered him a seat.

"Sit. Sit down." He gestured toward the empty chair in front of his desk.

He strolled forward like he was about to take him up on his offer.

"Tell me the details. I want to know what happened." Mafia Don climbed back to his feet and went toward the bar. "How did Midnight find her? When did this happen? How did you get away?" He plucked up a bottle of Hennessy and poured himself a drink. "You want one?" He finally glanced over his shoulder and spotted the gun capped with a silencer that Elijah had leveled on him.

"What the fuck?"

Before Mafia Don could ask another fuckin' question, Eli fired.

The bullets spun the don around, causing him to drop the Hennessy bottle. Stunned, his boss glanced down at the hole in his chest and then glanced back up at the man he raised like a son. "Why?"

"Is that a real question?" Eli asked, sliding his free hand into his pocket. Hell. Why not take his time with this muthafucka?

"Midnight," the don concluded, disgust curling his lips. "He got to you, didn't he? He told you some bullshit that got your head all spun around, didn't he?" Mafia Don shook his head. "After all these years . . . this is how you repay me? Where's your loyalty?"

"I could ask you the same for when you ordered the blackout on my family."

Mafia Don opened his mouth.

"Think before you start shoveling more bullshit my way. This gun has a hairline trigger. It could go off at any time." To prove his point, Eli fired two more shots that nailed the don in his other shoulder and then right kneecap.

His former boss toppled to the floor.

Calmly, Eli strolled forward until he was about a foot away and then squatted down with his weapon still ready to rock-a-bye this old nigga to sleep. "Tell me why. Don't I deserve that much?"

"I don't know what the fuck you're talkin' about," Mafia Don bluffed.

Elijah read the man's face and saw that his lips said one thing while his eyes said another. "All these fuckin' years, you played me for a fool. Had me looking up to you when you're the one who took *everything* from me." His finger started to move on the trigger again.

"Wait. Wait." Mafia Don lifted his bloody hand, asking for a time-out.

Eli allowed him to chug in a ragged breath so he could think of another lie.

"I don't know what that snake told you," he spat, blood leaking from the corners of his mouth, "but you gotta know that Midnight's playin' you. This is the only way he can break our bond. He needs you to take me out. You're one of the few who can get close to me. Don't fall for this shit. I'm beggin' you."

The lies floated around the room a few seconds before Eli spoke again. "The only one who has been playing me is *you.* Now all that shit is over. There's gonna be a new king ruling these streets, but it's not going to be Midnight. I chopped his ass up pretty good with his own toy. It was nice, but a gentleman like me prefers bullets, nah what I mean?"

"Please," Mafia Don whined. "Just tell me what you want. I can give you anything. Just name it."

"I already got what I want from you. And after this, I'm out. Time to make a fresh start out on the West Coast."

"What?"

"You heard me. I don't have any more love for this street shit. Figure I'll head out to Hollywood, write a script or some shit."

"You're crazy," the don said.

"Maybe. But you're about to be a dead muthafucka."

The office door swung open and Teardrop strolled in. "Hey, Boss, you're not going to believe—"

"T, shoot this muthafucka!"

Teardrop took in the scene and went for his gat, but the back of his head exploded before the gun cleared his waist.

"What the fuck?" Mafia Don barked with anguish.

A steady tattoo of heels hit the hardwood floor before Blake entered the room.

Mafia Don's eyes widened to the size of silver dollars.

"Blake?"

"Hello, Daddy." She waved her .38 at him. "I would love to say that you're looking well, but actually you kind of look like shit."

"I . . . I don't understand."

"It's fairly simple," Eli cut in. "My wife and I figured that in order to start our new life together, we first needed to make sure that you or anyone tryna to get at you don't endanger our lives."

"Your wife?"

Blake flashed her large Harry Winston rock. "Newlyweds."

As understanding dawned, Mafia Don's face purpled.

"Anyway, Daddy dearest, the way we see it, as long as you're alive, *our* lives will always be in jeopardy because of some street politics. And since Eli has a score to settle with you and I pretty much loathe the ground you walk on, this is the obvious solution for us to ride off into the sunset." She cocked her head. "You do want me to be happy, don't you, Daddy?"

Mafia Don bumped his gums, but no words came out.

"That's what I thought. I'm happy that you understand." Blake strolled up next to her husband as he stood.

Finally, the don found his voice. "You're not going to get away with this. My crew is going to come after you with everything they got."

"No, they won't," Elijah corrected. "Not after I tell them that you *are* the snitch they all think you are. You were responsible for the feds locking up Whitlock, Bell, and Graham. Nobody loves or respects a snitch."

Mafia Don took his case to his daughter. "Baby girl. Sweetheart. I know that we've had our differences, but I'm your father. We share the same blood."

"Which makes your sacrifice for my happiness all the more special," Blake said with a saccharin sweetness. She looked to Elijah as she slid her hand over his so that they both had their hands on the gun. "Shall we?"

"Absolutely."

They glanced down at the sniffling drug lord and together pulled the trigger.

Kiki Swinson, the bestselling author known for "fast, tension-packed" (Library Journal) novels featuring the glamour and grit of Virginia's most notorious streets, shows what happens when a criminal partnership takes a detour that puts its members on the road to jealousy, revenge, and murder . . .

THE SCORE

On Sale Now

LAUREN

Present Day

My feet moved at the speed of lightning. I could feel the wind beating on my skin so hard it made snot wet the inside of my nostrils. My entire body was covered with a thick sheen of sweat and I could feel it burning my armpits. My breath escaped my mouth in jagged, raggedy puffs and my chest burned. My heart felt like it would burst through the front of it. Even feeling as terrible as I did, I would not and could not stop moving.

"Move!"

"Get out of my fucking way!"

"Watch out!"

"Move!"

I screamed command after command at the nosy-ass people who were staring and gawking and being in my damn way. My legs were moving like those of a swift and agile cheetah as I swerved and swayed through the throngs of people on Virginia Beach Boulevard. I was met by more than one mouthful of gasps and groans and I could faintly see more than one wide-eyed, mouth-agape stare as people gawked at me like I was a crazy woman. I guess I did look crazy running through the high-end shopping area with no shoes on. I had run straight out of my Louboutins, my expensive embellished Balmain skirt was hitched up around my hips, my vixen weave was blowing in the wind, and my Chanel caviar bag was strapped around my arm like a slave chain. I could feel that my makeup was a cakey, smudged mess all over my face and eyes. But I didn't give a damn. I wasn't going to stop running. No matter what. Looking crazy was the least of my worries.

I had run track in high school and it was still paying off now, but clearly I wasn't in the same athletic shape. Still, I wasn't about to go out like this. I wasn't going to get captured on the street and probably murdered for something that wasn't totally my fault. I had been pushed and provoked to do everything that I did. All of the mistakes. All of the grimy shit I had done over the years. All of it was because I was born at a disadvantage from day fucking one.

I didn't want to die. I had always seen myself growing old with a few kids and grandkids surrounding me when I was ready to be settled. I would've given anything to be old and settled at this moment. But, of course, life threw me a curveball.

I could hear the thunderous footfalls of the three men chasing me. If they weren't so damn gorilla big and slower than me they would have caught me by now.

"Hey! Are you okay?" I heard a man on the street yell at me as I flew past him, nearly knocking him over. Why the hell was he asking me such a dumb question when you could clearly see that I was being chased by three hulking goons dressed in all black with their guns probably showing on their waists or maybe even in their hands. Thank goodness I am always so alert or they would've walked right up on me while I unsuspectingly ate my lunch at the posh restaurant and grabbed me. It was the fact that I had only been back in town for a few hours, the disappearance of my lunch companion, and the suspicious looks that had alerted me in the first place. How could I have been so trusting? So naïve and stupid, too.

I could feel the look of terror contorting my face, so I know damn well passersby could see the fear etched on every inch of it.

Finally, I dipped through a side alley and the first door I tried allowed me inside. Thank God! With my chest heaving up and down I rested my back against another cold metal door inside and slid down to the floor. My legs were still trembling and my muscles were on fire in places on my body I didn't even know existed. I tried to slow down my rapid breathing so I could hear whether the men had noticed me dipping into the alley but the more I tried to calm myself the more reality set in about the grave danger I was in. I was probably about to be murdered or worse, tortured and then murdered right in a dank alleyway in the place I thought I would never return to. If I hadn't gotten that call, it would have been years before I crept back here. I thought about Matt and wondered if he was the one who had sent these men after me. But how would he have known I was back? I knew Matt had a lot of selfish ways about him and although shit had gone south with us, I never thought he would try to do something like this to me. I expected that if he wanted to confront me, he would come himself. Even if it was Yancy who had sent the goons, I would think Matt would have tried to spare me.

CLANG!

A loud noise outside interrupted my thoughts and caused me to jump. I clasped both of my hands over my mouth and forced the scream that had crept up my throat back down. Sweat trickled down my face and burned my eyes. My heart jackhammered against my chest bone so hard it actually hurt. My stomach knotted up so tightly the cramps were almost unbearable. I dropped my head. Suddenly I felt like vomiting.

"I don't see her! She's not down here!" I heard one of the goons outside of the door scream to the others. I swallowed hard and started praying under my breath.

Dear God, I am sorry for all of the things I've done. I don't know how things got so far gone. I never meant anything by any of it. I just wanted to live a better life than I had as a child. I guess with the mother You gave me and the hand You dealt me, I should've just handled it. I should've worked harder and not try to take the easy way out all of the time. I knew stealing is wrong. Since the first time I stole a credit card from my foster mother's purse, I'd known it was wrong. But I got addicted to the feeling that I'd gotten over on someone. I felt powerful. I remember the times I'd hear her talking to my foster father about some of the fraud scams she witnessed by working as a bank manager. It was interesting to hear how bank and credit card frauds were being committed on a daily basis. It all seemed too easy, too intoxicating. I had to test the waters. . . .

So here I am today. I'm literally running for my life. Maybe this is Your way of teaching me a lesson. Trust me, I hear You loud and clear. If You let me get out of this, I swear I will change my life. I don't even know how things got this far . . .

Chapter 1

Our bodies arched, both of us reaching for that place of ultimate release we knew was coming. Yes! We screamed at the same time . . . except I kept screaming long after his moment had passed.

You've got to be kidding me, a cramp in my groin? The second time in the three times we had made love. Achieving pretzel positions these days came at a price, but man, how sweet the reward.

"What's the matter, baby? You cramping again?" he asked, looking down at me with genuine concern.

I was pissed, embarrassed, and in pain all at the same time. "Yeah," I answered meekly, grimacing.

"It's okay. It's okay, sugar," he said, sliding off me. He reached out and pulled me into the curvature of his body, leaving the wet spot to its own demise. I settled in. Gently, he massaged my thigh. His hands soothed me. Little by little, the cramp went away. Just as I dozed off, my cell phone rang.

"*Mph, mph, mph,*" I muttered. "Never a moment's peace."

Calvin stirred. "Huh?"

"Nothin', baby, shhhh," I whispered, easing from his grasp and reaching for the phone from the bedside table. As quietly as I could, I answered the phone the same way I always did.

"Muriel Mabley."

"Did I get you at a bad time, partner?" Laughton chuckled. He used the same line whenever he called. He never thought twice about waking me, no matter the hour. I worked to live and lived to work—at least that's been my story for twenty years, the last seventeen as a firearms forensics expert for the Philadelphia Police Department. I had the dubious distinction of being the first woman in the unit and one of two minorities. The other was my partner, Laughton McNair.

At forty-nine, I was beginning to think I was blocking the blessing God intended for me. I felt like I had blown past any hope of a true love in pursuit of a damn suspect.

"You there?" Laughton said, laughing louder.

"Hee hee, hell. I finally find someone and you runnin' my ass ragged, like you don't *even* want it to last. What now?" I said.

"Speak up. I can hardly hear you."

"I said . . ."

"I heard you." More chuckles from Laughton. "You might want to rethink a relationship. Word is we've got another dead wife and again the husband swears he didn't do it. Says she offed herself. That makes three dead wives in three weeks. Hell, must be the season or something in the water."

Not wanting to move much or turn the light on, I let my fingers search blindly through my bag on the nightstand until they landed on paper and a pen. Pulling my hand out of my bag with paper and pen was another story. I knocked over the half-filled champagne glass also on the nightstand. "Damn it!" I was like a freaking circus act, trying to save the paper, keep the bubbly from getting on the bed, stop the glass from breaking, and keep from dropping the phone.

"Sounds like you're fighting a war over there," Laughton said.

"Just give me the address."

"If you can't get away . . ."

"Laughton, just . . ."

"You don't have to yell."

He let a moment of silence pass before he said, "Thirteen ninety-one Berkhoff. I'll meet you there."

"I'm coming," I said and clicked off.

"You okay?" Calvin reached out to recapture me. I let him and fell back into the warmth of his embrace. Then I caught myself, sat up, and clicked the light on—but not without a sigh of protest.

Calvin rose. He rested his head in his palm and flashed that gorgeous smile at me. "Can't blame a guy for trying," he said.

"It's a pity I can't do you any more lovin' right now. I can't sugarcoat it. This is my life," I complained on my way to the bathroom.

"So you keep telling me."

I felt uptight about leaving Calvin in the house alone. My son, Travis, would be home from college in the morning, his first spring break from Lincoln University. He and Calvin had not met. In all the years before this night, I had not brought a man home, except Laughton, and at least a decade had passed since I'd had any form of a romantic relationship. The memory chip filled with that information had almost disintegrated. Then along came Calvin.

When I came out, Calvin was up and dressed. He was five foot ten, two hundred pounds of muscle, the kind of muscle that flexed at his slightest move. Pure lovely. He pulled me close and pressed his wet lips to mine. His breath, mixed with a hint of citrus from his cologne, made every nerve in my body pulsate.

"Next time we'll do my place. You can sing to me while I make you dinner," he whispered. "Soft, slow melodies." He crooned, "You Must Be a Special Lady," as he rocked me back and forth, slow and steady. His gooey caramel voice touched my every nerve ending, head to toe. Calvin is a singer and owns a nightclub, which is how we met. I was at his club with friends and Calvin and I—or rather, Calvin and my alter ego, spurred on by my friends, of course—entertained the crowd with duets all night.

He held me snugly against his chest and buried his face in the hollow of my neck while brushing his fingertips down the length of my body.

"Mmm . . . sounds luscious," was all I could muster.

The interstate was deserted, unusual no matter what time, day or night.

In the darkness, I could easily picture Calvin's face, bright with a satisfied smile. I could still feel his hot breath on my neck, the soft strumming of his fingers on my back. I had it bad. Butterflies reached down to my navel and made me shiver. I felt like I was nineteen again, first love or some such foolishness.

Flashing lights from an oncoming police car brought my thoughts around to what was ahead, a possible suicide. How anyone could think life was so bad that they would kill themselves never settled with me. Life's stuff enters pit territory sometimes, but then tomorrow comes and anything is possible again. Of course, the idea that the husband could be the killer could take one even deeper into pit territory. The man you once loved, who made you scream during lovemaking, now not only wants you gone, moved out, but dead.

When I rounded the corner to Berkhoff Street, the scene was chaotic, like the trappings of a major crime. I pulled curbside and rolled to a stop behind a news truck. After I turned off Bertha, my 2000 Saab gray convertible, she rattled in protest for a few moments before going quiet. As I got out, local news anchor Sheridan

Meriwether hustled from the front of the news truck and shoved a microphone in my face before I could shut the car door.

"Back off, Sheridan. You'll know when we know," I told her.

"True, it's a suicide?" Sheridan persisted.

"If you know that, then why the attack? You know we don't give out information in suicides."

"Confirmation. Especially since two other wives have been killed in the past few weeks."

"Won't be for a while. Not tonight anyway."

"Thanks, Muriel." She nodded toward Bertha. "Time you gave the old gray lady a permanent rest, don't you think?"

"Hey, she's dependable."

She chuckled her way back to the front of the news truck. Sheridan was the only newsperson I would give the time of day. We went back two decades, to rookie days when my mom and dad were killed in a car crash. Sheridan and several other newspeople had accompanied the police to inform me. She returned the next day, too, after the buzz had faded. A drunk driver sped through a red light and rammed my parents' car head-on. That was the story the police told the papers. The driver of the other car cooked to a crisp when his car exploded after hitting my parents' car, then a brick wall. My parents were on their way home from an Earth, Wind & Fire concert at the Tower Theater.

Sheridan produced a series on drunk drivers in Philadelphia, how their indiscretions affected families and children on both sides of the equation, which led to a national broadcast. Philadelphia police cracked down on drunk drivers and legislation passed with compulsory loss of licenses. Several other cities and states followed suit.

I showed my badge to the young cop guarding the front door and entered the small foyer. In front of me was a white-carpeted staircase. To the left was the living room. Laughton, his expression stonier than I expected, stood next to the detective questioning who I supposed was the husband. He sat on the couch, leaned forward with his elbows resting on his thighs, his head hanging down. Two girls clad in *Frozen* pajamas huddled next to him on the couch, one on either side.

The detective glanced at me, then back at the man. "Where were you?"

"I just got here, man," the man said. "Went upstairs and found her on the floor."

"And the kids?"

"My daughter spent the night with me. She had a sleepover at my house. This is Jeanne, lives a few blocks over. She got homesick and wouldn't stop crying, so I was bringing them back here. Marcy and I separated, but we're trying to work things out." He choked up, unable to speak any more.

"At three a.m."

"I told you, the child was having a fit. Wanted her mother."

A tank of a woman charged through the front door, "Oh my God. Baby, are you all right?" She pushed past the police officer there and clomped across the room, sending those close to look for cover. The red-striped flannel robe she wore and pink furry slippers, size thirteen at least, made her look like a giant candy cane with feet.

"Wade, what the hell is happenin' here?" She moved in and lifted the girl from the sofa by her arm. Without giving him a chance to answer, she continued, "C'mon, baby. You're coming with me."

An officer stepped sideways and blocked the way. "Ma'am, you can't take her—"

The woman's head snapped around like the devil possessed her, ready to spit out nasty words followed by green fluids. She never stopped stepping.

I expect she would have trampled the officer, but Laughton interceded. "It's all right, Jackson. Let her go," he said.

Jackson sidestepped out of the woman's way before Laughton's words settled.

Laughton nodded his head in my direction. "Body's upstairs."

The house was spotless. White was *the* color: white furniture, white walls, white drapes, white wall-to-wall carpet, white picture frames. The only real color came in the mass of throw pillows that adorned the couch and a wash of plants positioned around the room.

I went upstairs and headed to the right of the landing, into a bedroom where an officer I knew, Mark Hutchinson, was photographing the scene. Body funk permeated the air. I wrinkled my nose.

"Hey, M&M," Hutchinson said.

"That's Muriel to you." I hated when my colleagues took the liberty to call me that. Sometimes I wanted to nail Laughton with a front kick to the groin for starting the nickname.

He shook his head. "Ain't me or the victim. She smells like a violet." He tilted his head back, sniffed, and smiled.

Hutchinson waved his hand in another direction. "I'm about done here."

I stopped at the threshold of the bathroom and perused the scene. Marcy Taylor lay on the bathroom floor. A small hole in her temple still oozed blood. Her right arm was extended over her head, and she had a .22 pistol in that hand. Her fingernails and toenails looked freshly painted. When I bent over her body, the sulfur-like smell of hair relaxer backed me up a bit. Her hair was bone-straight. The white silk gown she wore flowed around her body as though staged. Her cocoa brown complexion looked ashen with a pasty, white film.

"Shame," Laughton said to my back. "She was a beautiful woman." I jerked around to see him standing in the doorway.

"Check this out," I said, pointing to the lay of the nightgown over the floor.

"I already did the scene. We'll talk later," he said.

"Damn it, Laughton. Come here and check this out." But when I turned my head, he was gone.

I finished checking out the scene and went outside for some fresh air. Laughton was on the front lawn talking to an officer. He beelined for his car when he saw me.

"What the hell is wrong with you?" I muttered, jogging to catch up with him. Louder. "Laughton, what the hell—"

He dropped anchor. Caught off guard, I plowed into him. He waited until I peeled myself off him and regained my footing, then said, "Nothing. Wade says they separated a few months ago and were trying to get it together, so he came over for some making up. He used his key to enter and found her dead on the bathroom floor."

"No, he said he was bringing the little girl home because she was homesick."

"Yeah, well, then you heard it all."

He about-faced.

I grabbed his arm and attempted to spin him around. "You act like you know this one or something," I practically screeched at him.

"I do."

I cringed and softened my tone five octaves at least when I managed to speak again. "How?"

"I was married to her . . . a long time ago."

He might as well have backhanded me upside the head. "You never—"

"I have an errand to run. I'll see you back at the lab."

I stared after him long after he got in his car and sped off.

The sun was rising by the time the scene was secured: body and evidence bagged, husband and daughter gone back home. It spewed warm tropical hues over the city. By the time I reached the station, the hues had turned cold metallic gray. I pulled into a parking spot and answered the persistent ring of my cell phone. It was Nareece.

"Hey, sis. My babies got you up this early?" I said, feigning a light mood. My babies were Nareece's eight-year-old twin daughters.

Nareece groaned. "No. Everyone's still sleeping."

"You should be, too."

"Couldn't sleep."

"Oh, so you figured you'd wake me up at this ungodly hour in the morning. Sure, why not? We're talkin' sisterly love here, right?" I said. We chuckled. "I've been up since three anyway, working a case." I waited for her to say something, but she stayed silent. "Reece?" More silence. "C'mon, Reecey, we've been through this so many times. Please don't tell me you're trippin' again."

"A bell goes off in my head every time this date rolls around. I believe I'll die with it going off," Nareece confessed.

"Therapy isn't helping?"

"You mean the shrink? She ain't worth the paper she prints her bills on. I get more from talking to you every day. It's all you, Muriel. What would I do without you?"

"I'd say we've helped each other through, Reecey."

Silence filled the space again. Meanwhile, Laughton pulled his Audi Quattro in next to my Bertha and got out. I knocked on the window to get his attention. He glanced in my direction and moved on with his gangster swagger as though he didn't see me.

"I have to go to work, Reece. I just pulled into the parking lot after being at a scene."

"Okay."

"Reece, you've got a great husband, two beautiful daughters, and a gorgeous home, baby. Concentrate on all that and quit lookin' behind you."

Nareece and John had ten years of marriage. John is Vietnamese. The twins were striking, inheritors of almond-shaped eyes, "good" curly black hair, and amber skin. Rose and Helen, named after our mother and grandmother. John balked at their names because they did not reflect his heritage. But he was mush where Nareece was concerned.

"You're right. I'm good except for two days out of the year, today and on Travis's birthday. And you're probably tired of hearing me."

"I'll listen as long as you need me to. It's you and me, Reecey. Always has been, always will be. I'll call you back later today. I promise."

I clicked off and stayed put for a few minutes, bogged down by the realization of Reece's growing obsession with my son, way more than in past years, which conjured up ugly scenes for me. I prayed for a quick passing, though a hint of guilt pierced my gut. Did I pray for her sake, my sake, or Travis's? What scared me anyway?